Broken Protector

AMBER WARDEN

PANDA LILY PRESS

Copyright © 2023 by Amber Warden

All rights reserved.

No portion of this book may be reproduced in any form without written permission from the publisher or author, except as permitted by U.S. copyright law.

This is a work of fiction. Any similarity between the characters and situations within its pages and places or persons, living or dead, is unintentional and coincidental.

https://amberwardenauthor.mailerpage.com

Contents

Book Description	VII
1. Chapter 1	1
2. Chapter 2	8
3. Chapter 3	14
4. Chapter 4	18
5. Chapter 5	27
6. Chapter 6	36
7. Chapter 7	43
8. Chapter 8	55
9. Chapter 9	64
10. Chapter 10	78
11. Chapter 11	85
12. Chapter 12	95
13. Chapter 13	102

14.	Chapter 14	109
15.	Chapter 15	120
16.	Chapter 16	130
17.	Chapter 17	138
18.	Chapter 18	145
19.	Chapter 19	152
20.	Chapter 20	159
21.	Chapter 21	166
22.	Chapter 22	175
23.	Chapter 23	182
24.	Chapter 24	188
25.	Chapter 25	196
26.	Chapter 26	205
27.	Chapter 27	213
28.	Chapter 28	222
29.	Chapter 29	229
30.	Chapter 30	235
31.	Chapter 31	243
32.	Chapter 32	252
33.	Chapter 33	257
34.	Chapter 34	267
35.	Chapter 35	275
36.	Chapter 36	281
Also By Amber Warden		287

About the Author 289

Book Description

Nera never wants to be a burden.

After an accident she can't remember leaves her partially blind, Nera struggles against her sheltered life. Acceptance to culinary school is an opportunity to test her limits. Her only regret is that she'll no longer catch glimpses of the man she's loved ever since she was a child. Giovanni is dangerous and gorgeous and out of her league.

Giovanni always watches over her.

During the shared dark incident in their past, Giovanni vowed to protect Nera as she once protected him. Someone sweet and kind like her was never meant to be touched by the mafia world he was born into. Soon she'll be out of reach and safe from his failures. Only when he goes to her family's bakery one last time, she does the unthinkable and saves him yet again, despite the painful consequences.

Hiding her at his estate brings a comfort that Giovanni has never known, but Nera pushes for more: a life at his side. Soon he spirals into an obsession for the less than innocent woman his savior has become.

But when they survive another mafia hit, Giovanni realizes that Nera has been the one targeted all along. A hidden enemy wants Giovanni to feel the devastating pain of losing the one he loves.

Nera isn't afraid. She revels in his need to kill anyone that might threaten her. She'll even strike first if it will keep them together a moment longer.

With wounded but vengeful heroines and protective, morally gray heroes, the Gentle Sinners series contains interconnected standalones with steamy, open door scenes and no cliff hangers.

Amber Warden's stories often include characters overcoming tragic pasts or current hardships and may include situations that not everyone would like to read. Please see below content information to help you decide if this story is for you.

Sexual Content: explicit and steamy

Language: includes profanity;

Violence: shootings; stabbings; kidnapping; torture; homicide; patricide; father murders mother; off page death of children; child abuse/neglect; marital rape (not between MCs)

Other: discussion of feelings of worthlessness and wanting to be unalive; death of a parent; partial blindness

Chapter 1

The sun wasn't yet edging above the horizon, but that was how Nera Carmen preferred to start her morning. The dim lighting set up around the kitchen let her fuzzy eyes make out shapes. Shapes had become enough, and she relied on familiarity and habits to get her through the day.

A brush of her fingers over the flaky crust let her know the croissants had come out perfectly, as usual. She set the tray on the cooling rack before reaching into the oven for the next. The comforting scents of baked bread wrapped around her. Her childhood had been filled with the same. Since Mylene had joined them, the daily offerings at Carmen Bakery had become decidedly French, but Nera wouldn't have changed that. She'd loved her parents. That hadn't prevented the time without them from adding up. A dozen years now outweighed the ten before.

Deeper in the house, a giggle turned into something lustier. Nera rolled her eyes as she continued to pull the finished bread. Mylene was awake, then. Switching rooms had helped, but Mylene had never been the shy type to hide her activities with Tommaso, Nera's guardian.

The bedroom closest to the kitchen suited Nera much better anyway. Tommaso had been against the change since it was smaller than her previous room, but after turning eighteen, the idea of the slightly separate living quarters had been too enticing for Nera. Besides, Mylene had stopped sleeping in the room closest to the kitchen shortly after she'd moved in.

Amber light filled the arching window above the sink, and Nera closed her eyes. She breathed through the wave of disorientation, letting the familiar spike of her pulse shift through her. Ever since the accident, which she didn't fully remember, dawn's glow had felt like an enemy. A nearly forgotten shout rang in her ears, causing her brow to furrow. Hair stood up along her arms from the dim memory. That was new. Nera sucked in another breath as she tried to search for something that wasn't there.

To avoid the growing frustration, Nera opened her eyes and let her gaze scan the brightened space. The shapes of her professionally designed kitchen shimmered in the sun's glow. Nera often wondered if full blindness would have served her better. Instead, for the past dozen years she'd lived with a too-bright vision that never seemed real, as if the world around her were an overexposed, black-and-white photo.

The shards of glass she had taken to the face during the accident had caused permanent damage. There'd been attempts at surgery over the years, but Nera hadn't been able to face any more failure.

"Sorry, *ma choupette*. I am late again." Nera heard Mylene enter, then turned to watch her outline stretch for her apron, which was hooked on the wall near the door. The French patisserie chef was a petite five-foot-one, but that had never stopped her from bossing around Nera's more than six-foot-tall guardian.

Nera was somewhere in between—on the taller side, though not as tall as Tommaso, with a love for butter and a need to cook by taste instead of measurement that added rounder curves to her hips and stomach.

"Did you wear out poor Tommaso again?" Nera asked, crossing toward another oven. The tarts should be done by now.

Laughter filled her ears. "Do not worry, ma choupette. I left him more than happy."

"Mylene!" Tommaso's shout came from the entryway. He crossed to Nera, placing a kiss on top of her head. His face swam into focus that close, hints of his darker gray eyes blending with the tan of his olive skin. He continued on to the coffee Nera already had waiting. "Do not say such things to our Nera."

Nera shook her head as she opened the oven door. "It's far too late to worry about that." Tommaso still treated her like she was a virgin. She wasn't, but knew better than to let on. The man she'd once called uncle, even though they weren't related by blood, would always see her as his little girl. He'd been big and gruff and caring even before she'd lost her parents. Nera considered herself lucky that he'd taken her in when she'd had no blood relations left.

"Let me have my lies," Tommaso said. "Are those my favorite tarts?"

Nera nodded as she added the tray to the others on the work surface.

Mylene slapped his hand before he could reach for one. "Let them cool." She leaned up, brushing a kiss along his chin. "They turned out perfectly, Nera." Mylene's professional gaze took in the room before she began helping Nera with the prep work.

They'd worked together long enough that it had become seamless. Tommaso had initially hired Mylene to help with the bakery he knew nothing about, wanting to maintain the business that had been such a cornerstone of Nera's life. That the two had fallen in love had surprised everyone. Tommaso had once proposed to Mylene, but she had declined, saying she didn't like to be tied down.

Tommaso had never been helpful in the kitchen. Anything he attempted turned out burned or lumpy or foul-tasting. He helped in his own way, like filling the van with the day's offerings.

Nera would miss their teasing voices the most when she left. She and Tommaso never spoke of her pending move to the prestigious culinary school in France, but the days until it became reality were winding down. On his last trip to the van, he paused like he sometimes did lately. The stillness of his shape watching her, as if memorizing the sight, made her throat tighten.

Her parents had prepared everything they sold in the kitchen at the bakery. Mylene had started out doing the same, living in the room above the shop for the first few years she was with them, but the newer kitchen that had been built off the house suited Nera better. As well it should. It had been designed for her despite her protests. Nera had balked at the expense, even at such a young age, and she still wondered how Tommaso could afford it. They never discussed money, but since becoming her guardian she had never known him to work outside of his help with the bakery.

Nera struggled to admit that she was grateful. Her morning transition was much easier to endure at home.

Mylene began organizing the pastry case, and Nera left her to it. The tiny French woman even waved her away from the baskets Nera had filled with cooled baguettes and croissants so she could tweak them just so. Nera had no issue admitting that she lacked the instinct for such things. When most of the world blended together, it was difficult to pay attention to aesthetics.

There was only one thing that added color to Nera's life. One person. She couldn't explain it, and hadn't told even her doctors for fear that they would convince her she was imagining things. The colored outline she saw wasn't possible or explainable. That didn't stop her from becoming excited when the flicker of red appeared in the bakery that morning.

Giovanni Di Salvo had come again. Nera froze mid-reach when the dark maroon caught her eye. She turned as if mesmerized, letting the outline of color dim her too-bright vision. It almost brought him into focus, even from so far away. The line of customers was as long as ever first thing in the morning, and Giovanni stood at the end of the line, staring at the phone in his hand as usual. His presence stirred something inside her. She'd long ago given up on overcoming her obsession with staring at him. Tommaso liked to tease her for it, and Mylene grumbled about not stroking a man's ego, but even that made her feel no shame.

There were few in the neighborhood who wouldn't recognize a Di Salvo, given that they were one of the prominent La Cosa Nostra families in the area, but Giovanni didn't look like the other Di Salvos Nera had encountered. He had olive skin similar to Tommaso's, but where other members of the family were broad-shouldered, Giovanni's form held a slimness that followed through down to his legs. Oh, his arms were toned, but the muscle was sleek instead of roped, and the glimpses of his collarbone did things to her stomach.

He also lacked the dark hair of the Di Salvo men. Giovanni's wavy locks were blond where they edged his face. The paleness offset his cobalt eyes, a color she used to appreciate. She'd heard other customers whisper about the cold hardness in his eyes, but she'd always found warmth there when she was close enough for her own eyes to focus.

She knew all of his features from before her accident. Besides the red aura around him, Nera no longer saw any color, only light and dark. She missed that particular blue of his eyes the most.

He'd gotten most of his features from his mother, but not his eyes. Inessa Di Salvo had been friendly, though not friends, with Nera's mother. Giovanni had often visited their bakery with her when they were children. His visits had increased after his mother's passing, as if the bakery was the place he could imagine her most clearly. After Nera's parents had joined Inessa in heaven, his brief visits had been one of the few recognizable things in Nera's life that made her feel safe, even as the words they exchanged dwindled to little more than a customer interaction. With him being older by enough years that they had never been playmates, it wasn't so surprising.

She didn't need words. The sight of his color was stimulation enough, but when they started to have their secret exchanges from either side of the pastry counter, his visits only grew more important to her. The Giovanni she remembered from the past had a sweet tooth, but he'd limited himself during his visits over more recent years to something savory, as if enjoying something sweet would make him less of a Di Salvo. Nera couldn't keep her eyes off him while he was there. She rarely saw him return her interest, no matter how much she craved it. Instead, he would fixate on a sweet treat that he never ordered. She'd made a game out of discovering what had caught his interest during his visits and slipping it into his bag anyway. They never talked about it, but during the brief moment when he ordered and his gaze lingered on her, there was a softening to his lips that told her he was aware of her attention.

Nera studied him as she returned to the other customers. She was relieved he had come. With the dwindling days before her flight, a part of her had already begun to panic that she wouldn't see him before she left. Giovanni was making it especially hard to guess what his sweet treat would be today, his gaze not shifting from the screen in his hands. She actually liked that he tried to make it difficult for her each time. If he'd catered to her inept vision instead, she would have been furious. Nera hated being treated like an invalid.

A brief shift of his chin led her to the tarts. It was the last one too. Tommaso wouldn't be pleased that he had missed out on his favorite treat.

When Giovanni was still three customers away from ordering, a stiffness entered his posture. Nera watched him step out of line and over to the front windows, raising the phone to his ear. The sudden increase in his distance from her had Nera closing her eyes against the blinding light.

When she opened her eyes, no maroon remained at all. Giovanni had slipped out as if he'd never been there. Nera's chest tightened as denial slid through her. He likely wouldn't visit again until after she was gone.

She turned away from the current customer mid-sentence, shoved the tart in a bag, and rushed around the counter. She jostled more than a few people as she raced through the crowded bakery to the door. The bright shapes of the world didn't fully process due to her haste. His maroon served as a beacon, though, so she gave into her need and sprinted toward it.

Chapter 2

Giovanni shouldn't have been going to see her. He stood in front of the windows, far enough to the side that he could gaze at her without being seen. The flow of customers eased past him without coming too close, just as he preferred.

If this was going to be the last time he'd see Nera for a while, he would drink his fill. Her auburn hair slithered over her shoulder as she tilted her head to listen to the older customer. The strands looked good against the dark red of her long-sleeved shirt. His fingers itched to brush it back, which was ridiculous. He never allowed himself to touch her, not since the incident.

Her smile formed and added a punch to his stomach. It was so bright. How many times had that smile dissipated all his other thoughts when he was a child? Giovanni had always been an overthinker, swirls of internalized toxicity that made the passive-aggressive jabs of his father pale in comparison. A single smile from her made it seem like none of that mattered.

When his gaze traced her lips, pink and full and parted in a laugh he wished he was inside the bakery to hear, heat slid up his neck. He loosened his scarf to allow in the cold bite of the wind. He'd been reacting to her strangely ever since Tommaso had told him about the culinary school.

Soon his silent protection would end. Perhaps it had never been necessary, but it was the least he could offer her after the part he'd played in the death of her parents. Not to mention her loss of full sight.

Giovanni's hand pressed against the bulletproof glass, wishing he could feel the chill through his glove. He watched her efficient movements despite her unfocused eyes. She'd refused any more surgeries years ago. Tommaso's latest report had mentioned a lessening of her headaches this past week. Giovanni hadn't been surprised. Nera loved the winter months, and the temperature had shifted recently.

She'd like it better in Paris. There were fewer hours of sunlight, especially in the winter, and a higher chance of cloudy days.

As the bell above the door chimed, he realized this would be the last time that certain stillness overtook her. She knew when he was present almost instantly. It was as if an invisible thread wove between them, vibrating like a spider's web. His chest squeezed as her face turned his way.

His phone's vibration was a welcome distraction as Giovanni joined the line of customers. He removed his glove before reaching for it, pretending that the sudden cold along his bared skin was what caused him to shiver. He ignored the notification, staring blankly at the screen as a wave of awareness spread over his skin. Nera was staring longer than usual.

Normally, her eyes shifted toward him and away. It was a game. He pretended not to notice, and she pretended not to look.

The ritual differed completely from the times before the incident, when she would come running to him as soon as he appeared. His teenaged self had been embarrassed by her enthusiasm.

Nera had never returned to that carefree girl, even if she was blessed with losing the memory that still prompted sweat-inducing nightmares for him.

Giovanni's eyes flicked to the case of pastries. She'd baked Tommaso's favorite tart today.

His phone vibrated in his hand. He finally opened the messages. He ignored the first one. Antonio knew full well where he had gone. His cousin understood Giovanni better than he understood himself. The second message reminding him of the meeting that had been called was more of the same: disapproval without being blatant.

'Noted,' was Giovanni's response.

'Available?' came back.

'What is it?' Giovanni asked, but when the screen changed to show an incoming call, he wanted to cuss. He hated a call when a text would serve well enough. Still, there were some things that were easier to leave unsaid that way. He accepted the call, stepping out of line. "Yes?"

"You better not be where I think you are." There was a sigh in his cousin's voice.

Giovanni let his silence be his answer.

"Well, it's not like I don't understand. You should have taken my advice long ago." A chuckle followed.

"Enough," Giovanni said. The advice had been ridiculous, and he didn't need to hear it again. Besides, Antonio wouldn't have called just to give him a hard time.

"I guess it is a bit too late. Just return. There's been movement." The click that followed made the urgency of the situation clear.

Giovanni glanced at the counter. Being denied one last interaction was for the best.

The jingle of the bell as he left sounded high and mournful. Giovanni shoved his phone in his pocket without bothering to pull out his removed glove. The bite of the wind was comforting in its way.

The bakery was located in their *borgata*, which should have been protection enough, but that promise had been broken once before. He'd left his car parked on another block like usual. He picked a new one each visit, never approaching the bakery at the same time or with any standard frequency. Twelve years, and only Antonio—and, of course, Tommaso—knew of his visits there.

Not that he was important enough for his presence to have registered for the other families; not anymore. The incident had made his family's position more than clear. Despite who his father was, Giovanni was useless as a target. While Antonio pushed him toward more, Giovanni was content as a capo. Antonio had better instinct for possible succession. His father had picked up on that truth long ago. His cousin even looked more like him, with his dark hair and larger build.

"Wait!"

A hand gripped Giovanni's naked one, jerking him to a stop. The warmth of it lingered even after Nera released him.

Her breath panted from between parted lips as her eyes traced his face. The tension at their corners eased as her pupils tightened with an intense focus reserved for him.

"Beautiful," she murmured.

Heat flared all the way up to Giovanni's ears at the term. People often commented on his looks, but none would have dared to describe him with that word. He should have been offended. He would be once he stopped feeling her husky tone reverberating in his chest.

A gust of wind swirled between them, bringing a brighter color to her cheeks and causing her to shiver.

Giovanni frowned at her lightweight, long-sleeved shirt and apron. She'd rushed after him without a jacket.

"Here." Nera thrust the paper bag into his hand. It freed up her own to buff her arms.

Giovanni glanced inside the bag, expecting to see the last of her decadent tarts. He was not disappointed.

"You'll have to start ordering what you really want," Nera said. Her tone held a note of scolding that reminded him of her mother. "I won't be around to indulge you anymore."

"Indulge me?" Giovanni repeated incredulously.

Her widening smile was his answer. "You've heard, haven't you? About the culinary school in France?"

He hesitated. "I may have."

"I'm glad I got to see you one more time before I left. If I'd known today was the day, I would have made panna cotta."

Giovanni wondered how he had become so transparent to her. He'd never admitted that panna cotta was his favorite. At least he suspected it was, but the taste was also mixed with memories.

Her fingers tightened around her arms as she focused on his eyes. "One of the bright spots in my life was our game. Thank you, Giovanni."

The sound of his name echoed in his ears even as he frowned. "Game?"

He often watched her laugh through the glass window but now he was hearing it for the first time in ages.

"You certainly made it challenging," Nera said. "I bet no one else would guess that Giovanni Di Salvo has the sweetest sweet tooth around. I enjoyed guessing which treat caught your eye and gifting it to you. How often was I right?"

His eyes fell to peer inside the bag. "Every time," he admitted.

"Oh," she gasped.

His gaze followed her fingers as they lifted to press against her lips, which weren't curved in the circle of surprise he'd expected. No, the soft sound she'd gifted him with wasn't one of astonishment. It was one of happiness. He skimmed over her flushed cheeks until he met her eyes.

"You admitted it," she said.

His pulsed raced, filling him with an overwhelming need to escape. His fingers gripped the pastry bag tightly. "Take care, Nera."

"Wait!" she cried, latching onto his hand again. "Giovanni, I—" Nera broke off her own words, her brow wrinkling as she tilted her head. The focus in her eyes scattered as they shifted to peer over his shoulder. Then she lunged at him, mimicking a memory he had never wanted to relive.

Giovanni stumbled into the wall as a shot rang out.

Chapter 3

Watching Nera's body jerk dragged a broken shout from deep inside Giovanni. "No!"

Denial never changed reality. Nera crumpled to the sidewalk.

Every cell in his body urged him to run to her. He shook with the effort to ignore it and pull his gun instead as he shoved off the wall and faced the threat.

The second bullet from the Bratva's gun dug into the brick where he had been. Giovanni's returning fire hit its mark. The Bratva soldier was dead before he hit the ground.

Like the cockroaches the Russian mafia were, the first shooter hadn't been alone. Screams from bystanders on the street rang out when the other two men fired. Giovanni dropped to his knees, using a parked car as a shield, even as he took them out as well.

He may have been less skilled in many things as a Di Salvo, but Giovanni had learned how to shoot. Practicing at the private range on the estate had become a type of therapy. The weight of the gun in his hand felt like it belonged there.

Even more Bratva soldiers rounded the corner, sending people running. Giovanni's jaw clenched as he held his fire. He had to make every bullet count. The open sidewalk offered very little cover. He squeezed off another shot, taking down one more *bratok* as he forced himself closer, drawing their fire to the nearest parked car so it wouldn't stray and hit the prone form that, his heart was reminding him with every painful pound, hadn't moved since the first gunshot.

He only grazed the next bratok, whose wild shot nicked the pavement beside Giovanni. Another squeeze of the trigger, and he plowed a bullet between the man's eyes before being forced flat to avoid the returning barrage from some very pissed-off Russians.

Sudden gunfire from a new direction forced them to stop. Tommaso continued to empty his weapon, his bulk in no way hiding behind the pole he was using for cover. His rapid distraction allowed Giovanni to take out the last three *bratkóv* that Tommaso managed to miss.

The sudden quiet along the street was deafening.

Giovanni scanned it one more time before rushing to Nera. Red stained the sidewalk next to her left ear, and Giovanni's legs folded beneath him. He crawled the last foot, his hands hovering over her body as he searched for where she was hit.

Nera still hadn't opened her eyes.

"Nera!" Tommaso's voice broke on her name. He stood over them, his gun still raised. "Where was she hit?"

Blood had soaked into the pavement, but Giovanni couldn't see the cause. His silence made Tommaso's jaw tighten.

"Goddammit, Di Salvo, get up!" Tommaso barked. He shoved his own gun into Giovanni's hands when his shaky legs obeyed, and they switched positions.

Giovanni's eyes darted down, taking in Nera's pallor before he forced them back to the street. He pressed his lips together more tightly, swallowing a swell of panicked words.

Tommaso's large hand coursed over her left arm, coming away sticky with her blood. "It was just blending with the color of her favorite shirt. An arm wound shouldn't be so bad." His clean hand moved to the back of her head, and he frowned. "No knot. Not sure why she's not conscious." He tucked his hands beneath her and lifted her in his arms.

Giovanni swallowed his fear of moving her. Tommaso loved Nera and had seen more wounds than Giovanni probably ever would. He started to fall into step with the bigger man, but the sudden glare he was skewered with froze his feet to the sidewalk.

"You around would be the worst thing. I should have accepted your choice instead of pushing you into coming to the bakery." A muscle ticked in Tommaso's cheek. "Go tell the Di Salvos I said to get their shit together. I'm too fucking old for this."

Giovanni's eyes flicked to him as he swallowed his retort. Taking Nera somewhere safe was their first priority. He stared down at the paper bag Nera had run out to give him. Broken grains of crust peeked at the edges of the opening, and a damp mess seeped into the bag from within, coloring the paper a darker shade.

Tommaso said nothing else as he left with Nera.

Giovanni took out his phone, forcing the urge to follow Tommaso deep down as he dialed. Antonio would know a discreet doctor to send to her. One with limited connections to others in La Cosa Nostra. His cousin's far-reaching tentacles came in handy sometimes.

Giovanni didn't expect silence from Antonio in response to his request. "Should I ask?" was the question that finally came.

The attempted hit wasn't something Giovanni could keep to himself. Only Nera's involvement needed to be kept secret. Giovanni crouched to check the last body. That was what the Bratva soldiers had become—bodies. His aim hadn't left a single one alive to interrogate.

Giovanni crossed toward where he'd parked his car. The hell with it. Let the Russians clean up their own mess. The deaths would serve as a message. "I'll return soon," he told his cousin before ending the call.

Even behind the steering wheel, Giovanni struggled to move forward. Nera lunging for him today was overlapping with a memory. A memory in which a ten-year-old girl had become his protector—and had lost nearly everything in exchange.

Chapter 4

Nera was only five when she was first captivated by Giovanni as he stood beside his mother in line at their bakery. Even as a child, he didn't smile. His lips remained pressed together, his cheekbones and chin already edging toward definition instead of the baby fat of youth. Morning sunlight filtered through the front windows, outlining his still form in what Nera's mind saw as the sparkling of the heaven place her momma had told her about.

"Angel!" Nera had cried, darting around the counter before her papa could catch her.

Hugs had never been in short supply in the Carmen household, so she saw nothing wrong with throwing her chubby little arms around the angelic cherub so he wouldn't escape.

The boy she hugged stiffened in her embrace. Nera's arms warmed where they remained curled around him, and her cheek rubbed against material that felt so soft. Now that the sunlight had shifted, she realized the angel was dressed as if it was time for one of those sermon things that made her sleepy. This made perfect sense if he came from heaven, though the boy's dressy clothes didn't scratch at her skin like her papa's.

Nera peeked up at his face, liking the way the pale hair framed his prettiness, but the eyes she stared into didn't put out that heavenly light that she expected. Their cobalt blue was dark and widened in surprise.

"Oh no, Nera! Let the boy go!" her momma had cried, pulling her away from the angel. She looked at the adult next to the boy. "I'm so sorry! She meant no harm."

Laughter tinkled from above Nera. Her childlike gaze shifted to the larger angel. Giovanni's mother was stunning, with her delicate, willowy build and long curls of blonde hair that shone with dawn's light. "What luck, Giovanni! Such a warm greeting you received."

The boy was still staring at Nera, his forehead scrunched as he blinked at her.

Nera grinned back, wishing her momma would release her so she could touch the angel again. She tried to wriggle free, but the grip on her tightened.

Her papa came around the counter with two plates of the custard treat Nera had just learned to make. Well, she'd mainly followed what her momma said to do and stirred, but that was a big help, or so she'd been told.

"Here," Nera's papa said as he gestured to the nearest table, the one in front of the windows that made Nera sleepy to sit at in the afternoon sun. "Please enjoy this as an apology for our daughter."

"Oh, panna cotta is my favorite!" Giovanni's mother had the warmest smile, one very like Nera's own momma's. "Come along, Giovanni. You're in for a treat."

The boy followed, sitting quietly across from his mother near a plate of *dolci*. He still hadn't said anything, but Nera didn't think that was strange for an angel.

Nera's momma tried to steer her toward the kitchen, but Nera ducked and managed to escape. "Nera!" her momma scolded, but Nera was quicker than spit, or so her papa always said, and crawled up onto one of the empty seats at their table before her momma could catch her again. She laid her head on her arms, pouting at her momma in the way that usually made her give in.

"We don't mind the company," Giovanni's mother said. Her hand patted Nera's own. "Not from such a friendly girl. Isn't that right, Giovanni?"

The boy looked away from Nera. Those pretty eyes of his focused on the custard dessert in front of him, but he didn't reach for the spoon.

Nera talked and talked as she sat there while Giovanni's mother ate the panna cotta. His mother nodded and smiled, encouraging the torrent of words with a word or two of her own. Not that Nera needed a lot of encouragement. While she found his mother stunning, her eyes kept returning to Giovanni, who hadn't touched the custard.

Having finished her story about the alley kitten her momma had let her pet, Nera rested her head on her hands again, shifting as close as the chair would let her and peering up into Giovanni's face. "Panna cotta is good. I promise."

Giovanni's mother had already finished her own dessert. "Try at least a bite. For me." Her smile faded as she tapped her spoon against the plate. "It really is my favorite."

A moment passed that felt like forever to Nera. Then Giovanni reached for his spoon. He froze after he took the first bite, as if absorbing the taste with every part of his body. Nera saw the moment the sparkle reached his eyes, proving he was an angel.

His mother's smile was dazzling as well. She leaned toward Nera, drawing her eyes away from Giovanni. "He likes it," his mother whispered to Nera.

Giovanni's shoulders hunched as he ducked his head, but the spoon scooped up a second bite.

"How old are you, Nera?" Giovanni's mother asked, and Nera straightened and held up her hand with all the fingers pointing out. Her words flowed again, and they talked while Giovanni ate in silence.

Nera decided his momma was right when his plate was empty by the end. Giovanni did like it.

Inessa Di Salvo began bringing her son to the bakery regularly after the first visit. Nera enjoyed picking out new things for Giovanni to try. If he left nothing on the plate, that meant he'd liked it. Often he and his mother ate panna cotta together.

Nera could never pinpoint when her heart accepted that they weren't angels. Over time, he became just Giovanni in her eyes.

It was nearly five years later that Nera came across her mother crying against her father's shoulder. Giovanni's mother had returned to heaven, or so she'd been told. Nera hadn't experienced loss before. Heaven was supposed to be a good thing, so she hadn't understood why it made her mother so sad at first, but when time passed without Nera seeing Inessa Di Salvo again, she began to understand the sadness.

Especially because she also hadn't seen Giovanni. He'd become older and hadn't accompanied his mother with every visit over the past year. Bubbles always rose in Nera's stomach when he did accompany her. After Inessa was gone, when he stopped coming, Nera became scared that he'd died as well and they just hadn't told her. Her father had been appalled when she asked and had denied the possibility. He said it was probably too hard for Giovanni to come to the bakery because he missed his mother so much.

Nera was helping her mother near closing time one day not long after that by sweeping up. She'd become a better helper. She'd already become a good baker as well, doing much more than just stirring each morning as her family prepared the treats for the day.

When she was finished, she moved to the propped-open outer door to remove the stopper. The bright sun had dazzled her eyes, and she lifted a hand to block it as she blinked in the warmth. Partway down the street, someone stumbled against the wall, slowly sliding down to sit.

Nera thought it was another homeless person, and she'd promised her father not to approach them. She didn't understand how it was dangerous to give them food, but a promise was a promise.

Nera didn't recognize him at first. His clothes were torn; dirt and blood caked his hair, hiding the normal, pale shine; and red smeared the cut on the side of his face. To her, Giovanni was beauty beyond words, had become even more so when he became a teenager. When he lifted his beaten face from his knees, he was gorgeous in a different way among the wounds.

The broom dropped from her hands as she ran to him. "Giovanni!"

His head shifted along the wall enough to turn her way, and his eyes opened to stare up at her as she hurried to his side.

Both of Nera's hands closed around one of his. When she saw the blood on the back of it, she didn't release him. Instead, she gently tugged him to his feet. "Come with me."

Her father helped Giovanni get cleaned up. Nera wasn't sure what they talked about. Giovanni never spoke much. Once he was sitting at the table he and his mother had always shared, Nera brought him a plate of dolci. Giovanni stared down at the panna cotta, his still face as gorgeous as any statue, with its chiseled cheekbones and the strong tilt of his chin.

"Your mother would want you to eat," Nera said, sitting down beside him.

Giovanni's hand had gone to the spoon. He only managed one bite before setting it down and swallowing hard. His dark eyes had seemed to shimmer with moisture.

Nera's hand had covered his over the spoon, and she'd started bawling for them both. She missed Giovanni's mother, so she knew he must miss her even more. She cried all the tears she imagined he'd never cried, and Giovanni sat beside her through it, his hand turning and linking with hers.

He began coming to their bakery again after that. It wasn't as often as he had with his mother, but somehow the decreased frequency made the bubbles in Nera's stomach stretch even farther when he appeared. Sometimes he wore bruises or cuts, but he never told her where he got them. Her father no longer smiled when Giovanni came to visit. He would pull the boy aside when the bruises were especially severe, and Giovanni would listen silently to the lecture that followed.

Nera was sweeping again on the day that had become, over time, a dull, dreamlike memory.

The hairs lifted along her arms, telling her he had come, and she lifted her eyes from the sidewalk. Giovanni was walking toward her. His lips tilted up at the edges, in the slight smile he reserved for her. She grinned in return, lifting her hand in a wave.

Just then, tires screeched as a car jerked to the side of the street beside Giovanni. Three strange men piled out. Giovanni fumbled for something at his waist as he turned, but they were already on him.

Nera released her grip on her broom as she ran toward him. "Giovanni!" she screamed, her legs pumping. She lunged at him with all her might, forcing him back and free of the men.

"Nera!" her father yelled somewhere behind her.

The strangers cursed, and then Nera heard gunshots and her mother's scream. A man hit Nera. Pain exploded in her cheek as she collapsed to the sidewalk.

"Don't hurt her!" Arms wrapped around Nera, shielding her from a kick. Giovanni grunted above her as his panicked eyes met hers. His body curled more tightly around her, protecting her even as his body jerked with every blow.

"No!" Nera screamed from the cocoon of his arms. "Giovanni!"

Her eyes popped open. Instead of the clear vision she had had as a child, a broken view of the world flashed above her. Nera's breath rushed out as she waited for her vision to settle. The grip on her hand loosened, and the room dimmed, the sunlight at the edges of her blackout curtains the brightest point in her swimming vision.

Instead of her cheek throbbing, it was her arm that seared with pain, disorienting her.

A familiar shadow sat beside her.

"Tommaso?" Nera asked.

"I'm here, Nera," he said, his hand closing over hers, the one attached to the arm that didn't hurt. "How are you feeling?"

Nera swallowed to wet her dry throat. "A bit of pain." She tried to shift to find relief from the ache, and something jostled along her arm.

She looked away from Tommaso's hand, squinting as she tried to focus on the cords attached to her.

"Here. For the pain." Tommaso pressed a pill against her lips, following it up with a water glass. "What do you remember?"

"I don't..." The sound of gunshots filled her mind, making her hand jerk against his arm and spilling drops of water on the bed. No, the gunshots had been in her dreams. But somehow they were overlapping with a different memory of the sidewalk outside the bakery. One where she heard metallic scuffling and saw a group of shifting shadows among her normal brightness. "Was Giovanni shot?" she asked.

Tommaso cleared his throat as he looked away. "No. You were."

"Oh." The cords took on another aspect, and she followed them up to what looked like an IV bag.

"We were lucky. The bullet went through and tore up mainly tissue and a bit of muscle. You'll have pain for a while, but you should heal well enough if you rest." Tommaso leaned down to press his forehead against the bed beside her. "When I heard the shots," he mumbled, "and then you were lying so still... I've never been so scared."

"I'm sorry," Nera said. Her hand shifted to pat the top of his head.

"Not your fault." He sighed, sitting up straight. "You've probably noticed you're not in the hospital. With the Di Salvos involved..." He looked away.

Nera nodded. "I'm aware. Giovanni really is okay?"

"Until I kill him, yeah." Tommaso shoved to his feet. "I need to let Mylene know you're awake. She'll want to feed you."

"I'm not hungry." No, Nera's head ached too much to think about eating.

"I'll try to tell her, Nera, but you know Mylene thinks the answer to everything is delicious food." He chuckled as he patted his stomach. "I should know."

Jumbled nightmares vied for her attention. Memories of Giovanni's mother blended with the made-up scenes and caused them to seem all too real. "Tommaso?"

He paused in the doorway, turning to face her. The light he'd allowed in filled her vision with bright shadows.

Nera swallowed, the saliva loosening her numb lips. "My parents. They were in an accident, right? They weren't shot?"

Tommaso didn't answer. He stared back at her, and the space between them stretched wider than she'd ever felt it had been before. His voice was gruff when he finally spoke. "The sound of gunshots can be a scary thing. Don't think about it too hard."

It wasn't an answer, but Tommaso had already slipped from the room before she could ask him again.

Chapter 5

The Di Salvo estate had once been a prison for Giovanni's mother. That was likely why Giovanni himself had always hated it, despite its elegant comfort. That and the fact that his father lived there. Still, with the gates and the number of Di Salvos prowling around, it was the safest place if the Bratva were planning another hit.

Besides, his father would expect a report. It was never in his best interest to keep Giovanni Sr. waiting.

Pushing open the massive front door raised an ache in Giovanni's shoulder that caused him to frown at his waiting cousin.

Antonio frowned back, his arms crossed as his eyes scanned Giovanni. "No need to scowl at me. I sent the doctor you requested, didn't I?"

Giovanni's fingers twitched at the reminder of how still Nera had been the last time he'd seen her. He hadn't doubted his cousin would come through; hearing the confirmation should have helped to settle him. It didn't.

Nera should have never tried to help him.

Antonio's gaze returned to his face. "At least this will remind her of the lesson she's forgotten."

Giovanni's hand had twisted in his cousin's shirt before he realized his intent. He swallowed down the emotional reaction, forcing himself to loosen his grip. Antonio was telling him a truth that he didn't need to hear, not when his own regrets were drumming in his head. "Don't."

"I've tried to tell you before. Your visits were the worst thing for her. Maybe now you'll accept that." Antonio smoothed his hands down his clothes. He had always looked more like a Di Salvo than Giovanni did. They wore the same type of suit, but Antonio's had a flair of color. Today's was red, like Nera's shirt, which set off his dark hair. The scar that ran along his chiseled jaw before dipping under, toward his throat, flashed white.

"Does he know?" Giovanni asked.

Antonio sighed. "Only about the hit. Your girl was left out of it since she was gone by the time the cleanup crew arrived."

The muscle pulsed beside Giovanni's eye. "I didn't ask for one." He'd killed all the Bratva. Leaving their bodies would have been message enough.

"I made the call. Don't be stubborn." Antonio moved closer to clap a hand on Giovanni's shoulder. "Come on. I'll go with you."

Giovanni hesitated, but then gave a single nod. Any buffer between him and his father would help more than it hurt. He'd given up long ago on impressing his father. "Any ideas?"

"I put out feelers." Antonio frowned as they fell into step together, his voice lowering. "The only thing that makes sense is they caught a whiff, but that still doesn't explain it. Hell, Gio, you were the only one there."

"Right." Giovanni didn't understand it either. Taking him out wouldn't stop anything the family did. The kidnapping from years before was more than fresh in his mind. As the son of the Di Salvo boss, the Bratva had considered him worth a prince's ransom. When his father responded that they should kill him, he'd sent a clear message about Giovanni's worth. He had none. Not to the Di Salvos, anyway.

"Get him the fuck in here!" his father yelled through his office door.

The soft murmur of another voice followed.

"At least Vittore's in there," Antonio muttered before opening the door.

A vase shattered against the wall, but Giovanni didn't let his steps falter. He was used to his father's tantrums. It would take more than some broken glass to make him flinch, though he didn't understand why Vittore ordered replacements every time.

A large, wooden desk took up a good portion of the office, but Giovanni Sr. stalked the space in front of it like a predator. Sitting behind a desk was more of his uncle's image. As consigliere, though, Vittore Di Salvo was often away, meeting with various people of interest to the family. His face remained calm as he watched Giovanni Sr. whirl.

Giovanni's father ran his hands through his thick, dark hair before pinning him with his eyes, so similar to Giovanni's own. Giovanni stood still and calm; he had learned early on that showing any emotion to his father only made things worse.

The veins on the sides of his father's neck bulged. "Do you understand what you've done?" he growled.

"I responded to a hit," Giovanni said, forcing his shoulders not to hunch under the continued glare.

"I'll say!" Antonio sauntered past Giovanni to lean a hip against one of the upholstered chairs. "The damn Bratva sent ten of their own, but Gio here doesn't have a scratch on him. Impressive, wouldn't you say?"

"You stay out of this, Antonio," Giovanni Sr. said, but his clenched jaw loosened. He sat on the corner of his desk as a frown took over his face. "They sent so many? What could be their game?"

The image of Nera, her blood seeping into the concrete, returned to Giovanni. "It wasn't a game."

His father batted the words away. "You were too hasty. Leaving at least one alive would have brought us more answers."

"I'm sorry my aim was so accurate," Giovanni said.

His father's jaw tightened again.

A chuckle rang out behind Giovanni, and an arm slid around his shoulders. "Don't be like that! I'm glad my efforts paid off."

"Back already, Enzo?" Antonio asked, grinning at their other uncle.

Enzo squeezed Giovanni's shoulder once more before releasing him. Enzo wasn't like his brothers. He cropped his dark hair close to his head and wore anything besides a suit—mostly jeans—and he stuck to dark colors because, as he said, they made it easier to mask bloodstains. He'd been cleaning up the family's messes for a long time, and was more lethal than the perpetual smile he wore let on. Giovanni had appreciated the lessons his uncle had given him over the years. On the rare occasion he asked for help, Enzo had never scorned him for it.

Now Enzo held out his hand, curling his fingers in a flicking motion. "Give it here, Gio."

Giovanni blinked before removing his Glock from his waistband and handing it over. He felt a ridiculous twinge of emotion. Becoming attached to a weapon wasn't necessary. The gun had served its purpose.

Enzo pulled the clip, nodding down at the few remaining bullets. "Matches the number of casings I found. I'm impressed. You didn't even need to reload." He tucked it into his own waistband and handed Giovanni another. "You should keep one on hand until the brainiac over there figures this all out." He grinned at Vittore before tilting his head to look back at Giovanni. "I found a lot more casings nearby, but from another weapon. You got something else?"

Giovanni shook his head. "Tommaso."

The crease on Enzo's forehead eased. "That explains it. Tommaso never could hit the broad side of a barn."

"I haven't heard that name in a while," Vittore mused.

Giovanni swallowed, but didn't offer an explanation.

Enzo clapped him on the shoulder. "Good job not getting dead," he said before leaving the office.

At least his uncle was glad he was still alive.

"Tell us exactly what happened," his father demanded.

Giovanni didn't have any details to add. "The Bratva shot first. No words were exchanged. They died."

Vittore frowned. "They said nothing?"

Giovanni Sr. scowled at his son. "Did you even try talking to them?"

"Their shots said enough." Giovanni kept his face blank. There was no need to admit to the fury that had coursed through him. They'd hurt Nera. He wished he could spill their blood all over again. This time, more slowly.

"I've canceled today's meeting. Let me work with my contacts in the Bratva. There must be some sort of misunderstanding behind this." Vittore crossed to the door, disappearing into the hallway.

With his brothers gone, Giovanni Sr. dropped all pretenses. "Get out," he growled at his son.

Giovanni turned to leave. He hadn't expected anything else. His father would never communicate relief over him turning up alive. He wasn't the type to say something he didn't feel. Besides their eyes, it was the one similarity they had.

Antonio straightened to follow him.

"No, you stay," Giovanni Sr. said, and Giovanni pulled the door closed behind him.

He didn't need the look Antonio threw his way. He trusted his cousin. Antonio would never tell his father about Nera.

Giovanni stared down at the new gun in his hands. His fingers tightened around it, and he gave in to the need, making his way to the gun range in the basement.

His grandfather had had it built for Enzo back in the day. Giovanni had never met his grandfather, but he had heard he was much like his father: quick to bursts of anger and final in his judgments. One of those judgments had resulted in his own death. Vengeance had been swift and brutal, and had paved the way for Giovanni's father to take over the family.

There was no such thing as heirs in La Cosa Nostra. The family was filled with made men, all with strength and ambition. When one leader fell, the next was picked from among the capos. The Di Salvos had been selected because of their actions.

Despite working his own way up to capo, Giovanni had no designs on becoming good enough to lead the family. His uncles, or hell, even Antonio, were all a much better fit. Blood was part of the requirement. It only had to be half Italian, which Giovanni had, but he didn't look it. His features reminded the family of his mother's betrayal.

The memory skewed the results of the first clip Giovanni emptied into a target. He reloaded, and soon the sound of steady gunfire brought him the quiet mind he craved. The ache in his tweaked shoulder gave him something other than his anger to focus on.

"I thought I'd find you here."

He turned to find Antonio leaning against the wall.

Silence stretched between them.

Antonio broke it. "Not going to ask?"

Giovanni waited. His cousin knew what he wanted.

Antonio sighed. "The doctor said no surgery is needed. Honestly, her wound wasn't bad at all. If she takes it easy for a couple of weeks, she'll be back at making dolci soon enough."

Giovanni frowned. "She lost consciousness."

"She swooned or something." Antonio shrugged. "There was no head injury or any other physical symptom the doctor could find. Taking a bullet was too much for her apparently. That girl's not the strongest."

Giovanni didn't bother correcting his cousin. Nera was strong. She'd proven that when they were kids. "She saved me again."

The tension eased from Antonio's face. "I realize that. And I'm grateful, really." He moved toward him, ruffling Giovanni's hair like he used to when they were kids. "I don't know what I'd do without you."

Giovanni scowled, ducking to escape him as he tried to smooth his hair. He hated that his skin wasn't quite dark enough to hide the heat crawling up his neck. "Same."

Antonio cleared his throat, looking away.

Giovanni studied his cousin. Antonio didn't often hesitate.

"I know you don't want to hear this," Antonio said, still not meeting his eyes, "but maybe God put that girl in your path for this purpose. Twice now, you didn't die because of her. It's like she was meant to be your shield all along."

Giovanni shook his head. "You don't believe in God." The two of them had only gone to services out of duty. Giovanni's own beliefs were more complicated. Living out hell in her lifetime should have been enough penance for his mother, and despite what his father said, he liked to imagine she was in heaven.

"Oops, you caught me," Antonio said, smirking as he faced him again. "But seriously, Gio, don't you think the girl's had enough?"

Giovanni couldn't argue against that fact. When Tommaso had called to urge him to see her one more time, he'd refused, but he still found himself outside the Carmen Bakery like he always had. "It was supposed to be the last time." He'd tried to convince himself that he was saying goodbye to the memories the place held for him, but his eyes had been full of her as soon as he'd looked through the glass.

"Yeah, that's the hell of it." Antonio raked a hand through his hair. "She'll need to heal now before she can leave for her culinary program in France. My recommendation? Wait for that, fuck her out of your system, and send her off to live her life."

Giovanni glared at his cousin. "It's not like that." He in no way wanted to fuck Nera. The idea of it made his fingers do the strange itching they'd been doing whenever he looked at her. Nera was beautiful, just as she called him, but his interest in her had never been sexual in nature. His mind was too full of the child she had been to think of her as a woman.

Besides, Giovanni wasn't as hot-blooded as the other Di Salvo men. He'd known too much about the pain his father had inflicted on his mother to ever want to do the same.

Antonio rolled his eyes. "You're lying to yourself, Gio, but whatever. Just let the poor girl go."

"That's my intention," Giovanni said. He turned to face the next target he'd set in place.

"Good," his cousin said. He left Giovanni in solitude soon enough. He knew that was what he preferred.

As he emptied his next round, Giovanni mulled over their conversation. Antonio had given him the update he'd been seeking, but the urge to see for himself that Nera was all right overwhelmed him. The quiet mind he'd achieved didn't return even after he emptied two more clips.

Chapter 6

Nera sat up in bed, the slight jostling of her arm causing her to bite her lip. The doctor had warned her that her arm would be sore and had left behind a sling. He'd removed the IV the night before and rebandaged the wound.

It was Nera's favorite time of the day, when she didn't have to strain against the too-bright shadows and there was only herself to worry about. That the scent of rising dough didn't fill the house, however, felt more than wrong. And sitting still was making her stir-crazy.

Nera struggled to reach for the strap of the sling. It was supposed to wrap over her shoulder snugly, preventing movement, but the doctor hadn't factored in the fact that she didn't have spaghetti arms. The fit was too snug and added to the ache. Nera fumbled with the buckle, annoyed that the manufacturers seemed not to have taken into account that the wearer would need to adjust it one-handed.

"Let me, ma choupette," Mylene murmured, crossing the room to perch on the bed beside her.

The too-tight feeling eased, but then the sling became too loose. Mylene hummed beneath her breath as she adjusted the strap again, her small fingers making quick work of it.

"How's that?" she murmured.

Nera rested her head briefly against Mylene's shoulder. The French woman was nothing like her mother physically. Her shoulder was thin and bony instead of sturdy like Nera's own, but the smallness was misleading.

"You should sleep more," Mylene advised. "Tommaso will not be happy if you do not get your rest."

Nera wrinkled her nose. "I've been in bed long enough."

"Very well." Mylene rose, heading toward the door. "But you sit only. No helping."

Nera perched on one of the stools at the kitchen's center island as Mylene got to work. The overhead lights made the space around her shimmer. Soon her home's regular morning scents wafted around her, and the knot in Nera's stomach loosened.

There was only one thing out of place before Mylene even got started. The large, black rifle didn't fit in among the bowls and mixers that began to accumulate on the work surface.

Tommaso had raised Nera around guns and taught her to respect them, but he hadn't taught her more than that. As a child, she'd never questioned their presence, even though her parents had never owned any. That was just Tommaso's way.

"Why are you not in bed?" Despite his gruff tone, Tommaso dropped a kiss on top of Nera's head before taking the stool beside her.

Nera had talked Mylene into letting her add the fruit to the tarts one-handed, and now glanced over at him guiltily.

Tommaso sighed, but his silence meant he didn't expect an answer. He glanced at the rifle, but didn't rise to put it away.

Mylene kissed his sulking mouth, long enough that Nera refocused on the tart in front of her. "Leave ma choupette alone. This is resting for her." The timer on the top oven went off, and she moved away to check on the croissants.

"True enough," Tommaso agreed. He eyed Nera's fingers where they poked out of the end of the sling. "But keep that arm still for now, you hear? Even a lucky wound can fester. And you're not coming to the bakery today."

Nera had no desire to argue. She was glad she wasn't lying prone, but she was used to listening to her body. A foggy fatigue lingered at the edges of her vision like it did at the end of a normal day. "I won't push."

Tommaso studied her face before nodding.

Nera picked up another strawberry, her hand hovering over the naked custard within the shell of the tart. Her flight was supposed to leave in two days, but she couldn't imagine the tight spaces and shaking of an airplane, not when shifting forward too fast sent a throb into her arm. She would have to call the airline. And the admissions office at the school. The doctor had recommended two weeks of healing. Nera had planned on having time to explore Paris before classes started, but not a full two weeks.

"Here, you eat this and let me finish," Mylene said, putting a warm croissant beside Nera's hand. She took the strawberry from Nera's still fingers, reaching for other fruit to finish the tarts.

The customers preferred Mylene's tarts over Nera's. It wasn't the taste, but rather the fact that Nera's eyesight meant she would never have the instincts for a pleasant mixture of color. She reminded herself to alternate fruits, but it wasn't the same.

"Where's my breakfast?" Tommaso asked, a pout in his voice.

"Good boys who put away their things get special treats," Mylene said, her chin jutting toward the gun.

Tommaso chuckled, reaching for it. "Scolded again. You're right, I should have put it away after cleaning it." He slipped off his stool, lifting the rifle into his hands.

Mylene nodded, satisfied. She lifted the finished tray of tarts. The sun had breached the sky, and the warm light outlined her figure as she crossed in front of the sliding glass door.

The sudden shattering of glass filled Nera's ears. It was a familiar echo of the nightmare she'd told herself to forget. She stared in confusion at the cracks that filled her vision. The tray of tarts fell to the ground, muted shades tumbling among the shards. Mylene's prone figure lay beside them.

Tommaso's shout cleared the daze from Nera's mind as he rushed to Mylene's side.

Nera shoved free from the island just before a flurry of bullets followed the first one through the broken glass.

"Get down! Get down!" Tommaso shouted, hauling Mylene to the opposite side of the kitchen and out of range of the sliding glass door.

Nera's arm protested when she dropped, but she ignored it, trying to squint through the brightness so she could see better.

"Oh, God, she's bleeding." Tommaso's voice broke, but he released Mylene to lift the rifle, his eyes intent on the sunlight streaming into the kitchen.

"Only glass, *mon grand*," Mylene said, lifting herself on shaky arms. "Don't worry about me."

"I'll always worry." Tommaso's gaze flicked toward where Nera lay prone. "Mylene, get out of the kitchen, but stay down."

Mylene scrambled for the entryway beside her.

Nera couldn't do the same. A bright path of light filled the space between where she huddled against the kitchen counters and the rest of the house. The light was broken by the kitchen island, but filled the tiled floor on both sides.

The shooting had stopped, suspended as if the gunmen were waiting.

"This shouldn't be. Giovanni is never here," Tommaso muttered as he crab-walked across the glass to get closer to the shattered door.

Nera listened to her heartbeat amid the continued silence.

Tommaso eased as close to the open space as he dared. His eyes were steady on Nera's. "I'm going to draw their fire. Use the island for cover as much as you can."

Without giving her time to protest, he faced out of the broken glass and began to shoot.

Nera scrambled for the island. The gunshots sounded so much louder coming from so close. She didn't hesitate but threw herself into the brighter shine on the other side and then past it.

Tommaso jerked back from the returning fire. "Good girl. Now, go find Mylene." He was no longer looking at her.

The kitchen knife Mylene had used to slice up the fruit had skidded into the entryway. Nera's hand closed around the hilt as she moved into the living area. It felt awkward in her nondominant hand, but familiar.

She found Mylene behind the sofa, her eyes trained on the front hallway. The doorknob there rattled, though the sound was muffled when more gunfire came from the kitchen.

Mylene grabbed Nera's uninjured arm. "We must hide, ma choupette." She tried to pull Nera with her as she darted toward the hallway, but her hand was slick with blood from her cuts, and she lost her grip.

Gunshots came from the front door, so much closer than the kitchen.

Nera threw herself back behind the sofa as she watched Mylene scramble out of sight behind the wall. Plaster flew off as a bullet slammed into the space where Mylene had been seconds before.

Nera closed her eyes as she pressed back against the hard column of the sofa's back. With the brightness dimmed, she could hear the footfalls of the intruder crossing the wooden floor. There was no time to think. They fell as close as she dared to let them get, and then she lunged up with a shout, her eyes opening again as she swung the kitchen knife.

The blade sank into the intruder's neck. He choked before he fell, and Nera found the sound somehow satisfying.

Behind the first intruder, another raised his gun.

The man she'd injured had taken her knife with him. Nera tried to throw herself back, even though she knew that the squeeze of his finger would likely be faster.

A gunshot rang out. Nera felt no pain. Instead, shadowed liquid splattered on her, and the second intruder's eyes went blank before he fell forward.

Behind him, a flash of red drew her gaze. Giovanni stared down at the man he'd shot as he stalked across the living room. His attention flicked to the other intruder, the one still gurgling around her kitchen knife, and he shot him in the head.

Nera didn't look at the two dead bodies. She couldn't look away from Giovanni's face. In all the visits he'd made to their bakery, he'd only ever looked calm. Sometimes, his lips would tilt into the most delicate of smiles, but usually his stoic mask was in place, holding a seriousness that Nera had associated with God's angels.

Now, his nostrils flared and his jaw tightened as he continued to point his gun, as if he wanted to shoot the dead men again.

"Are those the only ones inside?" Giovanni asked, his gaze scanning the room.

"Yes," Nera said.

Blood had run down one of the intruder's necks, coating his shirt beneath where she'd stabbed him. Nera knew it was blood, but the color was only a dark shadow.

Only Giovanni brought color into her life. The red of him helped to soothe her.

"And you're not hurt?" Giovanni's eyes dropped to her sling, and his eyes darkened. "Or hurt worse?"

A renewed flurry of bullets slammed into the kitchen. They both watched them carve into the wooden island from outside.

"I'm fine," Nera said. "Help Tommaso."

Giovanni backed toward the front door. Nera watched him scan the area before he slipped outside again.

She glanced down at the dead men. Crouching, she pulled the kitchen blade free. Then she darted for the hallway, where Mylene waited.

Chapter 7

Giovanni's hand tightened on the handle of his gun. Enzo would have another one to destroy. He tried not to think about what would have happened if he'd arrived a moment later. The time wasted attempting to talk himself out of checking on Nera was the worst kind of mistake. He hadn't brought the Bratva to her that morning. They'd already been there.

He couldn't help remembering the fierce expression Nera had worn as she'd driven the kitchen knife into her attacker's neck.

He paused after he slipped down the side alley, studying the quiet neighborhood along the street. As he'd already determined, no other Bratva moved within the rising dawn at the front of the house.

Gunfire continued toward the back, and he kept his gun raised as he raced through the alley. In the city, few neighborhoods had homes with yards. Nera's parents had chosen one that had an easy commute to the bakery. Or perhaps they had chosen the location of the bakery with their home in mind. They were dead before he'd ever thought to ask. He'd never known where their home was before their deaths.

Shouts reached his ears as he paused at the end of the alley. He didn't understand the words, but he recognized enough of the Russian language to determine they were cussing. Tommaso may not have been a crack shot, but he'd kept them at bay.

Giovanni listened through another round to determine their locations. Only three more besides the pair he had killed. Low numbers for the Bratva. Enzo would be bored by the cleanup this time.

He slipped out of the alleyway, taking out two before they even sensed he was there. Giovanni forced himself to shift his aim on the third, going for the gun arm instead. This time, his family would have answers.

The Bratva shouted and threw himself into the yard to avoid the shot. Giovanni followed. Four shots fired in quick succession, and he rounded the fence in time to watch the Bratva's chest jerk before he fell.

Giovanni swore in frustration.

Crack shot or not, Tommaso hadn't missed a target that close.

The man looked relieved even as his eyes struggled to focus on Giovanni. He slumped over among the broken glass.

The Bratva soldier Tommaso had shot was gasping from the wounds in his chest. Yet again, Giovanni would fail to bring someone home to the family for questioning. He ended the man's gasps with a head shot before rushing toward his friend.

Blood coated the front of Tommaso's shirt, and Giovanni cussed as he dragged out his phone.

"Sorry, Di Salvo," Tommaso muttered. "Should have been better than this."

"Be quiet," Giovanni told him, but there was no snap in the words. No, he just wanted his friend to save his strength. Tommaso may have chosen to no longer be part of the family, but Giovanni would always see him as blood.

"Do you know what fucking time it is?" Antonio grumbled in his ear. A sigh followed the complaint. "How bad is it?"

"A surgeon this time," Giovanni said. He glanced at the sprawled body of the bratok. "And send Enzo."

"He's not going to be happy. Enzo is less of a morning person than I am." Antonio didn't ask where to send him. Giovanni hadn't expected him to. His cousin knew him too well for that.

Giovanni grabbed one of the dish towels that lay crumpled among the glass, shaking the shards off it. "I'm bringing them to the estate. We'll meet the surgeon there."

Through the phone came a worried pause.

"The Bratva were here before me," Giovanni said.

"I'll try to ease your father into the idea," Antonio said. Then he hung up, and there was only silence.

A scream filled it. Mylene threw herself on top of Tommaso, already sobbing.

The man groaned. "I'm alive," he told her shakily, but he didn't shove her aside. His arm shook as he tried to lift it to hold her.

Nera filled the kitchen doorway, staring down at Tommaso.

"Don't move, you idiot man," Mylene reprimanded him, grabbing the towel from Giovanni and pressing it hard against the gunshot wound.

Tommaso groaned. "A little gentler."

"Gentle is not for you," Mylene muttered, applying more pressure as the towel began to soak through. She glared at Giovanni. "You. Do something."

Giovanni glanced at the woman who continued to try to stare him down, then looked back at Tommaso.

Tommaso's eyes struggled to focus. "I heard." His gruff voice shifted into a gasp. "Can't—" He swallowed, his head falling back. "Can't be helped." His eyes closed.

"Tommaso!" Mylene cried. "Don't you dare." The last word came out soft and keening.

Nera moved to a hook above Giovanni's shoulder, grabbing the keys to their bakery van and holding them out. "I'll help carry him."

"Absolutely not!" Mylene said, switching her glare to Nera. "Don't forget that you were also shot."

"I'll take the pain for Tommaso's life." She crouched among the glass.

Giovanni wondered how much pain he would bring her if he remained in her life. He pocketed the keys and gestured for her to move aside. "I'll support his torso." He wished he could say he could warry the man by himself.

When Nera cried out under the weight, Giovanni's body froze in panic, but she bit the inside of her cheek and moved forward.

The leg that the tiny French woman clutched lagged the most. "Move! Move!" she cried to urge them on.

Giovanni took in Tommaso's paling complexion and forced his tense body to continue.

Tommaso had been shot. For Nera, that seemed more unreal than her own injury. With his perpetual smile and his larger-than-life presence, Tommaso often made her forget the reality of death. He seemed too alive to ever die.

"This is his fault," Mylene muttered again. She'd been saying the same thing ever since the surgeon had kicked her out of the room where he was working on Tommaso.

Giovanni didn't deny it. He stood so very still across from them, as if separating himself from the situation.

Nera couldn't find any blame against him within her. She'd been the one to chase after him when he'd left the bakery without a word. She'd been the one to push him out of the way when she'd heard the first sounds of danger. It was her instincts that had caused this.

Instead of the blank face he so often showed the world, the one he wore even now, she kept remembering the fury that had filled it when he'd killed the intruder intent on shooting her. That expression had settled something within her. The maroon halo surrounding him had never been more soothing. Within its glow, not even the memory of the kitchen knife piercing the other man's throat could touch her.

Mylene continued to pace, and Giovanni's gaze scanned the hallway. The Di Salvo estate didn't fit him. Nera had thought that as they'd passed through the ground floor. Despite her angelic fantasy of him when she was younger, she'd come to understand that his pale blond hair and delicately carved features lent him a false persona. Giovanni hadn't been a happy child. She'd expected dark curtains and antique furnishings from his home. Expensive, of course, but more like an old Gothic movie, the kind her mother used to love.

Instead the Di Salvo manor was whitewashed and modern. Maybe white made the bloodstains easier to paint over, but the brightness was already beginning to give Nera a headache.

Which was why she continued to stare at Giovanni. His warm, red aura let some of the brightness fade.

Giovanni stiffened as his gaze latched onto her sling. He stepped forward, his hand hovering so close to her arm that the hair along it raised as if to reach for him. He let it drop to his side without making contact.

"That should be seen to," he said.

Nera frowned at the sling. A numbness had filled her arm, taking away the pain of her earlier effort.

Mylene gasped. "Oh, ma choupette, you've already bled through. I told you not to lift him." She scowled at Giovanni. "If you were more like my Tommaso, this—"

"There are bandages in the room at the end of the hall," Giovanni said.

Mylene bit her lip as her eyes settled on the closed door.

"I can handle it myself," Nera said. "The doctor showed me how."

"Don't be silly." Mylene's gaze dropped to her feet. "Besides, stepping away for a moment won't—" She swallowed, unable to finish her sentence.

"It doesn't hurt," Nera said. "I'd rather do it myself for the practice." She moved past her before Mylene could argue further.

"I'll show you." Giovanni pulled ahead to lead the way.

When Nera glanced back, Mylene was peering after them.

The restroom was even lavish. The open area held a sink and more first aid materials than Nera had seen. If anyone needed that many bandages, they would likely already be dead. The thought made Nera wince.

"Is it painful?" Giovanni asked, pausing in the act of gathering what he thought she might need.

"Not really." Nera slipped the strap of the sling down, laying it on the sink counter before returning to feel for the edge of the bandage. The material not covered in a gray stain flared brighter than anything else, blurring her sight. Anything white made things especially hard for her impaired vision. Her fingers continued to brush over the surface, an uncomfortable feeling filling her as Giovanni watched.

"Let me," he offered, his hand reaching for her.

"I can get it!" Nera snapped, her frustration growing when he flinched away. She knew she was being stubborn, but the damn thing was going to give.

"Do you not want me to touch you?" he asked.

Nera's fingers stopped moving as she stared at him in surprise. His face had that sharp quality that made him even more gorgeous, despite the frown he was wearing.

"Mylene is correct," he said. "I'm the reason—"

"Just do it!" Nera ordered, moving closer to him and turning so he had clearer access to her arm.

Giovanni blinked at her.

His hands lifted. Then his fingers replaced hers on the bandage. Dark splotches of material folded over the bright white as it came undone. She barely felt the warmth of his fingers against her skin before he released her to pick up the new bandages he'd set on the shelf beside them.

When he stared at her revealed injury, the hardness returned to his jaw, and his eyebrows drew together. She still didn't understand why other customers said his eyes were cold. That was the last description she would have used.

He wound the new bandage, careful to keep his fingers over it.

"You're the one who doesn't like to be touched," Nera observed.

Giovanni's eyes met hers again.

Nera didn't wait for him to deny it. "You've always been that way. My father used to scold me about it. Hugs were a thing in my family, and I would clamp onto you all the time. I'm sorry. It wasn't until after your mother passed away and you didn't come around as often that I realized—" She broke off, not wanting to say it. She'd realized she had always bothered him.

Giovanni shook his head as he rebandaged her arm. "I'd never been around someone like you before."

"Oh, come on. Your mother was the warmest person I'd ever met." Nera tried to picture them together, but the image she was searching for didn't rise in her memory. "Come to think of it," she amended, "I don't remember seeing her hug you. That's odd. The way she acted when I did it was one of the reasons I didn't catch on for so long. She would laugh so hard at the face you made."

Giovanni's tight jaw loosened. "My mother enjoyed the way I would get flustered."

Nera laughed. "I've got to admit, that was definitely part of it. I was a little disappointed when you started to get used to it, though I didn't understand why at the time." She reached out, poking his cheek. "You wore such a serious look, even as a child." She jerked her hand back when he froze. "Oh, sorry. There I go, forcing my touch on you again."

Giovanni reached for her hand, pulling it up to his cheek. His skin felt cold under her palm. He quickly released her, but Nera couldn't help cupping his face, her pinky sliding along the underside of his jaw.

"I never hated your touch, Nera. I just shouldn't be the one to touch you."

Her thumb tingled as it shifted down his face toward his lips. "Why?"

"I—"

"Here you two are," a cheerful voice called from the doorway.

Nera's hand fell away. She glanced over her good shoulder.

From what she could make out, the man standing there was more traditionally handsome than Giovanni was. He had wide shoulders that filled out a suit jacket, dark hair brushed back and curling along his ear, and a full smile that Giovanni would never think of wearing. His eyes were a similar tone, and Nera wondered if they were the same cobalt blue.

"This is my cousin, Antonio," Giovanni said. He had continued winding the bandage around her arm as if the moment before his cousin had come in had never happened.

Nera smiled toward the entryway. "Nice to meet you, Antonio. I'd offer my hand, but it's a bit occupied."

"Getting shot will do that to you," Giovanni's cousin agreed. "It's nice to put a face to the name, Nera. Giovanni has talked about you often over the years."

She tried to tamp down the happiness that spurted forth at the idea.

"Antonio is someone I trust," Giovanni said. There was something in his eyes as they stared at her that made her swallow.

"I'll also introduce you to Enzo when he returns. If I'm not available, either Antonio or Enzo will be close by while you're staying here with us." Giovanni finished attaching the bandage to her arm and reached for the sling.

Antonio sighed from the doorway. "You need to explain it better than that, Gio." He turned toward Nera. "What he's trying to say is, what happened at your house this morning... shouldn't have. Until we find some answers, and while Tommaso recovers, you're going to be staying here with us. But while you're here, you'll have either me, Enzo, or your boy here with you. Don't go anywhere without one of us."

Tommaso had talked a bit about his time with the Di Salvos over the years, never in detail, but Nera's stomach twisted as she nodded. "I'll try not to make a nuisance out of myself," she said. She looked up at Giovanni, who seemed worried. She'd only seen him actually look worried one time before, and that—

Her heart started racing as the thought hit a wall. When had she ever seen him worried? Giovanni only ever showed his blank face around the bakery unless something she did coaxed out that hint of a smile.

"It's only a precaution," he reassured her as he adjusted her sling, his fingers staying on the cloth. He stepped away from her when he was done.

"Speaking of, I'll take over here for now. You-know-who wants to see you." Antonio grinned at her when Nera looked toward him.

"I expected that," Giovanni said. Antonio backed out of the doorway to let him pass. Giovanni paused, glancing back at her. "I'll return soon."

"Thank you," Nera called.

The gratitude made him stiffen.

She tapped the strap of her sling. "Not just for the bandage. If you hadn't come this morning..." She swallowed, remembering the shadow of the gun pointed at her. Life was so fragile. How had she forgotten that for so long?

"Don't thank me."

When Nera focused on his face, the doll-like blankness had returned.

"Never thank me," Giovanni said. He stalked out of sight.

"Hey, Gio!" Antonio called after him. He sighed when Giovanni kept walking. "Don't worry about him," he told Nera. "He can be a bit too serious."

"I know," she agreed. That didn't mean she wasn't going to worry. He must be blaming himself for what had happened that morning. Or the other day.

"That's right, you do." Antonio leaned against the doorjamb. "Actually, I've always wanted to meet you. Giovanni never let me go with him to that bakery of yours."

Nera wasn't sure how to take his smile. "He should have. Or at least brought something back for you to try."

"I'm not much for sweets." Antonio's gaze slid over her. It started at her head and went all the way to her feet.

Nera shifted. Antonio was smiling still, but there was a tension in his casually crossed arms.

"Well, look at you," he murmured. "Softer-looking than I expected."

Nera forced her own lips to tilt up. "I think you mean plumper. I'm a baker, after all." Despite the amber of her hair, Nera had never been very fiery. She considered herself average when it came to looks, though her weight pushed her a tad under the edge of that for some people. "I can't imagine what you expected. I doubt Giovanni mentioned me much at all, but it was nice of you to say."

"You doubt it, huh?" Antonio straightened, moving toward her.

Nera forced herself not to step back.

Some of the exuberance faded from his smile, making it seem a bit more genuine. "Thank you for the other day. You saved him again."

"Again?" Nera asked, frowning.

The wattage of his grin moved back up a notch. "Well, it is what it is. Just know, Giovanni is very important to me." He nodded toward her bandaged arm. "That must have hurt."

Nera shook her head. "I don't remember much about it."

He laughed. "That must be a familiar sensation for you."

The edge to his tone made her fingers curl under the sling. "What—"

"Tommaso's surgery is done!" Mylene shouted from the doorway. She paused, studying them for a second, but her excitement shoved away any questions. "Come along. The doctor said we could sit with him."

Antonio sauntered toward the hallway. He paused, tilting his head as he looked back at Nera. "Didn't you want to join her?"

Nera nodded, swallowing her lingering question before she followed him.

Chapter 8

Giovanni didn't expect his father to be alone in his office. Vittore Di Salvo ran the business with a much cooler head than Giovanni Sr. Often over the years, Giovanni's uncle had intervened when his father was in a particular mood.

"What made you bring that damn family here?" Giovanni Sr. had shouted before Giovanni could even close the door.

He left it standing wide open instead. It wasn't like his voice would be the one to carry, and any Di Salvos in the house already knew what his father was like. As usual, the saliva in his mouth turned into a paste, making him swallow his words.

"Your mother and that fucking bakery," his father muttered. "I should have burned it to the ground long ago."

The usual fury rose in Giovanni at the mention of his mother. After what his father had done, he had no right to mention her. His hands clenched into fists at his sides.

His father's gaze raked over his face, and his frown turned into a scowl. "You look so much like her." He stomped toward Giovanni, his hand closing around his son's throat as he shoved him into the wall. "Is that what this is? Are you betraying me like her?"

Giovanni stared into his father's wide, paranoid eyes, knowing that they were exactly what his mother had seen before she died.

His father continued to squeeze. "That Tommaso—"

"Was shot in the chest and has yet to wake up," Vittore said as he walked through the door. "Really, brother. Release him."

Air returned to his lungs after his father did as he was told. Giovanni struggled to withhold the cough scratching against his windpipe for release as he remained against the wall a moment longer.

Vittore studied him before focusing on his father. "Just like I told you when he left the family, Tommaso is harmless."

"He's lucky he's not dead. Leaving the family, death is what he deserved." Giovanni Sr. stalked to his desk before whirling around, his energy turning into pacing. His glare returned to his son. "And you! I'm relieved your cock works, but your piece of ass has no business being here."

Giovanni flushed. "That's not—"

"She's like a daughter to Tommaso," Vittore said. He gestured at Giovanni. "Besides, she had a hand in keeping a bullet out of your son. That loyalty deserves an answer."

"They're not family," his father said.

"True." Vittore's quick agreement mollified Giovanni Sr. somewhat. He moved behind his desk, settling there with a grunt, and Vittore's posture relaxed. "Let them stay just until Tommaso recovers."

"Fine. We'll do as you say, Vittore." Giovanni Sr. then addressed his son without looking at him. "Get out."

Giovanni opened his mouth to raise his additional concerns, but a tilt of his uncle's head had him swallowing them instead. He followed Vittore into the hallway, where his uncle closed the door.

"Let's talk," Vittore said, leading him down the corridor to his own office.

The last of Giovanni's tension settled as the door clicked shut behind them. "Have you heard from Enzo?" he asked

"I want to hear from you," Vittore said, settling behind his own desk. Unlike Giovanni's father, his uncle better fit an office setting.

Giovanni laid out what he'd seen when he'd arrived at the Carmen home. He frowned as he finished. "I meant to leave the last one alive. The Bratva hadn't followed me."

"Their movements raise some questions. Even targeting you." Vittore winced after the words, his eyes darting away from Giovanni.

"There'd be no point," Giovanni agreed. "They learned that lesson years ago."

Vittore nodded, his hands folding in front of him. "The timing is odd. We were about to make a profitable venture with the Bratva. Money usually smooths the way. It doesn't draw this type of response. If it even is a response." He frowned again. "I'm beginning to wonder if you were the target yesterday. Could Tommaso have...?" He raised an eyebrow as he let the question linger.

Giovanni shook his head. There was no way Tommaso would have risked the Russians' attention, not while Mylene and Nera were in his life.

Vittore sighed. "It's almost as if the Bratva are targeting that girl. And you're certain she remembers nothing?"

Giovanni nodded. He'd been relieved when the trauma had taken Nera's memories so long ago. No child should have to remember that. "If she did, I don't see the risk in it." During the kidnapping, they'd both been held in an empty church, and Giovanni had kept the Bratva's attention from her as much as he'd been able to.

"We need more information." Vittore's lips pressed together as he stared at Giovanni.

Giovanni's stomach sank, but he knew what was expected of him. "I'll handle it."

"Take Enzo or Antonio with you," Vittore said.

It was another reminder that Giovanni hadn't earned the regard of the family. He didn't argue, though. He turned to leave.

"And, Giovanni?" Vittore called.

He paused at the door.

"I've disagreed with your father on most things lately, but he's right about that girl," Vittore warned. "I know you have a soft spot for her, but she's not family."

Giovanni nodded to let his uncle know he had heard. Vittore didn't call him back again, and he let the door close behind him.

Nera would never be a Di Salvo, and that was a good thing. Giovanni had already ruined her life enough.

Nera leaned against the headboard of the large guest bed, her eyes closed. She'd clicked off the bedroom lights long before. The later the day had grown, the more her arm had ached.

She'd forgotten the pain medication the doctor had prescribed. It likely still sat on the stand beside her bed at home. When they'd talked to the doctor earlier, she hadn't wanted to take the attention away from Tommaso's update. He still hadn't opened his eyes by the time Mylene had told her to go get some rest.

That was when Antonio had led her to the guest bedroom. Nera hadn't seen Giovanni since he'd changed her bandage. Not that she'd expected him to be at her side, but the fact that Antonio had remained had made her less than comfortable. Giovanni's cousin wasn't like him much at all. It seemed like there wasn't a silence Antonio wouldn't fill.

The Di Salvo estate was quiet outside of that, especially at night. No sounds drifted to her in the guest bedroom, and the silence made her racing thoughts even louder. No matter how hard she searched her memory, she couldn't remember when she'd seen Giovanni look worried.

Instead, her interrupted nightmare kept replaying in her mind. When the shots filled her ears yet again, she flinched against the headboard. Her tension made the ache in her arm flare hotter. For some reason, after she heard the dream's shots, she pictured Tommaso lying among the shattered glass in the kitchen.

The doctor said he would be all right, even though he hadn't woken up. His body needed rest to recover.

Nera slipped off the bed. She'd never pulled the sheets back, and besides a couple of wrinkles in the top comforter, there was no evidence that she'd even been there.

Nera had the feeling that was what her stay at the Di Salvo estate would be like.

If she had been home, she would have made herself some milk tea in the kitchen to help her sleep. She padded barefoot to the door, but hesitated with her hand on the handle. She didn't know where the kitchen was, and wandering among the Di Salvos could lead to trouble. In fact, she wouldn't be surprised if they had locked her inside the room.

The thought of that had her pushing down on the handle, but it turned without issue. She slid open the door.

Soothing maroon filled her vision. Nera blinked as she stared down at where Giovanni sat in the hallway, opposite her door. He looked back up at her. His brow wrinkled, and she waited, but the lecture she deserved didn't follow.

Of course it didn't. Giovanni wouldn't lecture her.

Nera crossed the hallway and lowered herself beside him. She'd moved a little too close, but the warmth of his arm pressing against hers eased the continued ache into a steady hum.

The hallway walls were still a bright white, and with nighttime falling, the hall sconces only seemed brighter. Nera's head turned toward Giovanni so that his red could dim the brightness around them.

She wanted to ask why he wasn't sleeping, but the steady silence between them added to her comfort. She wanted to make his presence outside of her door into more. Even as a child, she had never seen him as an older brother. She'd clung to him, hoping he'd finally accept her affection. He'd never looked at her romantically in return, though, and after his mother died, besides taking his hand that one time, any touching between them had stopped.

No, Giovanni wasn't out there, pining for her like she wished. He'd said it earlier. He only trusted two others.

Nera belatedly remembered that Antonio had asked her not to go anywhere without him, Giovanni, or some person named Enzo, whom she hadn't met yet. It hadn't been Giovanni who had asked, but he'd stood there as he'd said it, and she'd gotten the impression that Antonio was speaking for him. Guilt pinched at her chest. "Sorry. I was going to look for the kitchen. I couldn't sleep, but I thought a warm drink..." She trailed off, realizing she was making excuses.

Giovanni rose to his feet beside her. When he held out his hand, Nera hesitated, then reached up to take it. He helped her to her feet and led her away from the guest bedroom.

The kitchen was on the ground floor toward the rear of the house. It was larger than even her professional kitchen at home. Instead of the soothing black of the appliances she was used to, the bright metal ones at the Di Salvos' gleamed.

Giovanni crossed to the far cupboard, pulling down packets of tea before bending to fish out a tea kettle.

"I'll make it," Nera said, gripping the handle over his hand.

Giovanni paused before letting go. He moved to the kitchen island, leaning against it. The thing was huge. Eight chefs could work shoulder to shoulder and never brush against each other.

Nera could feel him watching her as she moved to the sink to fill the kettle. She didn't hate it.

She moved to the tea packets he'd laid out on the counter. Giovanni hadn't turned on the overhead light when they'd entered the kitchen, which she was grateful for. Even if he had, she would have struggled to read the labels. The brightness of her vision made words blur. The child who had once begged her momma to read to her was long gone. Not that her mother had been around to answer the call after the accident had impaired her vision.

"The right one is chamomile," Giovanni said. "The left, Earl Grey."

She pulled out one of each, moving back to the stove to wait.

"There you are," a voice said from the kitchen doorway.

Nera followed the newcomer's progress with her eyes. He was older than Giovanni, but didn't look as much like a Di Salvo either. His skin and hair were dark enough, but the latter was cropped close to his head, not a wavy cap like Antonio's. The man's chest was broad under the T-shirt, but paired with jeans, his clothes looked nothing like the suits the rest of the family preferred. Tattoos covered his arms and even the knuckles of the hand he held out to Giovanni.

"You've got another one for me, I assume," the man said.

Giovanni pulled a gun from his waistband. The memory of the last time she'd seen it made Nera's breath catch in her throat. She was more than grateful that Giovanni had shown up at her house armed, but after her earlier attempt, she knew not to try to thank him again.

She watched as Giovanni's handgun was exchanged for a new one that he tucked away.

The kettle reminded her of its presence with a shrill whistle, and Nera lifted it off the burner.

She crossed to grab a new tea packet and a third mug, pouring the hot water over the bags to steep. "Do either of you like milk in your tea?" she asked.

"Sure, doll, we both do," the man said. He was smiling at her when she returned from the fridge with the carton. "It's been quite a while since anyone's made milk tea in this kitchen, hasn't it, Gio?"

Giovanni's lips tightened before he nodded. "Nera, this is my uncle, Enzo Di Salvo."

"It's nice to meet you," Nera said over her shoulder as she stared down at the mug. With the sling on her other arm, she could only carry one.

"Likewise," Enzo said from behind her.

Giovanni crossed to her and took his mug, reaching out for his uncle's as well. "Thank you," he murmured.

Nera let her own mug warm her hands, focusing on that instead of the tingles from the slight brush of Giovanni's touch. She was being ridiculous. They weren't alone in the kitchen anymore, but still her heart thumped when he came close.

Not like it had when she'd chased after him at the bakery, but pretty close.

When she felt like she had her expression under control, she turned to face them, sipping at her tea.

To her surprise, Enzo had drained his own mug. "Thanks, doll," he said, setting it on the top of the island. He set a plastic bottle down beside it. "These are hers," he said to Giovanni. And then he was gone.

Giovanni frowned down at the pill bottle before setting his mug down. He opened the bottle and shook one of the giant pills out before crossing to her and holding it out on the palm of his hand.

Nera couldn't grab it with her hand full. Instead she opened her mouth and waited.

Giovanni stared at her lips. The way his eyes narrowed in thought made her pulse speed up. He relented, popping the pill in her mouth with only the slightest brush against her bottom lip.

Nera let the lift of her mug hide the shiver that ran through her. She chased the pill down her throat with most of her tea.

Silence fell between them again as they finished the warm drinks. Giovanni rinsed out the mugs, putting them on the rack to dry before leading her back to the guest room.

The brightness of the hallway blurred as a sleepy comfort enveloped her. Her footsteps became shorter, as if to draw out the time before she'd have to say good night.

Giovanni pushed open the bedroom door, scanning the inside. He stepped back, nodding at her to enter. "Sleep well," he murmured when she passed.

Nera nodded, knowing from the heaviness in her limbs that she would. She closed the door between them and soon fell into a deep and dreamless sleep.

Chapter 9

Tires screeched as a car jerked to the side of the street beside Giovanni, and three Bratva piled out. Giovanni fumbled to free the gun that Enzo had given him for his fifteenth birthday from his waistband, but the men were already on him.

"Giovanni!" Nera screamed. The voice of the adult he'd tried to stay away from mingled with that of the child, whose hero worship had seemed like a flash of warmth in an otherwise valueless existence.

It was the child's arms that shoved at him, pushing him away from his attackers. He heard her father call for her. His father would want him to save himself. A Di Salvo's life was worth all three of the lives before him. Antonio would have agreed.

But Nera had saved him from his fate in that moment.

He could have run.

Instead, Giovanni watched as the Bratva shot both of her parents. First her father, who had seemed larger than Giovanni's own, larger than life itself. When Nera's father lectured him, it was to build him up, not to tear him down, which he had struggled to understand until long after their deaths.

Then her mother, who screamed as the glass window of the bakery shattered. She lay still among the shards.

The young Nera cried out as one of the Bratva slugged her in the face. She fell to the sidewalk, and a different attacker drew his leg back for a kick.

Giovanni threw himself between them. He still didn't have any bulk as an adult, but his arms were the extra spindly ones of his teenaged self as he wrapped them around the young girl who had mistakenly called him an angel when she'd first seen him. "Don't hurt her!" he snarled as he absorbed the kick. More blows followed, and Giovanni grunted as a wave of panic washed over him. His body curled around her more tightly, protecting her even as he jerked with every blow.

Ever since he'd watched his father murder his mother, he'd often wondered if he'd share her fate. He had no intention of betraying the Di Salvo family, but neither had his mother. With a man like his father, there were no second chances.

A part of him had wished it was already over. Had always wished for that, ever since his father had first raged at him as a boy. While his mother was alive, he'd been biding his time. It was somehow freeing to admit he didn't want to be alive after she was gone.

He'd begun putting himself into situations that might lead to the death he craved. Often it was with the other Di Salvos, who inflicted pain but knew better than to cross a certain line. It was already clear that Giovanni Sr. didn't care for his namesake, but the boss of the Di Salvo family was a confusing man to understand, and no one wanted to cross him by killing his son.

It wasn't until he'd picked a fight with the Bratva that he edged closer to his goal.

But in that moment, with the warmth of Nera tucked against him, his to protect, things changed. Giovanni had a very clear understanding of what it meant to have something to live for.

He'd always hated his body, which was all arms and legs and edges instead of muscle and strength like the other men in his family. Comparison didn't matter anymore. All that mattered was making sure Nera survived. Even dazed and wounded, he'd used that pathetic body to shield her when the Bratva hauled them away together.

She didn't make it easy. Unlike him, Nera didn't quietly watch things progress in the church and wait for an opening. No, she was a force intent on making an opening all by herself. Not for her own escape. More than once she'd thrown herself at the Bratva, yelling at Giovanni to run.

It wasn't that Nera had a death wish. No, she just only ever had eyes for him.

The church's pulpit had a hollowed-out space underneath. Giovanni had often shoved her small body there and hovered over her. The Bratva would let out their rage until his own body was numb. When he could manage to say anything between blows, he would stare into Nera's eyes and whisper that things were going to be fine.

After the Bratva tired of their beatings, he'd rest with his shoulder against the podium and stare at the broken stained glass window that took up most of the upper wall above the pulpit. The image was more red than any other color, depicting the blood of Christ flowing for his people.

Nera would curl up against him, saying she was sorry over and over again. Giovanni got used to hearing an apology from her, but he never needed it.

Everything Nera attempted to do was to save him.

Giovanni himself was biding time. If the Bratva had wanted to kill him, they would have done it. No, they were trying to use him against his father, as if even the enemy understood how weak of a link he was.

Despite never feeling like he fit in, Giovanni was a Di Salvo. An injury against one was an injury against them all. He expected them to come for him. Likely it would be Enzo, who cleaned up all the messes. That was what Giovanni was, but he no longer cared—so long as Nera was saved.

But he'd underestimated how fed up with him his father had become. When the Bratvas returned the last time, their intentions were different. Their plan had failed. The Di Salvo boss wouldn't negotiate for his ransom.

Giovanni had begun to see himself as Nera's savior. Oh, he still knew he wasn't strong, but perhaps he had enough tenacity to pull her through the hell she'd rushed into.

The way they threw him like a rag doll in the end underlined how lenient they'd been when they intended to keep him alive. A Bratva lifted his gun, pointing it at Giovanni, where he lay curled against the ground, struggling to pull air into his lungs.

Nera had lunged at the bratok.

Giovanni could do nothing to stop it. He assumed she was throwing herself between them to take the bullet meant for him. If she had, then every single beating he'd endured had been as pointless as every other moment in his life.

Instead, her teeth sank into the bratok's wrist above where he held the gun.

The gun jerked up, and the shot went wild, shattering the glass above them.

The bratok she'd bitten shoved her free, and then they scrambled off the pulpit to avoid the falling glass.

Giovanni forced his body to move toward Nera, covering as much of her as he could.

He didn't realize that Nera would stare up at the falling glass in confusion. It was the last view filled with color she would see.

Her scream carved out the glimmer of purpose that had started to grow inside him.

Now, so many years later, Giovanni jerked against the sweaty, strangling sheets of his bed, her scream still ringing in his ears. His pulse thrummed as he remembered the blood that had run out of her eyes.

He'd killed all three Bratva that day. In his fury, what had seemed impossible had turned out to be rather simple. The large piece of glass he'd used had cut deep grooves into his hand, but it had ended them quickly enough.

Giovanni stared down at that hand, running his finger over the puckered scar.

He'd broken the Di Salvo code and rushed Nera to the hospital. It hadn't mattered. The damage was done.

Giovanni shoved free of the sheets and slipped out of bed despite having only crawled into it a few hours before. It wouldn't be his first night with little sleep.

The gun range was empty as usual. On the rare occasion Enzo would use it, but his uncle had taken over Giovanni's place outside of the guest bedroom.

Company was the last thing Giovanni wanted. He let loose shot after shot. The close clusters he made slowed his pulse, but there wasn't any number of shots that would allow the memory of her scream to fully dissipate.

When Nera opened the guest bedroom door, no color waited for her in the hallway. Instead, Enzo leaned against the wall, his arms crossed.

As she continued to stare at him, he chuckled.

"Disappointed?" he asked.

Nera looked away as warmth crept up her neck, but she shook her head. "Just surprised. You were up pretty late last night."

"So were you, but here you are, at the butt crack of dawn." He pushed off the wall, lifting an eyebrow as she continued to stare. "Don't worry, I know I'm not as good-looking as my nephews."

"That's not—" Nera swallowed the protest. Enzo Di Salvo wasn't as soothing to look at as Giovanni, but he also wasn't as bright and glaring as a lot of the people she'd come across. Maybe it was because he was wearing all black again. A long-sleeved T-shirt covered his inked arms, disappointing her. She would have enjoyed studying the tattoos. Not many people in her life had them. Tommaso had always said he had a thing against needles.

"Don't go falling for me or anything," Enzo said with a grin. He waved her along. "Want to check on Tommaso, I take it?"

"Yes, please," Nera said. He'd already decided he was right, and she jogged after him to catch up.

Tommaso had been carried to a room on the first floor the day before and hadn't been moved since. Even in the early hours of dawn, it seemed like the estate was crawling with Di Salvos. Nera nodded to those she passed as she followed Enzo, though it wasn't like she recognized any faces. It felt rude to ignore them, though they didn't feel the same.

The door to Tommaso's room was closed. Enzo ignored it, taking the same stance as he had outside her room. Nera reached for the handle, but the sounds from within reached her first.

Mylene was crying, full, gut-quaking sobs that made Nera's own stomach clench. That must mean Tommaso hadn't woken up yet. There was no way to mistake those kinds of sobs as happy tears.

She pushed her way inside, hurrying to where Mylene had collapsed on the floor and throwing her good arm around her.

Mylene clung to her, a little too tightly. Nera ignored the discomfort, guilt filling her for leaving the woman who had become like a mother to her alone the night before.

"I'm sorry," Nera murmured against her hair.

Mylene choked on her next sob. She pulled away, digging the heels of her hands into her puffy eyes. "Silly girl. I told you to go."

"But—"

"You know me, ma choupette. I'm emotional at all times." Mylene sighed as she leaned against the wall under the window. The rising sun made it impossible to read her face. "I thought he'd be awake by now, that's all. I was planning to yell at him good, but the energy released from me in another way."

"Yell at him?" Nera repeated. Her gaze found the bed, but all she saw from her angle on the floor was Tommaso's big hand. She'd never seen it so still. "Are you angry with him?"

"Well, of course!" Mylene shoved to her feet. Her hands gestured to the hallway, making Nera realize she hadn't closed the door. "Just look where we are! Tommaso promised me this was in his past."

Enzo lifted an eyebrow as he stared in at them.

Nera blinked at Mylene. "Giovanni is only trying to help."

"You see so little." To Nera's surprise, Mylene stalked to the bed and slapped at Tommaso's leg under the covers. "This man! The Russians were at our house long before that Di Salvo showed up. And him running out of the bakery with that gun the day before." She smacked the resting man again. "I am not so stupid."

Nera reached out and caught Mylene's arm before she could hit him again. "Don't! He was shot in the chest, Mylene." Renewed concern filled Nera when he continued to lie so still, despite the abuse.

The anger drained from the French woman. She stared at the bed. "That too. Oh, you idiot man!" She sank down on the edge of the bed and started to cry again.

Mylene had worn her emotions on her sleeve for as long as Nera had known her. As a young girl, she'd never seen anyone get so angry at Tommaso. She'd been upset by it at first and had told him he should send the patisserie chef away. Tommaso had laughed and ruffled her hair, saying he enjoyed a woman like that. Then he had riled Mylene even more.

Nera rubbed Mylene's back as she let her cry.

The window had brightened by the time Mylene wiped at her eyes. "I'm tired," she said. "It's difficult to rest, knowing how many people are about."

Nera let her have the excuse. "You didn't eat yesterday. Do you think you could, if I brought you something?"

"Don't forget, you're injured yourself, ma choupette." Mylene sighed. "Besides, I doubt the Di Salvos will let you near their kitchen."

Nera didn't bother arguing with her. "Well, I'm hungry." It wasn't a lie. Nera was as guilty as Mylene when it came to not touching the dinner tray Antonio had brought them the night before. "I'll see what I can find." She straightened away from her, refusing to admit she couldn't watch Tommaso lie there a second longer. It was as if she was watching every rise of his chest to make sure he breathed.

Mylene said nothing else as she frowned down at the man she loved. Nera pulled the door closed behind her.

Enzo led the way to the kitchen, not hiding the fact that he'd eavesdropped at all. Not that Nera had been quiet. He snapped on the overhead lights as they entered, which gleamed off the metallic appliances and light-colored stone counters. Nera squinted, willing her eyes to adjust faster.

"The Di Salvos have a cook. I can send someone to bring him in early if you're really hungry." Enzo glanced at her face.

Nera shook her head, moving toward the pantry that had held the tea the night before. "Do you like coffee, Enzo?"

"Who doesn't?" He hopped up to sit on the kitchen island.

The pantry was well stocked. Nera began taking out the things that she would need.

"You know, the Di Salvos aren't normally up this early in the day. Except maybe Giovanni."

Nera filed that bit of information away, though it didn't surprise her. Giovanni had often come to the bakery early in the morning. She hoped he was sleeping in, though; he'd been up late into the night.

Before long, she had more than the fixings for coffee spread out on the kitchen island. It had taken her more trips than usual since she only had one good hand.

Enzo lifted an eyebrow. "All that for coffee?"

"You know I own a bakery, don't you?" Nera laughed when he made a face. "Come on, be my spare hand. Despite what you've said, I saw quite a few Di Salvos already up, and the least I can do is make them breakfast."

"Oh, I'm not one for the kitchen," Enzo said, for the first time since she'd met him wearing a frown. He shifted uncomfortably on the kitchen island.

Nera laughed, but didn't push him. She wondered what it was Enzo did for the Di Salvos, since he'd been the one to bring her a suitcase of clothes from her house. The packet of ground coffee she'd found was a struggle to open. She'd looked in every cabinet, but hadn't found a coffee grinder hidden away anywhere. That didn't seem right. Coffee didn't taste quite the same unless the beans were ground fresh. She wondered if she could ask Giovanni for one, but for the time being, she gave in and used the fingers of her injured hand to try to pry apart the little plastic bag. The sudden flash of pain forced her to pause and breathe through it.

Enzo cursed and jumped to his feet. He crossed to her. "Give me that."

Nera smiled in thanks and handed over the packet. She made him coffee first, lifting an eyebrow when he admitted to liking his with a lot of cream but no sugar and filing away the information. Before her accident, one of the joys she'd had at the bakery was linking a face to an order. The customers had appreciated when she'd brought them something before they even asked. Recognition became harder, though, when so much blurred together in the brightness of her vision afterward.

Despite asking for help, Nera wasn't used to giving orders in the kitchen. Mylene would know what she needed after merely a glance. Enzo sighed again as he reached over her shoulder to help hold the bowl still for mixing.

"Just use me, doll," he said, pressing a finger to the side of the sling. "No more moving this. That face you make when you do upsets me."

"Sorry," Nera murmured as she let that arm rest against her side again.

Enzo cleared his throat. "None of that." He took the whisk from her to finish the mixing himself. When the batter ran smooth, he tapped it against the side of the bowl. "What's next?"

Nera talked through what she was doing. It wasn't exactly directions, but Enzo followed along easily enough. Speaking aloud that much reminded Nera of when she'd been a child and everything she'd thought had come out of her mouth.

Soon the kitchen filled with the scent of freshly baked bread.

"Wrapped around her finger already, Enzo?"

Nera recognized the tone, but the brightness of the kitchen prevented her from seeing Antonio's face. She imagined a sneer, not that he'd readily show it. No, he'd be wearing that smile that was a bit too hard and that never reached his voice.

Enzo didn't appear put out by the accusation. "Her arm's no good."

"Which is why she's supposed to be in her room resting. Whiling away the hours in the Di Salvos' good graces." Antonio sauntered into the kitchen to stare down at the offerings she'd made.

Nera had always been terrible at letting time pass without being productive. It had gotten worse after the accident. It wasn't like she could read, and even watching TV often gave her a headache. Doing something with her hands, especially something she could accomplish with her eyes closed, was best. She opened her mouth to tell Giovanni's cousin that, but then thought better of it.

Antonio reached out for a cooling croissant.

"Not that one!" Nera rushed over to the other batch, shifting one of the cheese-crusted ones onto a napkin and holding it out to him. "You said you didn't like things sweet, so this one will be better." She was close enough to see a quick flash of surprise cross his face before he took it from her.

"You made these for me?" Antonio asked, for once showing the more natural scowl she'd kept picturing when he'd hovered around her the day before.

Nera blinked at him, deciding not to admit that she'd had him in mind. "A lot of people prefer savory over sweet," she said instead, glad when the last buzz of the oven sounded, giving her an excuse to move away. She opened the oven with one hand, but Enzo beat her to the waiting oven mitt. She steered him to put the smallest batch on the closest counter, away from the others.

"I came looking for Giovanni," Antonio said, but he was speaking to Enzo.

"Sent him to sleep," Enzo said with a shrug.

Antonio shook his head, finishing the last bite of his cheese croissant. "His room was empty. I should have known where to go first." His hand curled around the empty napkin. "Not sure why I thought he'd be with her," he muttered before heading toward the door.

The disdain in his words made Nera's throat feel tight. He was gone before she could ask him to take Giovanni's croissants with him. She stared at the small batch of chocolate-filled ones before nodding to the others.

"Think the Di Salvos will eat what I baked?" she asked Enzo.

He grinned. "Come on if you're coming," he called, and a swarm of men filled the kitchen.

Nera's cheeks heated at the thought of so many watching her struggle to cook. Soon most of her offerings were gone. Most of the Di Salvos ignored her, though some nodded and thanked her on the way out.

Nera plated a mixture of what was left to take to Mylene, including the *pain au chocolat*. One she put on a separate plate. Giovanni never ate more than one of anything, no matter how much he liked it. She stared at the lone plate, wondering if Enzo also knew where Giovanni was.

"That for Giovanni?" Enzo asked, seeing right through her.

Nera nodded.

Enzo grinned. "Bring it then."

She grabbed the single plate, but didn't have the extra hand to pick up Mylene's. Her happiness dimmed. She was an idiot. Here she was, giddy over the thought of seeing Giovanni Di Salvo while Tommaso still hadn't woken up.

"Hurry it up, doll," Enzo said from the doorway.

Nera followed after him. Being happy or sad wouldn't do anything to change Tommaso's recovery, and he'd always told her to smile.

Enzo was talking to an older Di Salvo, one who was still finishing his croissant in the hallway. "Take that plate to Tommaso's lady. And no snacking on it."

The older Di Salvo laughed, and Nera recognized one of the few that had thanked her. "No promises. These were good," he said, nodding her way before moving past them into the kitchen.

The greatest joy in life was someone enjoying her food, and the last of Nera's confusion slipped away.

Enzo surprised her by leading the way down a set of stairs she hadn't seen along the hall. At the bottom, outside of a thick door, the muffled sound of gunshots came through, and Nera's pulse jumped. Enzo pulled open the heavy door when the shots paused. "Come on, while he's reloading," he said, gesturing for her to go inside. He followed her into the gun range, startling her when he called over her shoulder, "Take a break, crack shot!"

"I'm not in the mood, Enzo," Giovanni said, and Nera heard the scrape of metal before he paused. "Wait, why aren't—" He moved out of the cubby he'd been standing in, his words stopping when he saw her.

Nera stared back at him. Like usual, the maroon around him made his face clearer. His creased brow cleared as his expression went from irritation to surprise before returning to the steady blankness she was used to. The absence of his slight smile disappointed her, and she kicked herself for expecting it. Of course he was irritated. They'd interrupted him.

"See, I wasn't shirking," Enzo said. He stretched his arms over his head, letting out an exaggerated yawn. "But if you're not going to bother sleeping, I'm tagging you in. One of us might as well be rested for later."

Then he slipped out the door, leaving them alone.

Chapter 10

Giovanni set his gun down on the shelf in the range. Seeing the grown-up version of Nera was disconcerting when the child version had taken up much of his thoughts so recently. Target practice hadn't soothed his anger, and Antonio's visit hadn't helped his mood.

He moved out of the firing lane. The sight of her holding a plate of something she'd obviously baked added to his frustration. "You shouldn't push yourself."

Nera glanced down at the croissant. "Enzo did most of the work." She held it out toward him.

Giovanni decided that the lingering scent of gunpowder was a fitting taste to accompany what she had made, and he took the plate.

The fingers on Nera's injured side curled under the edge of the sling. There was a paleness to her face that worried him. The Nera he knew never liked to sit still, and a gunshot wound wouldn't stop that.

There were no chairs in the small gun range. That had never bothered Giovanni before, but now he needed a place where Nera could rest. He gestured to the far wall. "Sit with me?" he asked. There was one other thing he was sure of: Nera would never give up an opportunity to be by his side.

He helped her settle against the wall before joining her. The chocolate croissant was delicious, not that he'd expected anything less. Nera's skills had outshone her parents' before they'd died. With the arrival of the French pastry chef Giovanni had found to help, she'd only broadened her knowledge.

Nera knew his habits better than most. She'd brought a knife and fork. Giovanni hated eating anything by hand, even the things that were made for that. He felt Nera's eyes on him as he ate. She stared at his face, not trying to hide it. He wondered if she was thinking he was beautiful again. He hated that term, but he had to admit, with his high cheekbones, delicate brows, thick eyelashes, and silky, blond hair, handsome had never quite fit. His looks had led to a lot of his beatings as a teenager, but there was something in Nera's gaze that suggested the word "beautiful" was kind, not a punishment.

After he'd failed to protect her, that particular expression on her face was especially painful to look at.

"Both Enzo and Antonio were certain you'd be here." Nera finally looked away to scan the space around them. Her pupils contracted, and she lifted a hand to block some of the overhead lighting. "Do you practice shooting that often?"

Giovanni nodded as he took in the comforting familiarity of the indoor range. He wasn't surprised they'd known where he'd be. Target practice normally soothed him, though it hadn't this morning. Enzo liked to tease him, but he was glad he spent so much time there. Otherwise, the attacks by the Bratva might have ended differently.

"Tommaso took me to a range a few times. He wanted me familiar with the guns in the house, but he would never let me shoot." Nera closed her eyes, laying her head against the wall. "I guess, with my eyesight, he thought it was pretty pointless."

"You're not blind, Nera," Giovanni said. The specialists he had brought in had once called that fact a miracle after they'd tested the extent of her damage.

"No, I'm not." Her eyes remained shut, and her brows drew together as she frowned. "I often wonder if full blindness would have been easier. The way I see now, the brightness of it..." She opened her eyes. "It can be painful. I get a lot of headaches."

Tommaso had told him of her headaches. His stomach dropped at the reminder.

Nera's head turned toward him. "But every time I started wishing I was blind, you'd show up at the bakery." Her hand reached out, the fingers whispering along the skin of his cheek. He would have wondered if she'd touched him at all if tingles hadn't spread in their wake. "And I'd change my mind after you came. I would never give up being able to see you."

Giovanni's chest squeezed. It was painful, the sweetest of aches. He hated himself for it.

"Did you know I was supposed to fly to Paris today?" Nera's eyes traced his face. "I'd be lying if I said leaving didn't worry me. Without those brief glimpses of you, would I—" She swallowed the words, and her gaze met his.

Giovanni stared back. Even with how much he'd restricted himself over the years, he hadn't been able to stop going to the bakery altogether. The thought that she'd been waiting to see him every day shredded the rest of his resolve.

Her eyes dropped to his lips. "I had one other regret over leaving."

Nera had always been spontaneous, so it shouldn't have surprised him when she leaned in and kissed him.

Giovanni kept still. Her lips were soft and full where they pressed against his. They both kept their eyes open, staring at each other. He didn't want to push her away, but whatever she read in his expression had her lifting her lips off his. Her gaze dropped to her lap.

"I've never seen you that way," he explained. When her eyes grew moist, he wished he'd kept to his usual silence instead.

Nera wiped at a stray tear. "You idiot!" she shouted, making his eyes widen. "Don't you think I know that?"

For the first time, Giovanni had the thought that he might not fully understand her. The idea created a roiling in his stomach. "Then why—"

"It's not so surprising. You met me as a child. It's like that's all you've ever seen." She grabbed his empty plate from him, setting it aside before shocking him by straddling his lap. Her breasts pressed against his chest above her sling, and her good hand wrapped around to caress the back of his neck. "I'm all grown up. Try to think about that this time," she murmured.

Giovanni's hands moved to her waist, but he hesitated to move her, scared he'd hurt her. "Nera—"

She took that moment to kiss him again, while his lips were parted. Nera deepened the kiss this time, her tongue thrusting inside to tangle with his own.

The sudden flash of sensation had his eyes closing. Nera continued her assault, her open-mouthed kisses hot, decadent. She tasted of chocolate and something unique, something he'd never had before.

Her flesh under his hands was warm and soft, and she shimmied against him with every thrust of her tongue. Her movements also shifted her breasts along his chest, where her nipples were hardening as she cried out against his mouth.

Giovanni swallowed the sexy gasp before closing his mouth against hers, though he didn't pull away. He tried to wrap his head around his confusion. He'd never been a very sexual person, but the feel of her rocking against him was doing things to him that he'd never expected to feel. Especially not with Nera.

She licked his bottom lip before biting down. His body tightened from the sudden sensation, and his lips parted in shock, allowing Nera to deepen the kiss again.

His eyes opened, and her intent gaze captured him. Staring into her heavy-lidded eyes, he couldn't deny that the woman in his arms was his Nera. The fingers sending electric sparks into his skin belonged to her. It was her tongue stroking along his, making him pant for breath.

Nera was kissing him, and it was that thought that sent a wave of heat unlike anything he'd ever felt before through his body.

She cradled his growing erection between her thighs, rocking against him and adding to the ache that throbbed there.

Giovanni's hands slid to her back, urging her closer as his tongue tangled with hers.

Her sling was squashed between them, and she cried out—not in a good way. Giovanni quickly created some distance between their chests.

"Giovanni, no—"

He cut off her protest by initiating another kiss. At first it was hard, but his pressure softened so he could cherish the lips under his. He lifted his head to see her blink at him.

"I see you, Nera," he murmured. She still cradled his erection, so he didn't doubt she understood what he meant. "That's enough for now." He hated that he had hurt her, first with his words, then again when he had wanted her closer. Giovanni needed time to get his head on straight and figure out what the hell to do about the foreign feelings inside of him.

Her hand trailed up from his neck, leaving tingles in its wake. The backs of her fingers brushed along his jaw, where her eyes traced the outside of his face. "I've always loved your color."

The admission only added to his confusion. "Color?" Tommaso and the doctors had told him she could no longer see color, only in black and white. Mostly white, like an overexposed picture.

Her cheeks flushed as she met his eyes. "It's been my secret. Only you have an outline of color. It's how I always know when you're near."

Giovanni remembered the way her eyes would lift toward him, no matter how far back he stayed, trying to avoid her notice. "Only me?" His heartbeat thrummed in his chest.

"Yes, only you." Nera's expression softened as she continued to trace him with her gaze. "It's the prettiest shade of red."

Red. A chill rushed through him, wiping away all the lingering heat. He reminded himself that the warm woman before him was the same girl he'd failed so long ago. The girl that he'd tried to protect with his body. While the Bratva had beaten him, she'd stared up at him. And above him had been that damn stained glass window, the one depicting red, red blood more than anything else.

Giovanni helped her to her feet, creating distance between them as soon as she was steady.

"Is something wrong?" she asked.

He shook his head even though every part of him wanted to run away. He'd taken so much from her over the years. If he wasn't careful, he'd allow her to give more of herself to him before he was through.

"You regret it, don't you?" Nera scowled at him. "Well, you shouldn't. That was all me. I forced that kiss on you, so there's nothing for you to regret." Her hand clenched at her side. "And you enjoyed it, no matter what you tell yourself." She turned away from him for the first time he could remember. "I need to check on Tommaso," she said as she struggled to open the heavy sealed door that helped to soundproof the indoor gun range.

Giovanni silently reached over her to help, careful not to touch her. He followed behind her as they ascended the steps.

She was right. He had enjoyed kissing her. That was the worst part.

Chapter 11

Nera led the way to Tommaso's room, trying her hardest not to be annoyed. She'd just experienced one of the best moments of her life. She'd always wanted to kiss Giovanni. Sure, it had taken a while for her to get a response from him, but for a brief, stunning moment, he had kissed her back.

Then she'd reminded him about her disability, and all that lovely interest had faded away. She should have never mentioned his color. The euphoria she'd been feeling had made her the idiot, not Giovanni.

Nera had known he kept coming around the bakery out of pity. Like he'd said, he'd never seen her as a possible sex partner. She'd known that and had given up a few years before. She wasn't as innocent as he wanted to think.

There had been a time around when she'd turned eighteen that Giovanni had stopped coming to the bakery. Enough days passed that she'd decided he'd stopped coming altogether. She'd asked Tommaso, but he said he hadn't heard about anything bad happening. Tommaso had been frank about his time in the Mafia, so she knew the world of the Di Salvos wasn't safe. If Tommaso was right, then Giovanni hadn't stopped visiting because he was hurt.

She'd decided he'd finally gotten over his sympathy for the orphaned, partially blind child she had become. Which was good, she'd told herself. Because she was no longer a child.

Then she had snuck out of the house to attend the party some college kids had mentioned at the bakery that day.

For someone who was normally so isolated, to the point of being homeschooled after the accident, the sounds and the press of bodies at the party were overwhelming, not to mention the flashing strobe lights that dazzled her already muddled vision. She'd found a quiet corner to give herself time to acclimate.

One of the frat boys had found her there. Nera had known that he only wanted one thing from her, but that fact didn't bother her. She'd gone to the party for that very reason. He knew nothing about her and didn't treat her any differently from any of the other girls at the party. He'd found her curves fuckable, and that was all that mattered to him.

She didn't remember his name, but he hadn't been too muscular or tall, and he had had blond hair. She let her sight go blurry and pretended he was Giovanni when she let him take her virginity. The frat boy was skilled enough to get her going and made it enjoyable enough that it didn't hurt.

She had been a little embarrassed when Giovanni began visiting the bakery again, but not so much that she wanted him to stop. She knew better than to wait around for him to realize she was no longer the little kid who'd cried on his shoulder as it finally sank in, months after the accident, that she'd lost both her parents and her sight. He'd never see past that.

So whenever the time between Giovanni's visits to the bakery stretched, she'd sneak out for a hookup at the college. She had a particular type she was looking for, one that was easy enough to imagine as someone else. It wasn't until the third hookup that she learned what an orgasm was. Nera finally understood why Mylene seemed so chipper all the time.

And she realized she really enjoyed sex.

That hookup was the first person she had repeated encounters with, but when he told her he wanted to date her, she'd used his graduation as an excuse for distance. After that, she had been more careful about saying yes more than once to anyone else.

Giovanni could treat her like a child all he wanted, but she knew exactly what she wanted. Unfortunately, it had always been him. And for a brief moment that morning, he'd wanted her in return.

Nera glanced at him before she opened the door to Tommaso's room. Giovanni's normal, stoic expression was in place, as if he hadn't stuck his tongue down her throat and pulled her against him.

Maybe, out of the two of them, he really was the idiot.

When she opened the door, Tommaso's tired but smiling face turned toward her.

All her disappointment morphed into joyful butterflies that carried her swiftly to his side. She called his name as she carefully hugged him with her good arm.

"My silly girl," Tommaso said, his voice husky with sleep. "Were you worried? You should have known better."

"He's much too stubborn to die," Mylene agreed.

Tommaso's laugh switched to a groan, and he pressed a hand to the bandage on his chest.

Nera pulled away to study him. His skin was still too pale, and he'd clenched his jaw against the pain.

"It'll take more than one bullet to take me out," Tommaso said once he had his breath back.

"Two were removed from your chest, you idiot, idiot man!" Mylene shouted at him. Then she burst into tears.

Tommaso reached out, his fingers linking with Mylene's in a squeeze. "See? You love me. Ready to marry me yet?"

Mylene cursed at him in French.

It hurt Tommaso to laugh. Though he teased Mylene to soothe her, Tommaso's eyes slid to Giovanni, a question there. Nera watched Giovanni shake his head in answer, and the smile left Tommaso's face.

Giovanni walked Nera to the guest room late in the evening. Tommaso waking up had eased part of his tension, though a full recovery would take time. He still slept more than he was awake, and Nera had remained by his bedside for the rest of the day.

She paused outside the bedroom door, frowning down at the floor as she bit her lip.

"You could have stayed," Giovanni said.

Nera shook her head. "He was tired. And that wouldn't be fair to Mylene." Her eyes lifted, some of the lines there easing as she traced Giovanni's face. "It was good to see him awake and laughing."

Giovanni wondered if it was him she was seeing or if she was just absorbing his color. His hands clenched at his sides. All the times she'd stared at him, was a part of her remembering? "You should rest," he managed to say.

Nera's gaze latched onto his. "So we're not going to talk about what happened?"

Giovanni remembered the moment of heat he had felt, but when he traced her figure with his eyes, he still couldn't understand it. Oh, Nera was beautiful, with her rounded curves and her auburn hair trailing over a shoulder. Maybe someone else would see her differently, but there was a softness to her that appealed to him. Just seeing her often soothed something inside him. It had never brought that heat before.

He forced his gaze to her lips. They were a little too wide for her face, but often curved up in a smile when she saw him. She wasn't smiling now, and that was his fault, but when no wave of lust swamped him as he remembered how her lips felt against his, he finally relaxed.

"There's nothing to talk about," he said, meeting her eyes.

She stared back, her brow furrowing. Then she stepped forward, close enough that he saw the rapid beat of the pulse in her neck and the quick rise and fall of her chest as she dragged in a breath.

"What if I invited you in?" she asked.

And she was Nera. The girl who had cried for him after his mother died. The one who had grabbed his hand when he wondered if he could move forward. The woman who had run after him, even though they barely spoke, and saved him yet again.

The memory of their kiss was different when he remembered how much he cared for this person who should have never been a part of his life. Having her tight against him had felt right, even though he didn't do those kinds of things. He'd never wanted to before.

Her hand reached out, closing over his. Her lips parted, and he suddenly had the insane desire to cover them with his own. "My arm hurts a little," she murmured, dousing the budding flame. "Come in and help me with my bandages?"

"Nera…" He swallowed as he stared down at their linked hands. The steady footsteps of a third party approached, and a hand clapped him on the shoulder.

"I'll help her," Antonio said. He smiled at Nera as she pulled her hand away from Giovanni and frowned. Antonio's grin widened at her annoyed expression. "I've got a soft touch. Don't worry."

"I'll take care of it myself," Nera muttered.

Giovanni blinked at her. He'd never heard that tone before.

"You sure?" Antonio asked. "I wouldn't want you to struggle."

"Yeah, right." When Nera turned her eyes to Giovanni, the irritation there softened as she traced his face. "Good night, Giovanni," she murmured, and moved into her room.

Antonio's perpetual smile slipped away when they were alone.

Giovanni should have realized Nera would pick up on his cousin's falseness. Nera didn't like it when people weren't honest.

"None of this is her fault," he reminded his cousin.

Antonio switched his scowl from the door to him. "No, it's yours. How long are we going to keep this up?"

Giovanni shrugged the hand off his shoulder. "The Di Salvos have no reason to protect her. My say-so has never had sway on any of them."

He sighed. "This is a mess. Tommaso woke up. Couldn't he—"

"Not yet. He was shot in the chest, Antonio."

"Shit, yeah." Antonio ran his hand over his hair. "I guess that'd take down even someone like him. I still don't like it." He shifted his glare to the closed bedroom door. "I should be going with you tonight, not babysitting."

"Enzo will be there," Giovanni reminded him.

"Fucking Enzo," Antonio said. "Make him sit on her instead. He's better at cleanup than taking action."

"I heard that." Enzo had crept into the hall on silent feet. He slipped his hands into the pockets of his jeans, but didn't bother defending himself. "We doing this or what?" he asked.

"I'll meet you down there," Giovanni said, then watched his uncle nod as he moved to the stairs.

Antonio stared after his retreating figure as well. "Seriously, Gio. Let me do this with you. I know you're worried, but the kid will be fine for one night."

"She's not a kid," Giovanni said. He pictured the way he'd seen her last, with her lips parted and her hands reaching toward him. "She's not a child," he repeated to himself.

He found his cousin studying him. "I interrupted something, didn't I? You had a certain look."

Giovanni shook his head. "It's fine." He'd been relieved, actually, when Antonio strolled up. He couldn't afford the distraction.

"Tonight is dangerous. You—"

Giovanni raised his hand to halt the words. His eyes returned to the guest bedroom door. Nera was partially blind. She wasn't deaf. He waved Antonio toward the stairs.

His cousin's scowl was back, and fiercer than ever. "Don't want her to know? This is the life, Gio."

"She'd worry," Giovanni said, but he couldn't meet his eyes. As much as the way Nera looked at him, with that hero worship he didn't deserve, tore him up inside, he didn't want to taint her image of him either. He was the furthest thing from the angel she'd once compared him to.

"Fuck that. You're the one worried." Antonio's face softened. "That look you had before surprised me. I've never seen it on you. I was the one that told you to fuck her out of your system, but—"

"Don't, Antonio." Giovanni's hard tone stopped his cousin. "Just don't."

Antonio's lips pressed together. "Fine." He glanced up the hallway. "You know, some of the family already have a soft spot for her. Because of her fucking baking, sure, but there's also Tommaso. I don't think they'll do anything. I really can't come?"

Giovanni closed his eyes. "This Bratva thing makes little sense. I can't rule out..." He swallowed, unwilling to say it. His jaw clenched, and the skin near his eye began to twitch. He forced himself to take a breath deep into his lungs, opening his eyes again to see his cousin's serious face. "I need you here," Giovanni finished.

Antonio nodded. "Then I'll be here." He clapped Giovanni on the shoulder again.

The warmth there was familiar. "We'll know more after tonight."

His cousin released him. "Yeah. We will," he murmured as Giovanni headed to the stairs.

Enzo was waiting for him in the driver's seat. Giovanni didn't argue over it, even though he hated Enzo's driving. At least they'd get there faster.

He half expected the tires to screech when they reached the warehouse, but his uncle was smarter than that. They parked far enough away to check out the security. It was the same as they'd confirmed before. Only four men on a normal night.

Nothing like the crowd that would have been there the night after the Bratva had opened fire in broad daylight. Giovanni had suspected his and Antonio's plan had gone awry. Hitting the warehouse would have always been risky, since for some reason the Di Salvos had been attempting to generate an alliance with the Russians. Ruining those plans would likely be seen as a betrayal, if they were caught.

Giovanni had never been on board with an alliance. A Di Salvo didn't forget, even if the pain the Bratva had caused him had happened a decade before. His own retaliation over the years had helped him earn the capo position in spite of his father's desire for the opposite. That an alliance would be attempted at all just showed that his father still didn't consider him a worthy family member.

When the Bratva shot at him, he and Antonio had suspected they'd uncovered the secret hit they had planned. One that would ruin any chances of an alliance between the families. He would have been grateful the Bratva shot first, but they'd hit Nera and then they'd been at the Carmen house before him. He couldn't find the logic in it.

The Bratva had no reason to target Nera. Giovanni had worried they would want to silence her back when he'd killed their kidnappers, but she wasn't part of the life. He'd offered his protection, made sure Tommaso was in place, and replaced the damaged bakery window with bulletproof glass, which he should have had done to the Carmen house as well, damn it. But nothing had happened after a dozen years. Why was it happening now?

Giovanni was going to get answers.

He and Enzo took their time, listening to one pair of guards bitch about the cold.

Enzo pointed toward the younger one, but Giovanni shook his head. He pointed at the older bratok. Enzo rolled his eyes, but nodded.

His uncle waited until they were out of earshot to murmur, "Don't be soft. Not like you're doing a favor, letting him have a bit more life as a Bratva."

Giovanni didn't waste his breath arguing. They moved together, taking the older Bratva alive. He made a point of shooting the younger bratok in the head after they'd knocked him out.

Enzo stared at him, then moved to the side of the door as the second set of guards came running. They were careful, but not careful enough. Giovanni killed the younger of them as well. The other might bleed out, but he was alive for the moment.

"Feeling bloodthirsty?" Enzo asked as he lifted the torso of the first bound Bratva.

"No." Giovanni grunted as he helped. He still hated that he'd look weak trying to carry one out himself. The progress was swifter than it had been when Nera helped to carry Tommaso, though.

They returned for the bleeder.

"This one will force me to dump the car," Enzo complained. "Do we need him?"

Giovanni only had the breath to nod. The trunk was big enough. Besides, some people broke quicker after listening to the person next to them scream.

Chapter 12

Nera had always known Giovanni was a Di Salvo. She hadn't always known exactly what that meant, but her parents had treated him and his mother with respect. She'd thought their mothers had been friends, but when she'd said it aloud, her mother had been uncomfortable as she'd denied it. Her mother said they were friendly, but that she'd never call a Di Salvo a friend.

Tommaso had begun visiting the bakery whenever Inessa Di Salvo did. He'd been loud and boisterous and liked to pretend to tell Nera secrets about Giovanni, whose face would go stiff when he heard him whisper. That only made Tommaso laugh louder, but Nera would feel bad and quickly admit that there never was a secret. Giovanni would look away, but some of his stiffness would leave.

She was more certain that Tommaso was a friend. He'd often go off with her father to the back of the bakery, as if they were telling each other secrets too. But when she'd called him a friend one morning, her father wore the same expression that her mother had, as if he smelled a burned tart.

Tommaso was the one that had come to the bakery to tell her parents Giovanni's mother had died. He'd come a lot less for a while after that. Her father would call him when Giovanni's bruises were particularly bad, but Giovanni began catching on. Tommaso and her father would talk on occasion, but they didn't say much. Tommaso had stopped laughing as often. Then her parents had joined Giovanni's mother in heaven, and Tommaso had been at the hospital, telling her he was going to take care of her for a while.

It wasn't until after Tommaso became her guardian that she had learned more about the Di Salvos. A few of the family members had been angry with him and had shown up at the bakery. It had scared Nera. Most things had scared her. On top of losing almost everyone she had known, adapting to her new vision was disconcerting. Giovanni only came by once around that time, right after the threats to Tommaso. That was the first time she'd seen his color. The first time since the accident that she'd been able to take a full breath of air.

The angry Di Salvos no longer came around after that, but neither did Giovanni. Tommaso had tried to explain that it wasn't safe for her to be around a Di Salvo, but she'd only known that she missed him. Tommaso had held her while she cried. Eventually she'd seen a flash of soothing maroon at the bakery, one that had returned from time to time; her chest wasn't so tight whenever she saw it.

A dozen years later, and Tommaso had been part of her life longer than her parents had been—Giovanni for longer than that. As she'd gotten older, Tommaso had explained as much as he could about the Di Salvos. Nothing he told her changed a thing about how she felt whenever she caught a glimpse of Giovanni.

So when she heard the muffled conversation through the door about how dangerous the evening would be, she hadn't been able to sleep. Instead, she took the time to pray.

The night passed, and it was shortly before dawn when she'd had enough of her own thoughts. Normally she'd begin baking, which would at least keep her hands occupied. Nera cracked open the door to the guest room.

Antonio leaned against the opposite wall, his ankles crossed and his eyes closed. "I bet you wish I was someone else." He moved his hand to his lips before letting out a puff of smoke that smelled sweeter than a cigarette.

"That's right." Nera had already picked up on the fact that Giovanni's cousin didn't like her, so she figured there was no reason to lie.

His laugh made the rest of the smoke leave his mouth. When he opened his eyes to appraise her, for once his smile seemed to reach his voice. "You know, some would say I'm better looking than Giovanni." He slipped something inside his inner jacket pocket. "Less... delicate."

Nera's worry for Giovanni grew. If his cousin was one of the people he could trust, it didn't seem like he could really trust anyone. She let her disgust show. "He's not delicate."

"He's small-boned, like his mother. Add that soft hair and the high cheekbones on his pretty, pretty face, and you can't call him anything else." The humor faded from his voice even as his lips spread wider. "He's the spitting image of Inessa. If not for his eyes, his father wouldn't have believed the paternity test."

Nera studied the man before her.

"A lot of people wondered about it. Giovanni never has looked like a Di Salvo. It's only one of the burdens he's always been under." Antonio tilted his head, his gaze fixed on her. "No one was surprised when his mother was killed. They assumed the son would be next." He crossed his arms as he tilted his head back again. "Some even tried to speed it along."

Giovanni had shown up with more than just fresh bruises that time outside the bakery when she'd taken his hand and led him inside. Nera stepped out of her room, squinting against the fluorescent lights to better study Antonio's face. His jaw was clenched tight.

"Not you," she murmured.

Antonio's eyes opened wide. "No, not me. I love my cousin. He's always been a Di Salvo."

Nera nodded.

When Antonio pushed off the wall, she scuttled backward a step. He closed the distance she created until her back hit the wall.

Nera glared up at him. Unlike Giovanni, Antonio was taller than her, and she stared at the scar along his throat. She hated how he hovered so close, his bulky shoulders blocking out the nearest bulb and creating a shadow in her too-bright field of vision.

"So I don't do it for you?" His head lowered toward her until his breath grazed her ear. "I've got more experience than Giovanni. Are you sure you don't want to try me?"

Nera turned her face away from him. "Why?" She had to swallow to find more words. "Why do this? You don't even like me."

His chuckle sent a tremor through her, so different from the one she felt with Giovanni. He lifted away, letting her breathe again. "True. The way you crawled into his lap was hot, though. Even got my cousin stirred up, and Giovanni can be a bit strange about that."

"Don't talk about him that way," Nera snapped before frowning at him in confusion. The door to the gun range had been shut. Were there cameras in there? She flushed at the idea that someone had watched her throw herself at Giovanni. It hadn't been a failure, but it also hadn't been a success.

Antonio shrugged. "Made me curious, is all." He backed off, his gaze tracing down her body dismissively. "You want to see him, right? Come along." He turned and started walking down the hall.

Nera hesitated, the space between them stretching. "I didn't know he was back," she said, her feet moving despite her reservations.

Antonio made a noncommittal sound in his throat before leading her to the stairs. She recognized the path she'd taken the day before. Giovanni's face had looked calm when he'd sat next to her in the gun range. Well, before she'd tried to jump him, anyway. His relaxed expression was subtly different from his normal blank face, and both Enzo and Antonio had indicated they'd find him at the range more often than not.

Only Antonio didn't reach for the heavy door. Instead, he turned down another corridor she hadn't noticed the day before. One that led to another staircase down.

She'd thought the gun range was in the basement, but there was another sub-level.

Less light illuminated the second half of the flight of stairs. The shadows that gathered made seeing the steps more difficult, and she nearly missed the next one. They were strangely irregular. She clutched at the railing to steady herself against her mounting vertigo. She had once been more than familiar with that feeling, but she hadn't experienced it in a while.

"What's wrong?" Antonio murmured, a few steps below her. "You don't want to see him?"

Past his shoulder, she could make out a door that looked similar to the one that led into the gun range.

Nera pressed her lips together and felt for the next step with her foot. She forced a deep breath to try to slow her heartbeat. Dislike for Giovanni's cousin grew within her. She hoped he really was down there. Just seeing him would help to steady her.

Antonio opened the heavy door, and noises reached her ears, guttural groans of pain that made the hairs on her arms stand up. Nera froze, but Antonio's hand clamped around her forearm, dragging her inside the dim space.

Acid roiled in her stomach at the smell—blood and sweat and defecation. She tried to breathe through her mouth instead, but that made her saliva curdle in her throat.

A dark maroon drew her gaze. Her eyes flew to Giovanni, and the lurching in her stomach faded. He hadn't seen her yet. His face held its usual stoic calm as he stared down at someone strapped to a chair. Normally, his dress shirt was a bright white, but shadowy stains spread across it, keeping the light at bay.

"Perhaps you didn't hear the question," Giovanni said. He reached for a man. The knife in his hand also appeared shadowed. He didn't immediately withdraw, but carved at the man.

The tied-up man choked on his scream, the sound tightening Nera's own throat as she watched Giovanni step back with the man's ear in his hand, easier to see against his maroon glow. He held it in front of his victim's panicked eyes as the man's mouth opened and closed. Then he dropped the bloody flesh. The sound of it hitting the floor finally forced her to swallow.

"I'll ask again," Giovanni said. "Who ordered the hit on the house on Mead Street?" Then he paused, his head lifting and turning toward her.

Nera stared at the darkened knife in his hand. In her mind's eye, it brightened into a long, colorful shard of glass. That image made the last of her revulsion fade. Giovanni's bloody hand with glass in it meant safety.

She slowly blinked as she met Giovanni's gaze.

"Antonio," Giovanni said, but his eyes didn't leave hers.

His cousin said nothing.

Enzo shifted forward from the corner, but she couldn't look away from the blood that should have been a deep, dark crimson. It was all just shades of gray. Only Giovanni was allowed to be red.

Nera straightened her posture and cleared her throat. "I'll have panna cotta waiting when you're finished," she said. Her eyes traced his color once more, letting in the calm it always filled her with. She turned toward the door.

Not because she couldn't stomach seeing more. No, Giovanni wouldn't be able to keep going if she was there.

Antonio closed the door behind her, and Nera paused at the foot of the stairs.

"Fucking panna cotta!" Antonio spat. "You're so—"

Nera turned and shoved him in the chest, hard. She used both hands even though it caused her injured arm to flare with pain. He stumbled, his back hitting the wall as she closed in. Nera's good hand fisted in the top of his shirt, wishing she could pull it tight enough to choke him while she dragged his face down until their noses almost touched.

"Don't you ever use me to hurt Giovanni again." The words didn't come out as a shout. They were calm and hard as she glared at him.

Antonio wasn't glaring back. His eyes seemed to be searching hers for something. They narrowed at whatever he saw there.

Nera released him, turning to the steps. "And yes, fucking panna cotta." The image of Giovanni with a bloody shard of glass in his hand returned. It felt clearer than the brightness of the stairwell above as her feet found each step. "Come on. I'll need a hand."

Antonio said nothing as he followed along behind her.

Chapter 13

Giovanni's hands felt numb as he set the knife down. The second Bratva was dead. He'd killed the first too quickly after Nera's sudden appearance, but it had loosened the other man's tongue. Nothing he'd learned had been quite enough. The information was more like slowly revealed portions of an unfinished painting.

"I'll take Antonio with me tonight," he told Enzo.

His uncle paused where he'd crouched beside the first body. "No, you fucking won't."

Giovanni frowned. "Enzo—"

"You did good work here."

Giovanni blinked at him. He and his uncle had always gotten along well enough, but no Di Salvo had ever praised him.

"You surprised me. Asking about what happened so long ago." Enzo nodded as he stared at the mutilated hand in front of him. "Got some things to chew on."

"We need more." Giovanni had suspected the Bratva were being used. Neither man had offered up a name, though.

"Sure, but we can't get sloppy about this." Enzo's smile had faded ever since Nera had stood before them. "You need to sleep. A couple of days without can make you sharp. Too much more, and mistakes are made."

"I'm fine," Giovanni said.

Enzo grunted his dissent, but started to clean up.

Giovanni felt the fatigue, but it was shoved behind the memory of the calm nod Nera had given him. Someone like her, who wore every thought on her face, couldn't have faked that confusing calm. Had she not clearly seen what he was doing? There was no way in hell she'd left him to torture someone and gone off to make dolci for him to eat afterward. That wasn't possible.

"I'll talk to Vittore. Scout a few things out." Enzo moved to the second victim, emptying his pockets. His eyes flicked toward Giovanni. "I can take Antonio. Could be he gets shot."

Giovanni shook his head.

"Just a little shot," Enzo said, rolling the body over.

"I'm not upset with him." He'd known what his cousin was trying to do. Based on the way Antonio had stared at Nera, she'd surprised him as well. That was a difficult feat. Confusion had kept his own expression contained when his heart stopped at the sudden sight of her.

Giovanni's fingers itched. It was probably just the drying blood.

Enzo paused again. His normal grin returned. "I like her. Save me some panna cotta."

It took a while for Giovanni to remove all the blood from his skin. By the time he made his way to the kitchen, he expected to find it empty. Instead, Nera was really there, opening the freezer door.

Antonio scowled at the tray she tried to remove one-handed. "Give it here," he said, stomping toward her and taking the tray to set on the counter himself.

The custard had had the proper time to set. Giovanni could practically taste it. His tongue tingled. Nera had actually left that room spattered with blood and made panna cotta.

She thought it was his favorite. The dessert was so wrapped up in the memories of his mother, Giovanni wasn't as certain.

Nera's face turned toward him with a smile. "Perfect timing."

Her smile didn't look forced. Giovanni didn't know what to say. He watched her plate the custard. She walked it to him, handing him the plate with a spoon.

Giovanni swallowed.

"Gio—" Antonio began, but he shut up when Giovanni's gaze skewered him.

Nera grabbed Giovanni's hand. "We should talk." She tugged on his hand to move him forward.

They left Antonio glaring down at the rest of the panna cotta.

Nera led him all the way to her guest room. Even after the door was closed behind them, she didn't let it go.

Giovanni set the plate on the table in the small sitting area before turning to face her. He still hadn't found any words. An apology wouldn't be appropriate. He wasn't sorry about what he'd done. He wasn't even sorry she had seen what she had. It was better that she understood what kind of man he was.

Nera turned his hand over, staring at it intently. She hadn't linked their fingers. "This feeling is so strange," she murmured. Then she brought his hand close to her face and kissed his palm.

The heat of her lips slipped inside him, chasing away the numbness. Giovanni closed his eyes to absorb the intense spike of heat that raced through him.

Nera released his hand. "You should eat."

Giovanni opened his eyes again. Nera stood before him. Her gaze was the same one she'd always given him—filled with warmth and affection. What Nera had seen hadn't changed the way she looked at him.

He moved closer to her, using the hand she had kissed to stroke her face. "Nera." He shivered when he said her name. The heat continued to spread. His gaze dropped to her lips. He wanted to taste them far more than the panna cotta. "I want to kiss you." He'd never said those words to anyone before.

Nera's tongue flicked over her lips before they parted. "Go ahead."

Giovanni slowly brought his face closer to hers, savoring the puff of air, a shared breath, before their lips met. The first brush made his skin feel too tight. The heat inside him expanded. He wanted to be gentle, but her lips clung to his, and soon his mouth was slanting over hers again and again.

He reminded himself not to pull her against him—that had hurt her arm—but her hand found its way to the back of his neck and each stroke of her fingers made him shudder. His tongue stroked hers in return, and the gasped sound he swallowed made his head spin.

Nera returned his kiss stroke for stroke. It was as if her mouth was made for him. He never would have guessed that. His thoughts began to slip away as he lost himself in her. "Nera." Her name sounded different to him now.

It was her turn to shudder. She pressed herself against him, and he shuffled back, remembering her injured arm. His legs collided with the bed. He lifted his head to get his bearings only for her to shove him with her good hand, completing his tumble onto the mattress.

Nera's face was flushed with need as she stared down at him. She licked her lips, which looked redder than before, then climbed onto the bed after him. She was a little awkward with one arm tucked in her sling. He wanted to ask if she was okay, but her gaze was impossible to look away from.

"More." Her voice had a huskiness he'd never heard before, and the word described exactly what he wanted. His arms cushioned her body to lie over him so their lips could meet again. Something about kissing her lying down made the heat spread faster. Or maybe it was the way her lower body rocked against his erection.

He'd never been so hard. The reality of it was difficult to process with her tongue in his mouth. The idea of having her was taking over everything else. He'd never desired anyone in this way.

He hadn't confessed his lack of sexual interest to anyone. The Di Salvos were known for their Casanovas, and he didn't need one more strike against him. His worry over his lack of libido had faded once he realized none of the family would believe that he was still a virgin so late into his twenties.

Giovanni opened his eyes to study the woman in his arms. He had hoped it would help him regain control, but it was Nera who was doing this to his body—the person who had meant so much to him for so long. His chest squeezed as he saw her glazed eyes.

Their lips parted as she continued to rock against his erection. Her hand caressed his face. "Giovanni." Nera had always said his name in just that way. Like he was everything precious to her.

She tried to press closer to him, but bit her lip as if she was in pain.

He wrapped his arms around her, careful as he switched their positions. Being on top let him brace himself better to protect her arm. Her skirt fell around them as she bent her knees, her legs pressing against the sides of his hips through his slacks. Giovanni couldn't control the sudden thrust of his hips. He pressed his erection against her, the intensity of it making him lose his thoughts.

"Nera." His control was slipping through his fingers like water. Giovanni held himself still as he closed his eyes. He'd only meant to kiss her. He needed to shove himself away from her and create some distance.

Her hand slipped between them. Even through his slacks, one stroke had him groaning before he stole her lips again.

Nera was nimble for being one-handed. She slid his button free. He didn't hear his zipper over the thudding of his heart. Then her hand found him, wrapping around his bare cock.

Giovanni had masturbated over the years. He'd found the process clinical. Enough stimulation would get him there, but he didn't resort to it often.

Nothing about Nera's hand felt clinical.

He thrust into her tight grip, and the sensation was unlike anything he'd ever experienced. Until she moved her hand into his next thrust, and then it was even better. He froze, and his body shook as their lips parted. He stared down into her eyes.

He swallowed, opening his mouth to speak. But then Nera's hand stroked him again, squeezing the breath out of him.

"Giovanni, let go," Nera murmured against his lips before sealing them with her own.

He cried out into her mouth as her hand worked him over in earnest. Each firm stroke pulled his foreskin down more until the air swirled around the sensitive head of his straining cock. Her words reverberated in his mind, urging him to give in to his body's intense need. He thrust into her strokes until a euphoria flooded through him. He called her name as he came all over her fucking skirt.

He collapsed to his side beside her with her hand still on his cock.

Nera pressed a gentle kiss to his lips before she released him. Then she slipped off the bed.

Drowsiness swamped him as he watched her change her skirt. It was as if the last of his strength had just been pumped out of his body. Two days of insomnia had finally caught up to him.

Nera crawled back onto the bed beside him, propping herself up with the pillows. She patted her lap, and Giovanni didn't resist the siren's call. His head found her soft stomach, careful to avoid the sling. His arm rested over her thighs, his fingers curling against the fabric of her skirt as he closed his eyes.

The scent of her arousal drifted to him from so close. He knew he should touch her like she had done for him, only his eyelids wouldn't lift. He was a selfish prick like his father, giving in to his own pleasure like that, even if it had caught him off guard.

"Sleep," Nera told him, her hand sifting through his hair. His self-loathing scattered into nothingness as he slipped into the oblivion of her gentle care.

Chapter 14

Nera didn't expect to fall asleep. Her heart was pounding in her ears, and she ached with unfulfilled need.

Not that she hadn't enjoyed herself.

Giovanni never lost control like that. Never. It was as if he'd always had a shell around him, one that kept everyone at a distance. When she'd been a child, she'd cracked that shell with her hugs.

He'd looked almost vulnerable hovering above her, with his eyes squeezed shut and his jaw clenched so tightly. He'd been trying to stop himself from going any further with her sexually.

The evidence of how much he wanted her had been too tantalizing to resist. She'd watched his control shatter after she'd given him permission to let go, and the way he'd called her name as he came had flooded her with her own intense need.

Despite how much she ached, a smile of joy slid across her face. She'd wrecked him. Her. And the way he'd called for her meant he knew exactly who was doing it to him.

Her eyes dropped to his hand. Before he'd fallen asleep, he'd clung to her. Now his hand lay limply on top of the bedspread.

Giovanni was the type of man who didn't bat an eye while he tortured someone. The thought didn't disgust her. It made her want to bring him to climax again. She'd been enough for someone like Giovanni.

He likely hadn't stopped at torture. No, Giovanni was a killer as well. The realization made the last of her tension ease. It made no sense, but the thought that he killed people made her feel safe.

She recalled the image she'd been confused by before. Giovanni with a long shard of glass in his hand, not a knife. The glass hadn't been clear, but colored red. Maybe red with blood. Only that didn't seem right.

The memory pulled at her, and she closed her eyes to focus. Giovanni's face filled her mind. Not the one she'd seen soft with sleep, but a thinner, teenaged version.

"It's okay," Giovanni said. It wasn't in a soft whisper, but a broken gust. His eyes were so blue where he hovered over her.

She cried, making her view of him shimmer through her tears. Nothing was okay. The angry men were hitting him again, and it was all her fault. Her wet eyes tried to glare at the men past his shoulder. Giovanni had tucked her away, and she couldn't see much besides wood, him, and shadows. When the shadows shifted, she saw a picture of Christ, but He just stared down at her. He didn't save her like her mother had always said He would.

No, He'd sent Giovanni instead. But Giovanni kept getting hurt. Because of her.

"It's okay," he grunted again before another kick had him slumping forward. The men stopped, backing off.

Nera edged closer, scared to touch him. She pressed her forehead against his and squeezed her eyes shut. Her eyes and nose were running, but she knew Giovanni wouldn't say anything about that. All he ever said were those same words over and over, but they were a lie.

It wasn't okay.

He couldn't do anything to save himself. Because of her. The men who beat him said it all the time. If he caused trouble, they would hurt her.

But Nera always caused trouble. Her father said she was a trouble magnet. She was older, and should have been better able to control her impulses. In a few years, she'd even be a teenager like Giovanni.

When one of the men pointed a gun at him, the idea that he might die filled her with rage. She attacked the man the only way she could, with teeth and nails. The gun fired anyway, and panic filled her. She had failed. But when she stumbled back, Giovanni caught her, holding her tight, so he couldn't be dead.

Nera opened her eyes, needing to see for herself, but he was too close for her to see him. Then there was shocking pain, and she couldn't see properly as the tinkle of falling glass filled her ears.

She tried to squeeze her eyes shut against the pain, but that only made it worse, so she opened them wide.

Giovanni was staring down at her through her wavering vision. She searched his expression. If he showed he was worried, then it was bad, but besides a tightening of his jaw, his face remained stoic. He stood with a long, colorful shard of the fallen glass in his hand.

Nera tried not to blink. Blinking made the pain in her eyes spike. So she saw when Giovanni stabbed the glass into the first man's neck. Sometimes her vision wavered, as if the world went dark. Giovanni remained silent as he killed all three of the men. Then he stood above her with that glass clutched in his hand. It was as if he couldn't open his fist.

He bent with it still in his hand, curling his arm under her legs and lifting her. Nera knew the glass should hold color, but it was too bright to see.

"I'm sorry, Nera," the teenaged Giovanni had said as he carried her out of the church.

Fingers trailed down the side of her face, and Nera opened her eyes.

Giovanni stared down at her, his face fuller than it had once been, but still bordered by elegant angles. He had only become more stunning with age. His blond hair was messy from her running her hand through it while he slept. "I'm sorry," he repeated.

Nera shook her head even as she tried to wrap her arms around him. She grimaced as the sling tightened against her bad arm.

Giovanni's hand rested over it and helped the ache to become less important.

Confusion filled her. She hadn't been sleeping. That had been a memory.

"We should talk," Giovanni said before pulling away. His jaw clenched and the skin near it pulsed. "We never did."

Nera struggled to sit up beside him, finally grabbing his forearm with her good hand to pull herself up. He tensed beneath her touch, and his eyes had no color besides gray where they stared into hers. She drew closer to him, practically in his lap, until she could press her forehead gently against his. She closed her eyes, worried he'd misunderstand the dampness there.

His skin was so warm against hers.

"I was never in an accident, was I?"

Giovanni's sigh moved against her lips. "No."

She hadn't really needed an answer.

They stayed like that, just as they'd once sat together under the stained glass window of a church.

Nera took in a shuddering breath and opened her eyes.

Giovanni had never stopped looking at her.

"Thank you," she said.

Giovanni jerked his head back like she'd hit him. "What are you thanking me for?" If she hadn't been clutching at his arm, she was sure he would have moved as far away from her as he could.

Nera blinked at him.

"Are you thanking me for failing to protect you? Or for getting you kidnapped in the first place?" He closed his eyes, and more words poured out, like the flood behind a broken dam. "Your parents were killed because I was there. Not in an accident, but shot."

Nera remembered the sound of the shots in her nightmare, her mother's scream.

"And they hit you. The Bratva hit you, there on the sidewalk. Every day after that, they managed to hit you, no matter what I did. And still, you would smile at me. You would press your forehead against mine like you just did." Giovanni's hand came up, shaking as he brushed her hair from her face. His hand stayed there as he closed the distance between them, their foreheads touching again. Her skin tingled where they pressed together, his eyes staring so intently into hers. "You were always the one saving me, Nera."

"Giovanni..." No other words would come. Just his name. She wished she could see the color of his eyes. Blue would be the perfect hue for the emotion that seemed to shatter there.

Giovanni made a pained sound before his lips captured hers. He started out gentle, like he always did with her. Her arm wrapped around his neck as she bit his lower lip. She didn't have a chance to lick it after, not when his tongue had already found hers.

He lowered her back to the bed as he continued to devour her. He kept his chest off her bad arm, protecting her. That was just like him, she told herself, though she still worried it meant he wasn't as into this as she was.

He caught her hand before she could check if he had an erection, and he pinned it beside her head on the pillow.

Giovanni lifted his face from hers. He swallowed, and her eyes followed the motion, liking the way his Adam's apple bobbed. She wanted to lick his throat.

"Were you thanking me for that as well?" he asked. "For using you earlier? For being selfish?"

Shock ran through her. Her eyes flew back to his, hating what she saw there.

"No, I—"

His lips smothered the denial. Despite being on top of her, he hadn't pressed against her. No, he was keeping his hips away instead of proving to her that he wanted her.

His grip on her hand changed. The pressure eased as he linked his fingers with hers, making it impossible for her to touch him in any way besides that.

His lips finally freed hers, sliding down her jaw instead. She wanted to tell him he was wrong, but he kissed her neck and she lost her breath. She turned her head, and he answered the silent plea with another caress. He nipped her neck like she had his lip, and she shuddered. He did it again, as if to verify she liked it.

"Let me make it up to you," he murmured, kissing his way to her open collar. He nipped there as well before sucking on the skin.

Nera's thoughts fled. All she could do was feel.

His mouth was a miracle. Hot and teasing, and he'd only made it to the top of her chest. The barest slope of her breast.

Nera tried to touch him with the fingers peeking out of her sling. He lifted away, watching them curl. He dropped a kiss onto each one before nipping her index finger, a harder nip than before.

"Be a good girl," he murmured. Then he shifted his head and kissed her breast over the nipple.

Nera hated the sling and her shirt and her bra. If they weren't there, she'd be able to feel that kiss better instead of the frustrating hint of pressure.

Giovanni sat up. He hadn't released her good hand, as if he knew she wouldn't be able to stop herself from reaching for him. He used his free hand to shift up the tail of her shirt until it bunched gently against her sling. His head lowered to kiss her quivering stomach.

Her stomach wasn't flat and sleek and sexy. No, she was soft and round, which he knew because his head had used her as a pillow. Having him kiss her there brought a flash of embarrassment, but it faded as the sensations continued and his kisses lowered. He paused at the elastic waistband of her skirt. His teeth scraped her skin as he bit the waistband and dragged her skirt lower on her hips with his teeth.

She'd always thought Giovanni was beautiful. Seeing him be sexy as hell ruined her.

He sucked at the dip under her stomach. She'd never known the skin there was so sensitive. She cried out, her hand trying to tug free from his so she could fist it in his hair and shove him that inch or two lower where she really needed him.

Instead he licked and sucked and nipped right above her lowered waistband and she lost her ability to breathe with the way her body clenched below. She wanted to spread her legs, but his weight held her still.

He released her hand so that both of his could drag her skirt and underwear down her legs and all the way off. He crouched at the end of the bed, staring at the juncture of her thighs. His face was still, the expression there unreadable like usual.

Nera finally had her hand free, but he was too far away for it to do her any good. It felt strange to be bare only from her stomach and below. Her legs pressed tight together to ward off the sudden chill against all the heat that had gathered.

"No, let me see." Giovanni's hands moved to her legs, pushing them wider. Her whole body shuddered when his skimming hands brushed the inside of her thighs, and he paused. He repeated the motion. Her legs drew apart even more, and her hips lifted.

He crawled between her opened legs, his hands rising higher. The blank expression on his face somehow made it appear more intent as he brushed over the hair covering her first. Then the fingers on his other hand slid right over her center. Self-consciousness hit her at the intensity of his stare as he found out just how wet she had become.

She reached for him, her hand twisting into the sleeve of his shirt.

His eyes lifted to hers. "You want to stop?" he asked.

Her legs tried to clench together at the thought, but he was between them.

"N-no!" She struggled to swallow. "I want you to touch me more. Really touch me."

His hand moved to where hers twisted his sleeve. He pulled it free. His eyes switched to stare at it. "Have you ever touched yourself?"

"Giovanni!" She wasn't sure why he was trying to embarrass her.

He moved her hand to replace his. "Show me."

He was staring down at her hand. His own moved away, both of his palms skimming over the tops of her thighs.

The idea of him watching her touch herself was embarrassing, especially with the way Giovanni stared. Like he wouldn't miss anything about it. Her hips lifted, brushing against her own hand.

"Please, Nera." His eyes met hers. "Show me how you like to be touched."

The ache she felt had become almost too intense. Her hand moved on its own, her fingers swirling around her soaked entrance. She really was wet. She dipped her index finger inside.

His gaze had dropped. He watched her hand move up, her wet finger slide over her clit. Something about him watching made even the softest pressure too much. Tremors started in her legs as she stroked her clit. It was too intense. She dipped below again, using her own wetness to ease the pressure as she began the back-and-forth motion that helped her orgasm build when she was alone.

Only she wasn't alone.

She gasped as her desire spiked, her shoulders quaking now.

Giovanni captured her hand, pulling it away as his fingers linked with hers. He forced their hands above her head, lying next to her on the bed.

She'd been so close. Her hips lifted against nothing as frustrated tears filled her eyes. "Giovanni, please!"

His other hand moved between her legs. His finger dipped inside her, slightly bigger than hers. His eyes were on her face as his finger slid up and stroked over her clit. His touch was firmer than hers had been.

Her clit throbbed before tugging pulses took over. She cried out as the orgasm hit. Giovanni's finger continued to stroke her through it, drawing out the sensation longer than she had known was possible.

She had melted into the bed. A part of her was disappointed it had happened so quickly. She didn't want it to be over.

Only it wasn't. Giovanni's finger dipped inside her before he brought it up to resume his strokes.

Her eyes flew wide. She hadn't meant to close them. He was still staring at her, and she couldn't look away. Her clit throbbed under his touch, but it wasn't usual for her to orgasm that quickly. She didn't want to disappoint him.

"I—"

He captured her mouth in a kiss. His lips were harder than before. His tongue thrust inside even as his finger pushed inside her down below. Then he was stroking her clit again. Nera's focus splintered as his tongue stroked in time with his finger. His touch down below was rougher than she ever touched herself, or maybe she was more sensitive. The pressure began to build. Her hips lifted, as if trying to throw off the touch that suddenly felt like too much. Giovanni wouldn't be deterred. He swirled and rubbed and stroked. His lips captured the sudden sounds she was making as her hips bucked against the throbbing. The second orgasm made her vision brighter than ever before.

He lifted his head as his fingers thrust inside her.

"Ah!" Her strangled cry filled the room around them as her hips lifted into his thrusting fingers. It was as if her pulsing was trying to suck his hand deeper as he worked her through her orgasm.

She lay quiet in the aftershocks, little jerking motions below making her clench around his fingers before he slid them out. She protested their loss with another sound.

Her body no longer seemed to have any bones in it. Giovanni's hand squeezed hers, reminding her that she did. He kissed her again, the kiss gentle this time even though his whole body had stiffened.

She had to swallow twice to get her voice to work. "What about you?" she asked.

"Nera—"

There was a knock on the bedroom door.

Giovanni's jaw hardened as he looked at it.

The air in the room chilled her half-naked body, despite how hot she had been only moments before.

A voice she didn't recognize spoke through the door. "It's important, Giovanni."

She almost missed the flash of surprise that loosened his tension. Giovanni rolled off the bed. He pulled the covers over her before crossing to the door, cracking it just enough for him to slip from the room.

Nera sank into the bed again. She sighed when she realized she and Giovanni hadn't really talked. It was hard to regret that with the aftershocks reminding her what they'd done instead.

Chapter 15

Vittore Di Salvo was the last person Giovanni expected to encounter outside the room Nera had been given. He respected his uncle more than his father. While Giovanni Sr. led the Di Salvos with emotion and spontaneous violence, Vittore stood behind him with a calm strategy that Giovanni envied.

Giovanni only pretended to have that kind of calm. Inside, he was a roiling mess.

It didn't help that he'd never been so disheveled in front of his uncle. Or that he could smell Nera on himself.

He'd plunged his fingers inside of her to prevent his instinct from taking over and making him thrust something else inside of her instead. Watching her fall apart had been spellbinding. And good God, he was thinking about sex while staring at his uncle.

Vittore studied him, and a flash of amusement brightened his Di Salvo eyes even while his lips remained straight. "I'm sorry to interrupt."

Giovanni cleared his throat. "You said it was important."

The amusement faded from Vittore's eyes. "Your father would like a word. I thought it would be better if I came to collect you."

Giovanni's mind raced as he glanced toward the closed guest room door. Nera was naked and vulnerable. His hand clenched at his side as he wondered how long he'd been asleep. Enzo was probably still on cleanup and Antonio—

"This can't wait, Giovanni. You know how your father gets." Vittore glanced at the door. "She'll be fine. The Di Salvos—"

"Have no reason to protect her, just as my father said." Giovanni forced himself to take a deep breath. It had been a mistake to bring her to the estate, but the Bratva had attacked her twice, and he hadn't known what else to do.

Vittore sighed. "I prefer to play interference with your father, but I can stay here if that will ease your burden." His hand closed over Giovanni's shoulder. "I must warn you, though, he's in one of his worst moods."

The idea of his uncle standing outside Nera's bedroom made Giovanni's stomach twist. The heat from the squeeze on his shoulder almost burned.

Footsteps clamored up the stairs. Giovanni looked past his uncle, relieved and annoyed at his cousin's appearance.

Antonio's gaze didn't miss the tension between them. "Well, it's not often we see you down here, uncle. Letting the boss off his leash?"

"Hold your tongue, Antonio." Vittore's hand dropped from Giovanni's shoulder. "Giovanni Di Salvo is no one's puppet."

Antonio lifted an eyebrow. "You here to do his dirty work then?"

Vittore didn't answer. He studied Giovanni. "Don't keep him waiting longer than you have to," he said before striding toward the stairs.

The cousins watched him until he moved out of sight.

Antonio let his false grin drop. "Sometimes I wonder whether it was your father or Vittore himself who killed my father."

Giovanni said nothing. Vittore had been kind to him over the years. His own hesitation to leave Nera's safety to his uncle had surprised him.

Antonio turned and slid his gaze over Giovanni. "Well, well. This is a new look for you." His eyes flicked toward the closed door. "I didn't know you had it in you."

Giovanni refused to feel embarrassed. He took a threatening step toward his cousin. "I haven't forgotten." He still remembered the way his throat had closed when he'd stared back at Nera past his bloody hand. "How the hell am I supposed to trust her with you?"

"What choice do you have?" Antonio's face tensed. "Look, I did you a favor."

Giovanni stared at him.

"I figured she'd run screaming, but at least you'd fucking know." His own frustration slid across his face. "I didn't expect fucking panna cotta."

Giovanni's relief at her steady gaze in the basement flooded back, along with another emotion. One that made his stomach swoop in a sickening way.

"I hope you enjoyed the dessert." Antonio ran a hand through his hair. "I got rid of the rest before anyone could see it. Your father would lose his shit."

Giovanni remembered he hadn't even tasted it. "Thank you," he said.

"Sure. I'm here. Anything you need." Antonio waved him away with a flash of his smile. "Now go on. You can't keep him waiting. But swing by your room first. It's way too obvious what you were up to."

Giovanni glanced down at his hand. "Nothing happened."

"Liar." He laughed. "It's about time you got your cock inside of her."

Giovanni's heartbeat quickened. "That's not what happened." He'd made sure he hadn't gone that far. He was too scared to. He'd failed to protect her before, but he wouldn't again. Even if it was from himself.

"Then you're an idiot."

Giovanni stared at his cousin.

"On top of being batshit crazy like all us Di Salvos." Antonio sighed. "Now, are you really intent on pissing off the boss? Get out of here."

Giovanni felt the pressure of the passing time weigh down his shoulders. His footsteps were heavy as he swung by his room. As he washed his hands, he tried not to remember the way Nera had looked when she'd orgasmed. While he changed his clothes, he tried not to recall the way her hand had gripped his erection, how it had felt to give in to his orgasm. He was beginning to think he'd been lucky not to experience sexual attraction in the past. It splintered his focus.

He would need his normal shell of calm in front of his father.

It was too bad cracks formed in it as soon as he stepped out of his room.

"Get out of there, Giovanni," Vittore said. Giovanni had never heard his uncle use that particular tone, but it wasn't directed at him. Vittore wasn't outside of his own room. No, he was down the hall, in front of a door that was never opened.

It was open now.

The last memory Giovanni had of his mother's bedroom sent ice through his veins. His jaw clenched as his feet carried him down the hall, even as the child within him wanted to run away.

A part of him would always want to run away from his father.

Vittore's hands shook where he stood in the doorway. "You said you wanted to speak to your son. Here? You meant here!" he snapped. "What the hell are you thinking?"

Giovanni forced his hand to remain at his side instead of reaching for the gun in his waistband. The cold inside him had spread, slowing his last step as he reached the open door. His breath held as he scanned the bedroom.

His worst fear wasn't inside. Nera didn't lay where his mother once had.

But his father's gaze burned with an emotion he'd seen before, standing in that spot, the exact position he'd been in the night he'd shot Giovanni's mother.

Giovanni's jaw worked. When the words came, they were even, void even of the terror that hadn't gone away. "You have something to say to me?"

Giovanni Sr. waved his hand. "Come here."

Giovanni's feet moved him forward until he stood before his father.

"Vittore, leave." His father's eyes never left his.

"I don't think I should," his uncle said from the doorway.

Giovanni Sr. glared at his brother. "And close the door behind you."

Silence followed the order. Then the snick of the door as it latched.

His father said nothing. His hands opened and closed at his sides, but Giovanni couldn't break away from his eyes. Blue shouldn't appear as dark as black.

He was almost relieved when his father's hand closed around his throat and slammed him into the wall. "What the fuck are you thinking?" Giovanni Sr. screamed in his face, squeezing the air out of him.

At least Giovanni didn't have to struggle to find the right words. Not when his father wouldn't let him breathe.

His father's size had always overwhelmed him. Giovanni's body was slighter, much more like his mother's.

He wondered how often she had been pressed against this same wall. It couldn't have been only the last night, the one that his father had made certain Giovanni had seen.

His father's other fist found his gut. Pain radiated through Giovanni's body as he repeated the blow twice more. Giovanni's fingers twitched, but he forced himself not to reach for the gun. Instead, his fingers went numb.

His father released his neck so he could crumple to the floor. The breath shuddered into his lungs, but he hadn't been given a reprieve. His father's hand fisted in his hair instead, twisting his face to shove his nose into the carpet.

"Enzo does a good job. You probably can't even smell the blood, but you remember it, don't you?" His father's voice was even more terrifying in that hard and even tone. Giovanni Sr. hadn't shouted on the night he killed his wife either.

Giovanni remembered everything about that night. His mother had told him she loved him right before his father had shot her in the face.

His father ground his own face into the carpet. "That fucking traitorous bitch bled out right here. I never thought you'd need that lesson again."

Giovanni's cheek felt raw. Not only from the rug burn, but from the way his teeth had bitten into the inside of it.

His father released him, stepping away. "Tell me what I heard isn't true."

Giovanni pushed his torso off the carpet with shaking limbs. His jaw worked again, but this time he couldn't force out any words.

"Tell me that a woman with no link to the Di Salvos didn't watch you torture someone. You can't be that stupid."

The carpet beneath Giovanni blurred in his vision. Neither Antonio nor Enzo would have told his father. He squeezed his eyes shut. The how wasn't important. He forced himself to speak. "She's no risk to us."

His father's laugh was a deep, humorless bray.

Giovanni shoved off the carpet, dragging himself to his feet to face his father. "You're not going to touch her." His hand reached for the small of his back.

His father was on him before he could pull the gun loose. He wrapped his hand around Giovanni's neck as he slammed him into the wall again. His father's other hand took away his gun, tossing it onto the bed. "Still so weak." He sighed, his hand tightening on Giovanni's throat. "It won't be me. I'm not the one who should kill her. You're going to take care of this, aren't you?" He pulled him forward only to slam him into the wall harder, pain lancing across the back of his head.

Giovanni slid to the ground when his father released him.

"You have a week. Unless I hear she's anywhere near a Bratva. I'll end the traitor myself then." His father's foot landed on his hand. The heel ground down, forcing Giovanni to bite back a cry. "Attempt to pull a gun on me again, and you'll lose this hand."

His bones and tendons continued to throb after his father moved away. Giovanni refused to cradle his hand against his chest. He didn't look up as his father left. The light from the hallway played across his throbbing hand.

Giovanni stared down at it. His fingers twitched, as if to confirm nothing was broken.

Panic made his mind blank.

The light flickered as Vittore moved into the doorway.

Giovanni looked up at his uncle.

Vittore crossed the room, sinking down to sit beside him.

Giovanni stared at where his gun rested on the bed. "He expects me to kill her." The words still didn't sound real when he said them aloud. He closed his eyes. Images of Nera flashed through his mind. The joyful smile of the small child who had clung to him in his first ever hugs. The smile didn't seem to fade as he saw her laughing with his mother, with her parents, with Tommaso, all while calling his name. He'd seen anger from her before as well. He'd seen the way it had flashed when she'd thrown herself at his attackers.

And, so recently, he'd seen a woman's face flushed with passion. Nera had absolute trust in him. Even while she watched him carve off someone's ear.

"I'll talk to your father," Vittore said.

Giovanni's hand curled into a fist. It hurt. "What good will that do?"

"I warned you. He's in a mood today, though lately that always seems to be the case." Vittore let his head fall back against the wall. "I know your Nera isn't a risk to us."

"How do you know?" Giovanni asked. Not because he questioned Nera. No, he had no doubt that she would only ever think of him. He should have stayed far away from her long ago.

"I'm not a fool, Giovanni. I was the one that cleaned up that mess of a kidnapping years ago. Not physically, Enzo handles that, but the fallout after " His uncle stared at his legs, extended in front of him. "Your father refused to lift a finger, but he was proud of the way you handled yourself. I didn't tell him about the girl back then. Maybe if I had, he'd see what I see."

Giovanni turned to face his uncle.

"I've stopped by the bakery myself a few times since. Never when you would see. I knew you were keeping an eye on her, but I respected that." A sad smile lifted his lips. "I like her for you. You looked so happy earlier. I've never seen you look like that."

Giovanni stared at the gun. He opened and closed his hand, relieved when the pain was less sharp each time. "If I have to kill someone, it won't be her."

The smile faded. "Sometimes you are exactly like your father. So, what, you're going to kill the head of the Di Salvo family now? You? The boy who was just thrown around like a rag doll?"

Giovanni hated that his words were nothing but the truth.

Vittore rose to his feet. "There's one thing you haven't mentioned. My brother is worried because there's no reason for the girl to be loyal to us. Give her that reason."

Giovanni's heartbeat throbbed in his chest. "No."

Vittore ignored his protest. "Marry the girl. That will provide her with Di Salvo protection."

"Like it did my mother?" Giovanni asked. He could picture her broken body so easily, lying right where he sat on the carpet.

"Your mother was a Bratva." Vittore's tone had gone cold. "I thought the marriage would form an alliance, but she betrayed us. Your father wasn't wrong to call her a traitor."

Giovanni swallowed the denial his father and uncles never listened to. He'd never been able to convince them that his mother wouldn't turn on the Di Salvos. Just as she hadn't been able to.

Because she'd hated his father. That much had always been true.

Giovanni closed his eyes against the memory of her pleading her case.

"Your bakery girl has no such ties. It's completely different."

Giovanni opened his eyes again to find his uncle holding a hand down to him. He gripped it, allowing Vittore to help him to his feet. He crossed to the bed and picked up his gun. No dust resettled on the coverlet. In fact, as he looked around, Giovanni realized the room was spotless. He didn't understand. Why would his father maintain the room of the woman he'd never cared for?

Giovanni let his gun rest in his hands.

Vittore clapped him on the shoulder, just as he'd done outside of Nera's bedroom. "Marry the girl, and I'll work on your father. He can be volatile, but he sees reason. At least, he used to." With that, he left him alone in the room.

Giovanni continued to stare at the gun. He couldn't agree with his uncle's perception.

His father was never one to see reason.

And a moment of volatility could change everything.

Chapter 16

Nera paced the bedroom, wondering when Giovanni would return. Her eyes strayed to the untouched panna cotta. The custard had melted, and the plate appeared as if it held a slosh of white goop. She sighed as she crossed to pick it up.

Antonio was waiting for her when she opened the door.

His eyebrow lifted at what she carried in her hand, but for once he remained silent as he fell into place beside her.

The kitchen was as bright as usual, but outside the windows dusk had fallen. The state of the panna cotta further underscored that time had passed. At least Giovanni had rested.

Antonio cleared his throat behind her as she washed out the bowl. "I'm not sure whether I should tell you this..."

Nera let the warm water continue to flow over her hands. "Would that really stop you?"

He leaned against the counter next to her. Despite the harsh tone of her words, he was smiling. That only irritated her more.

"Oh, everything I do has a purpose." Antonio stared down at the single dish she continued to wash.

Nera gave up on the distraction. The plate was already clean. She turned off the water, placing it on the nearby rack to dry with all the others.

Antonio grabbed her hand, drawing her attention back to his face. "Panna cotta isn't Giovanni's favorite."

Nera snorted. "I think I'd know better than you." She tugged on her hand, but Antonio's hold tightened on her wrist.

"It was his mother's favorite."

"I know that!"

Footsteps paused in the doorway. It was the Di Salvos' cook. Nera smiled at him, pulling free from Antonio as she moved away from the counter. The cook hadn't liked her in the kitchen during lunchtime, when she first made the panna cotta, but his frown had eased when she'd respected his space. She greeted him before heading toward the exit.

"Hold on," Antonio said, jogging after her. He glanced over at the cook and lowered his voice. "Don't make it again."

Nera's brows drew together. "But—"

Antonio's fist smacked into the wall beside her, causing her to flinch. "Goddammit!" He glanced through the open archway.

As usual, a group of Di Salvos had gathered near the entrance. Nera didn't understand why they seemed to have so much time on their hands. In her mind, they should have been off doing something much more Mafia-like.

"Look." Antonio leaned closer to her ear. "Any reminder of Giovanni's mother is not welcome in this house," he whispered. His head lifted, and there was no hint of a smile as he stared at her. "Do you understand?"

Nera didn't. She nodded anyway, better able to breathe when Antonio gave her space. Even so, her chest still felt too tight.

Antonio's hands slid into his jacket pockets as he leaned into the arch of the entryway. "Where to next?"

"I should check on Tommaso," Nera said.

Antonio nodded, leading the way.

Tommaso was sleeping. Nera stayed with Mylene, keeping her company and helping her to coax Tommaso into eating when the dinner trays arrived.

Eventually Nera returned to her room. It was impossible to sleep. The sheets smelled of Giovanni, who still hadn't returned.

Antonio's muffled voice reached her through the door. "Goddammit!" His frustration sounded similar.

Nera slipped out of bed, padding over to the door.

Antonio's voice had lowered to the point that she strained to hear it. "I knew I should have gone with you. Didn't Vittore—"

"Don't," Giovanni interrupted. She'd never heard that exact tone from him before. "I'm going with Enzo tonight. You good here?"

"For fuck's sake, Gio." Antonio's voice had gone even softer. "I can tell you're favoring one hand. Let me go."

Silence followed, and Nera reached for the doorknob.

"I need this," Giovanni said. The emotion from before had faded. His words sounded hollow through the wood between them.

"Fine," Antonio said. "Don't worry about the girl. Consider me her perpetual babysitter. Whatever you need."

Footsteps followed, and Nera realized she'd waited too long. She pulled open the door, moving into the hallway.

Giovanni's back stiffened at the sound of the door opening. Then he continued to walk away.

Nera didn't call after him. All she could do was watch him go. She stood there long after he'd disappeared down the stairs.

"You should get some sleep," Antonio said.

Nera couldn't see his expression clearly, but his voice sounded tired.

She went back inside the guest room and closed the door. Her talk with Giovanni was going to need to wait.

She didn't expect that she wouldn't see him at all the next day. Or the day after that.

It was earlier than usual when she slipped out of her room. Her hope faded when no red glow waited for her. She'd thought maybe he disappeared before she woke up. It had been days since she'd seen him.

Antonio said nothing as she crossed to sit down next to him against the hallway wall.

Nera stared back toward the room. She was beginning to think that what had happened inside it was all a fever dream. Even Giovanni's scent on the blankets had faded.

"No sling?" Antonio asked.

Nera had chosen not to put it on. Her arm ached a little where the bullet wound was, but the straps of the sling were a pain to get right on her own. "It's been a week, I'm healing."

Antonio leaned his head against the wall. "Giovanni won't like it."

Nera didn't admit that she agreed and hoped he'd notice. Maybe then he'd come talk to her.

She wasn't sure how she felt about Giovanni's cousin. His attitude toward her hadn't changed much, despite the additional time they'd been spending together. But that extra time meant she saw more resemblances between him and Giovanni than she'd like to admit. Especially in their eyes.

The hallway lights were too bright. Nera searched for any other lurking Di Salvos, but all seemed quiet, which wasn't a surprise. It was well before sunrise.

"Can you explain?" Nera asked. "About Giovanni's mother?" She bit her lip as she avoided looking at Antonio. She'd been holding off to ask Giovanni himself, and part of her wanted to withdraw the question.

Antonio remained silent. He squinted up at the light fixture above them.

"I liked her." Nera easily pictured the delicate woman who had looked so much like Giovanni. Or really the other way around. "She came to the bakery often, and she was so warm. She loved Giovanni. That much was obvious." His mother had doted on him, though she was careful to respect his boundaries, unlike Nera. "I know she died."

"Died isn't quite right," Antonio said. His legs stretched out on the floor in front of him. "She was executed."

Nera's heart beat hard in her chest.

"She betrayed us," Antonio continued.

"She would never!" Nera closed her mouth when she realized she'd shouted the words. Her gaze fell to her lap, unable to meet Antonio's eyes. "She wouldn't hurt Giovanni."

Antonio didn't respond at first. Then he acted like Nera had said nothing at all. "Giovanni's mother was killed as a traitor. And that's something the Di Salvos never forgive." Antonio's head shifted along the wall. Nera felt the weight of his gaze as he studied her. "It's important that you understand that."

It wasn't the first time Nera had been told something like this. Tommaso had spoken about loyalty when he'd explained what the Di Salvos were all about.

"Giovanni was there when she was killed." Antonio stared up at the light fixture again. "I'd hate for that to happen to him again."

Words pushed at Nera's lips, but she swallowed them, letting the silence remain.

The hallway windows were still dark when she pushed to her feet. Antonio rose beside her, resigned to her typical day as he followed her to the kitchen.

Nera hated having nothing to do. Mylene and Tommaso had taken to bickering more in his room now that he didn't sleep all day. The kitchen had become Nera's escape, like usual.

She decided to bake tarts in addition to croissants that morning. She had the extra time, and Tommaso's favorite might improve his mood.

Without the sling, it was much easier to work. She'd almost memorized her way around the kitchen. Over the last three days, she'd even begun helping the Di Salvos' cook during lunch and dinner. He hadn't liked it at first, cursing at her in French. During the dinner service, when she'd cursed back in the same language, he'd grinned at her. Soon he was showing her pictures of his half a dozen kids, and they'd become fast friends. She was much more comfortable baking than cooking meals, and he had a lot he could teach her.

Even so, she preferred her time alone in the kitchen best. Well, mostly alone. Antonio had complained when she'd left off the lights the first morning, but he no longer mentioned it. The shine of the metal appliances and the overhead fluorescent lights gave her a headache later in the day.

When she lifted the first tray of tarts, her bad arm protested. She would have dropped the metal tray if Antonio hadn't steadied it. "Give me that." He took it to the preheated oven, slipping it inside. "You're using the arm too much."

She studied him. "Are you worried about me?"

Antonio shook his head. "Not you." That was true enough. Antonio only ever worried about Giovanni. It had taken Nera a while, but she'd finally realized that was what drove most of his actions.

She still hadn't figured out how forcing her to watch Giovanni torture someone had been for Giovanni's benefit. She'd almost begun to hope Antonio would do it again just so she could see Giovanni, but his cousin seemed to be respecting his wishes. She wouldn't fool herself into believing she had an ally in Antonio.

After the baking was done, Nera plated more than a few tarts to take to Tommaso's room. Antonio beat her to it, carrying the plate himself.

"Get going," he said.

The Di Salvos had been hovering outside the kitchen, waiting for her to leave. More said good morning to her as they moved inside to grab her treats than they had the first time. Nera liked to believe they were getting used to her being around. There was one older Di Salvo that always voiced his appreciation for her baking.

She knocked lightly on Tommaso's door, waiting a moment before opening it. There were some things between Mylene and Tommaso that she didn't want to see.

But when she pushed open the door, it was Giovanni she saw standing closest to Tommaso.

Nera blinked. Whenever she encountered that maroon glow after she hadn't seen it in a while, she was struck all over again by how much it truly eased her tension. "Giovanni."

His hand fisted as she said his name.

The remnants of a bruise darkened the back of it, just enough to create a shadow that her vision picked up. Giovanni wasn't looking at her, she realized. Not really. He stared at the open doorway behind her instead.

"Excuse me," he murmured to Tommaso and crossed the room.

When Nera refused to move out of the way, Giovanni's eyes fixed on her arm. *Good*, she thought. He'd have to say something to her now. She waited for the flash to cross his face, not wanting to miss it before he forced himself to remain calm.

His face remained blank. "I'm glad you're healing," he said. Then he slipped past her. Their shoulders brushed, and Nera warmed from even that slight pressure.

She whirled in the doorway. "Giovanni, wait!" she called, reaching for him.

"Nera!" Tommaso called from the bed.

Nera hadn't heard that tone from him very often, and it stopped her forward momentum. She turned to look at the man who had been a father to her for longer than her real one.

"We need to talk, Nera," he said.

Antonio nudged her inside the room, handing her the plate of tarts before pulling the door shut behind him.

Chapter 17

Giovanni paused when Antonio chased him down the hallway. Now more than ever, one of them needed to stay as close to Nera as possible.

Until he personally saw her board the plane to France, he was going to worry. Giovanni's hands tingled as he wondered again whether that would be far enough out of his father's reach.

He never should have brought her to the Di Salvo estate.

Antonio stared at him expectantly, and Giovanni realized he'd missed what his cousin had said. "Are you sure about this?" he asked again. "I mean, I was the one that said you should fuck her out of your system, but I didn't expect you to actually do it."

Giovanni's fingers tingled like they did every time he failed to keep from imagining how Nera had looked when he'd touched her. His shoulder still burned from brushing past her in the doorway.

"I'm impressed, to be honest. Using her like that to then ignore her for days is cold. I didn't know you had it in you." Antonio clapped a hand on his shoulder and squeezed.

Unfortunately, it was the shoulder he'd scraped during the raid against the Bratva the night before. Giovanni bit his cheek to keep his hiss of pain inside. The calculating look on Antonio's face meant he was more than aware of what he'd done.

Between his raw, healing throat, the slight fracture to his hand, and now his shoulder, Giovanni didn't need the reminder of how weak he was. He shoved his cousin's hand away. "I told you, nothing happened."

Antonio glared back. "I'm not an idiot. Even if all you did was get hard around her, that's a big deal for you."

Giovanni's stomach sank.

"I've been aware for a while now that you're a little bent when it comes to that stuff. So when you said you didn't see her that way, I was disappointed, but I believed you." Antonio ran a hand through his hair. "But hell, Gio, you had an erection when you were standing all disheveled in the hallway. One even talking to Vittore didn't soften. I wanted to shove you back into the room so you'd use it right then, but—"

Giovanni shoved his cousin into the wall. "Enough!" He froze before he dragged his hands away from Antonio's chest. He was reminding himself of his father.

Antonio glanced toward the closed door to Tommaso's recovery room before looking back at Giovanni. "Are you running? Is that what this is?"

Giovanni took another step away, his hands starting to shake. "My father told me to kill her."

Antonio's anger receded at that. "Well, fuck."

The panic that had been lurking inside him was much too close to the surface. "She was supposed to fly to France." He closed his eyes, forcing himself to pull in a deeper breath. "There's a culinary school there."

"And no Di Salvos. Not that I'm aware of, anyway." Antonio cussed under his breath. "What did Vittore say?"

Giovanni felt lightheaded remembering his uncle's words. "I haven't mentioned France. He had a different solution."

"What solution?"

"Vittore told me to marry her." It still didn't sound real.

Antonio stared at him.

"It's not a solution." Giovanni's hand ached where it clenched into a fist at his side. The pain was a steady reminder that he couldn't protect Nera from his father.

"She'd be a Di Salvo," Antonio said, though he looked doubtful. His gaze moved to the closed door. "She's been getting phone calls, but she hasn't picked up. You sure the culinary school is what she wants?"

Giovanni didn't bother answering. He knew all too well that Nera's obsession with him rivaled his own for her. It didn't matter. His father wasn't the only enemy.

Despite torturing more Bratva over the last few days, no new information had come to light. None of the Russian *bratkóv* appeared to know why Nera was targeted or who could have done it. His questions confused them.

Giovanni was beginning to think that if he wanted answers, he was going to have to meet with their lunatic *pakhan* he'd heard so much about. He hadn't been able to figure out how to do it and return alive. The Bratva had been more scared of their boss than of him, no matter what he did to them.

All the dying men had said the same thing: There was no reason for the Bratva to target him or Nera.

Giovanni ground his teeth together. The sooner he could put Nera on her plane to France, the sooner he'd be able to think clearly again.

Nera stared at Tommaso.

"Don't look at me that way. This was always the plan." He tried to sit up straighter, groaning as he did.

Mylene rushed forward to push at his shoulders until he lay back against the pillows again.

"I'm fine, Mylene, love," Tommaso said, but the words came out in a less than convincing pant.

Suddenly, the way the admissions office had been insistent about getting ahold of her made sense. They'd been understanding when she'd called to tell them she was recovering from an illness nearly a week ago and had offered various options.

Nera had been waiting until after she talked to Giovanni to call them back. Only, apparently, Giovanni had never intended to talk to her. She wondered how much he had donated to the school for them to be so persistent.

"Let us have the room for a while, Mylene," Tommaso said. His tone was back to the gruff, low murmur Nera was so familiar with.

Mylene blew out a breath, but straightened away from him. "I don't like this," she said. She crossed to Nera, putting a hand on her good arm. "You! Don't put your dreams aside for any man." She shot a glare at Tommaso. "They're not worth it."

The door slammed behind her as she left.

Tommaso held his arms wide for Nera. "Come over here."

Nera stared at the bandages wrapped around his torso. "You were shot."

His fingers curled all the same, beckoning her forward. "That's nothing. I'm still a big bear of a man. And I want to hug my daughter."

Only she wasn't his daughter. Nera crossed to him anyway, easing herself onto the bed, careful to keep her weight off his chest. He might think he was invincible, but he was only a man.

A man who had been protecting her ever since her parents had been killed in the Mafia's crossfire.

Nera listened to his heartbeat beneath the bandages. It had always been a little slow, as far back as she could remember. She would close her eyes and listen to it when she was afraid of how the world continued to look in her broken vision.

"Why didn't you tell me what really happened?" Nera asked. His arms tightened on her back. "I can't believe I didn't remember." On closed eyelids the images of Giovanni in the church would be so clear.

"Trauma does strange things. I guess I assumed your mind knew best." He sighed. "Besides, it made things easier on Giovanni. That boy has had it tough."

Nera didn't have a response to that. Even when she'd thought he was an angel, he'd looked like an especially sad one.

"How much do you remember?" Tommaso asked.

Nera carefully sat up, and Tommaso's arms fell away. "Giovanni protected me. I think he's always done that. Is he the reason you became my guardian?"

He shook his head. "I volunteered. Giovanni kept the Di Salvos from killing me for leaving, though. Persuaded his uncle it wasn't a betrayal."

The word made her remember Giovanni's mother. "Giovanni feels responsible for my parents' deaths, and for what happened to me, but

I was the one that got involved that day. I couldn't stand the idea of Giovanni getting hurt." She frowned down at her hands. "I still can't."

Tommaso brushed her hair behind her ear. "Have you told the boy that you love him yet?"

Nera's eyes filled with tears. It made the world blur in a gentler way. "You just told me that he wants me to go to France." She closed her eyes. "I could tell him, but I doubt it would change anything."

"I understand why he's doing what he's doing. France would be safer for you." Tommaso's voice grew gruffer. "Things are a mess right now, Nera. And in my condition, I can't help to protect you like I should."

She took a breath, trying to steady her voice. "I told you. He feels responsible for everything bad that's happened. This too." Her lips trembled. "What would me telling him I love him do? It'd be a burden. I don't need more of his pity."

Tommaso's rough fingers pinched her nose closed.

Nera blinked her eyes open to stare into his angry face.

"Don't be a ninny. What Giovanni feels isn't pity." He released her so she could breathe, then sighed. "He's got it all figured out, so I didn't bother him with my truth either."

"What truth?"

"My time with you was limited. I always knew it. I was biding my time until he got his head out of his ass and came to collect you." Tommaso shook his head. "When I used to be his momma's bodyguard, I saw it. You two were it for each other. Even his momma knew it, God rest her soul." He frowned, but the expression eased as he reached out to rough up Nera's hair.

"Hey!" she protested.

Another groan escaped him as he collapsed against the pillow. "Damn, they made a mess of me. Hard to keep my eyes open." He forced them wide, but they almost immediately began to droop again. "Tell him or don't tell him, Nera, that's your choice. But don't fret about going to France. It'll just be a few more years of you two biding time." His big hand blocked most of his yawn before resting on the bed again. "You two were meant for each other. It'll happen eventually."

Nera watched the tension leave Tommaso as he slipped into sleep, a sign of how close he'd come to death.

She couldn't tell him all she was thinking anyway. Eventually wasn't good enough. Not when she craved Giovanni's hands on her. Her cheeks flushed, and she scrambled off of Tommaso's bed.

At least the memory let her accept the opposite of what her inner voice had been trying to tell her. Tommaso was right. Giovanni's touch hadn't been about pity.

Mylene thought culinary school in France was her dream. It had been Mylene's dream, once upon a time. That was part of why Nera had chosen it. The woman had become like a mother to her.

But culinary school, for Nera, had always been about running away from a dream she'd seen as an impossibility. Now France would no longer be running away.

Like Tommaso said, it would just be biding time.

Chapter 18

Giovanni continued to avoid her into the next day, so Nera grumpily made her way to the kitchen.

"Hey, none of that." Antonio stretched as he walked beside her.

Enzo had taken over for him during the night, so for the first time in a while, Antonio had gotten enough sleep. Nera had forced herself to move away from the door when Antonio mentioned the Bratva to his uncle.

Not that she minded knowing things. She'd had her suspicions about what Giovanni was up to. Listening at doors wasn't an honest way to get information, though. She was a long way off from Giovanni wanting to share things with her, if he ever wanted to.

Without Giovanni taking a shift outside her door, she'd become a bigger burden on the other two. The rest of the Di Salvos seemed friendly enough. They'd complained when Enzo ate more than his fair share of what she'd baked that morning, but it had been good-natured ribbing. Nera didn't fully understand Giovanni's concern over her safety with them, but she trusted his judgment.

She'd called the school late the night before, which had been morning hours for them. Tommaso had told her what time the flight was that Giovanni had scheduled for her. He had said none of the other Di Salvos were to know, so she hadn't mentioned it to Enzo or Antonio.

Nera was starting to resign herself to the idea that Giovanni wouldn't talk to her at all before he saw her off.

"You know you don't have to help with lunch or dinner, right?" Antonio asked as they drew closer to the kitchen.

The French cook was inside, already muttering curses.

"I like to keep busy," Nera reminded Antonio.

"Just don't overdo it with the arm!" he called after her.

Nera thought he might have lied before. He was a bit of a worrywart, even toward her. While she was helping the cook, Antonio often shoved her aside to take over. He wasn't nice about it, despite his smile, but she'd started to believe he was well-intentioned, if still an ass.

Halfway through preparing lunch, Nera let Antonio take over lifting the tray and pulled out her vibrating phone.

"Sneaky, sneaky," the cook said, more than obvious in his attempt to peer over her shoulder. "Is that another lover? Be careful, the Di Salvo men can be possessive."

Nera stared down at the incoming call from the school. If she waited to call back, it would be too late in their time zone. She accepted the call, moving to the side of the kitchen.

They wanted to verify her start date. Very aware of Antonio's presence and what Tommaso had told her, she kept an eye on him as she answered their questions with single-syllable words.

The cook helped by asking Antonio to pull something out of the far oven.

"Tomorrow," Nera murmured in response to their question about her flight. "No, thank you." She declined their offer of help getting from the airport to her lodgings and ended the call as soon as she could.

"Going off to France?" the Frenchman asked in a low murmur.

Nera wasn't surprised he'd recognized the culinary school's name. She'd been proud to be accepted into such a prestigious program. She glanced at Antonio even as she shook her head. "No," she lied. The strained smile she tried to flash reminded her how bad she was at lying. "I'll go stir the sauce," she offered, giving Antonio a wide berth as she crossed the kitchen.

She stared into the sauce as she stirred, telling her heartbeat to settle. The cook wasn't a Di Salvo. He was an amazing chef with half a dozen kids, who liked to curse in French while he created his culinary masterpieces.

Her gut twisted anyway. Her sight made it impossible to tell if the color of the sauce was right. She pulled up a spoonful and blew to cool it enough to taste.

An odd thudding sounded behind her, and she whirled, the hot sauce splashing against her arm. She tried to focus her eyes in the overly bright kitchen, but what they told her she was seeing made no sense. Antonio lay crumpled on the ground, and the French cook was bringing the skillet down on his head with another sickening thud.

Nera's hand reached behind her, patting along the cutting board on the counter as she watched the cook place the skillet on the kitchen island. He fumbled under his apron, and Nera threw herself to the side, knocking the cutting board to the floor with her as the French cook brought up a gun.

The shot didn't sound like any of the ones she'd heard before, either on the street both times she'd saved Giovanni or outside the gun range in the basement. It was more of a coughing hiccup as it pierced the saucepan she'd left on the stove.

The knife she'd been searching for before nicked her hand as she scrambled for safety. She closed her hand on the blade as the next bullet cracked the tile behind her, then the island was between them.

"I'm sorry, ma choupette."

Nera hated that he used the endearment Mylene had always used for her. She scuttled faster around the island, using her injured arm to grab the handle of the knife. It was her dominant hand anyway, and the cut in her other hand burned. She almost tripped over Antonio, who was still prone on the floor. He would be clearly visible if anyone bothered to look through the entryway, and she prayed for one of the Di Salvos to see him and come help.

She pushed herself up to her feet behind the chef, staggering in her haste.

It sounded like the cook was crying. "They have my kids," he sobbed as he turned.

Nera sliced the knife across the Frenchman's throat.

He'd always been particular about the sharpness of his knives. Blood spurted, and his eyes went wide in shock.

Nera grappled with him for the gun he held. His finger squeezed the trigger before she could rip it away. The bottle of cooking wine they'd been using shattered. Then she had the gun, and the cook lay on the ground, gurgling as he stared up at her.

Nera turned her back on him, dropping beside Antonio to check his pulse. It felt strong beneath her wet fingers. She was careful to keep the knife edge away from him, but she couldn't bring herself to drop it. Her other hand gripped the handle of the gun. She'd never held a gun besides when Tommaso had made her, and she made certain she pointed it away from Antonio. Her fingers fumbled for the safety she remembered, but they were slick in blood and struggled with the mechanism.

In fact, Antonio's shirt was covered in the gray color. He hadn't been bleeding, but she'd smeared it all over him.

A shout from the entryway pulled her attention there. A Di Salvo stared back. It was the older one who had always called good morning and thanked her for breakfast. Nera started to sag in relief, but then she realized he was pointing a gun at her.

Her throat closed on any words that might have stopped him.

His arm was shoved to the side even as he pulled the trigger. This shot was the sound she remembered. It tore into what remained of the saucepan. The dark liquid splattered the ground.

"Let's just calm down," Enzo said. His voice sounded like it always did: amused and bored all at the same time.

Nera's throat loosened. "I didn't—" Her eyes flew to the staring blankness that the Frenchman's had become. "Well, I did. The cook was me. But not Antonio!" She swallowed as she carefully placed the gun on the floor. "I'd never hurt Antonio," she whispered.

She moved away from where he lay. Her palm wouldn't uncurl from around the kitchen knife, even though her healing bullet wound ached from the intense pressure.

Enzo crossed the kitchen to crouch down beside her. "Can I?" he asked, moving his hand toward the knife.

Nera nodded. "I'm sorry. I can't seem to..." Her eyes found the wide, accusing, dead ones of the cook, and her hand finally loosened.

"I understand." Enzo took the knife away. "Don't worry. I never liked his cooking." His touch was gentle as he turned her hands over. "Cut yourself good. Giovanni won't be happy."

"Sorry," Nera mumbled around the sudden constriction in her throat. Her lips became too numb for any other words to slip through.

His fingers smoothed over the backs of her hands, and he gave her a quick squeeze. "Nothing to be sorry about. You did good." His eyes narrowed as they moved to the entryway. "Bring Giovanni here," he ordered the other Di Salvo. "Junior, not Senior."

The man who had come close to shooting her nodded and fled.

Enzo's gaze flicked over the rest of the kitchen. "Only casualties were a saucepan, a bottle, and a stupid Frenchman. You did better than good." They settled on where Antonio lay. "And that casualty, I guess."

Antonio let out a curse, his hand reaching for his head.

"But see? His head is hard. No damage there." Enzo squeezed her hands again before releasing her to help Antonio sit up. "You were supposed to be protecting her, you idiot," he said, his tone light.

Antonio's eyes opened to glare at Enzo. "Where the fuck is he?" He grew still when he found the dead man bleeding out from his throat.

"This is your mess. Help me with cleanup." Enzo moved to the body, pushing the apron aside to pat at the cook's pockets.

"Fuck, my head hurts," Antonio complained, his fingers gingerly searching over the back of his head. "That cast-iron packed a punch." His fingers came away clean. "Huh," he grunted, staring down at the blood on his shirt.

Enzo's eyes flicked to him. "That was all her." He rolled the body over. "Might need stitches."

Antonio crawled toward her. "Here, let me see." His hands were just as gentle as Enzo's had been, but then they squeezed too tightly to counter his body's sway. "Damn, I'm seeing double." He stared at her face as his eyes struggled to focus. Then he smiled. "You're not dead." He glanced over at the cook. "Fuck, I'm getting soft. Never saw that one coming. He say anything?"

"His kids." Nera closed her eyes. The pictures the French cook had shown her flashed in her memory. All chubby and smiling and way too young. "They have his kids. I don't know who." She'd killed him before he could tell her. Nera's stomach lurched as she wondered if that meant she'd killed all those children.

"That helps. He didn't seem like the type." Antonio patted the top of her head. "You, though." He shrugged, his hand falling away. "I've got to keep my eye on you."

"Nera!" The way Giovanni called her name was familiar. His face was all hard angles and clenched jaw when he took Antonio's place in front of her. His color brought a shadow to the too-bright light that helped her breathing to slow. Giovanni reached for her hands.

The blood that smeared them wasn't all her own. Nera had the stupid urge to pull free to hide that, but she let him touch her instead. At least with him filling her vision she couldn't see the dead eyes of the Frenchman staring at her anymore.

Chapter 19

Giovanni's hands shook as he studied the blood on Nera. It shouldn't have been there.

The deep cut was in her nondominant hand. There was a bloody knife nearby. He wanted to use it on the blubbery body until the Frenchman's face was no longer recognizable. Maybe then he'd find the calm inside that used to be so easy to obtain.

"I'm sorry, *padrino*," a voice said from the doorway.

Nera's eyes shifted past Giovanni to the Di Salvo soldier. Her shoulders tensed, and she looked toward the metal door of the oven instead.

The soldier's gaze wouldn't meet Giovanni's. It flicked toward Nera, but inside was only guilt. "I'm sorry," the older Di Salvo said again, this time to her. "If Enzo hadn't…" He swallowed, looking away.

Giovanni released Nera's hand as he stood, a different chill running through his body.

"Leave off," Enzo told him from where he continued to search the cook's body. "It couldn't have been helped, the way she looked."

Giovanni forced himself to look away from the man who had been a Di Salvo for longer than he'd been alive.

His uncle smiled. "Good thing I like that look on a woman."

"Get out of here," Antonio ordered the soldier, who fled the kitchen. He moved in front of Giovanni, forcing his eyes to focus on him. "It's my fault. I fucked up." His hand moved to the back of his head, and he winced.

Giovanni looked at the dead cook. His neck continued to seep blood onto the tile below him. The wound differed from the one Nera had given the Bratva in her living room; a slice instead of a stab.

He crouched down in front of her. "Can you stand?" he asked, wishing he could carry her. His pathetic body wouldn't make it up the flight of stairs to her room.

Nera stood on her own.

Giovanni reached for her injured hand, careful not to squeeze the cut as he led her out of the room—and right into his waiting father.

"What's all this?" Giovanni Sr. asked. He stared past Giovanni to study Nera, a blankness in his eyes that was more terrifying than heat.

Ice trickled through Giovanni's body, numbing him until he no longer felt his grip on Nera's hand.

His father's gaze shifted to him. "I warned you."

Giovanni moved in front of her. "There was no Bratva," he forced out. That Nera's attacker hadn't been part of the Bratva made no sense to him, but that wasn't important in that moment. His heart had slowed until he could barely feel the thump.

The old, familiar heat entered his father's hard, blue eyes as he stared down his son.

"Uh, brother, the doll is bleeding. Get out of the way," Enzo said from the kitchen doorway.

The staring contest between them was broken, and Giovanni followed his father's gaze as it shifted to his uncle.

"She's tons better than that French cook. You should have her replace him." For once there wasn't a smile on Enzo's face. "I bet even you would like her panna cotta."

Giovanni Sr.'s jaw tightened as a message passed between him and his brother. Then he turned away, his tread heavy on the stairs.

"For fuck's sake, Enzo," Antonio muttered from behind him.

Giovanni stood frozen in place.

Enzo scowled at him. "Get her tended to." His face softened as it drifted to Nera. His smile had returned before he disappeared back into the kitchen.

Giovanni took her to the same bathroom where he'd bandaged her once before. He was afraid it would become a habit. It couldn't. That was why he had to send her away.

He didn't speak as she let him wash the blood off her hands. Nera followed his directions without words. Luckily, the cut along her palm wasn't as deep as he had first assumed. Butterfly bandages worked well enough to seal it before he wrapped it in the same type of gauze he'd used for her gunshot wound.

"That was your father?" Nera asked. Her uncut palm came up to cup his face, lifting his gaze from the bandage to meet hers. "Your eyes are the same," she murmured.

"Yes," Giovanni said. That was the only physical trait he shared with his father. His skin, while it looked similar, bruised much more easily.

"Can I hug you?" Nera asked.

She'd never asked before. As a child, she'd forced her arms around him and squeezed him tighter than he'd ever been held before. The experience hadn't always been pleasant, given the skittering nerves that flooded over his skin. Every hug had caused a tightening in his chest, as if he couldn't breathe. He'd worried that he would somehow break her.

Giovanni nodded. Her arms wrapped around him, so much stronger than they used to be. She was soft and warm where they touched.

Her forehead was at the perfect height to press gently against his.

The numbness from the encounter with his father faded as her warmth took over. It wasn't the biting heat he'd experienced with her before. He wasn't aroused.

How could he be when he knew his father would prefer it if he killed her?

Nera's eyes stared into his own. They didn't glimmer with her recent scare. They weren't blank. The warmth that was all Nera resided there.

"Can I kiss you?" Her question was a whisper against his lips.

Together, they closed the space between them. This time the kiss remained gentle, as if they were each verifying that the other was still there. The soft brush of her lips returned the ache to Giovanni's chest. He felt like he had slipped within a sun-warmed lake, where the air was just above his lips; only he had no desire to reach for it, not if he had to leave this comforting embrace.

Nera's lips parted from his.

"Can I love you?" The murmured words added to his disorientation. Her breath brushed over the dampness she'd left on his mouth as she searched his eyes. "Is that okay? Because I already do. I always have." Her eyes filled before closing, so that a tear slid free. "I don't know how to stop."

Giovanni couldn't move his arms from where they had wrapped around her, even to wipe the tear away. "Do you want to stop?" he asked.

He'd always known she'd loved him, even as a child. That was why it had hurt so much to be near her. No one had ever loved him. Not even his mother, despite what she'd said at the end.

His mother had named him Giovanni for a reason. To remind herself exactly where he'd come from.

His breath held as he waited for Nera's answer.

"No." Then she kissed him again. It started gentle, like the one before, but her lips slowly began to demand a response. Her tongue stroked inside him as she pressed tighter, pushing him back against the door.

Giovanni's lips slanted over hers in return. Her lips were soft and stroking and perfect. The way her tongue tangled with his sent the same heat in as before to destroy him. She cuddled his growing erection against her own heat, her sexy murmur in his mouth pulling out his own groan of response.

Nera was in his arms, and his body reacted because she had been put on this earth just for him. He never wanted to let her go.

Panic slid through him at the thought. He lifted his head and pressed it against the door, closing his eyes so he couldn't see more temptation. He needed to grip hard to the control that he was known for.

Nera's lips grazed his neck, sending a delicious shiver through him. The fading bruises there added to his sensitivity. Her hands slid down to his ass as she pulled him right where he wanted to be.

Only Nera had forgotten about her injuries. She tried to muffle a gasp of pain against his throat.

Suddenly control was easy, as the heat fled from his body.

Nera noticed the change. Her head lifted, and they stared into each other's eyes again.

"Don't send me away." It was a plea. One he'd expected. That was why he'd avoided her for days.

Giovanni swallowed hard. "It's not safe." That was even clearer after the attack in the kitchen. Giovanni hadn't been nearby. There was no question that Nera had been the target. He still didn't know why.

"I don't need safety." Nera bit her lip before words rushed free. "He was French, Giovanni. He knew about the school."

Giovanni closed his eyes as his panic grew. He pulled her more tightly against him. The thought of something happening with her so far away was excruciating, but so was the image of his mother, broken at his father's feet. "If you stay with me, you'll die, Nera. Probably at my father's hands."

But still he couldn't let go of her. He opened his eyes, forcing himself to look at the fear that would be there on her face.

There was no fear. Nera glared at him instead. "I'm not afraid of death, Giovanni. If I'm going to die, I want my blood to be on your hands."

"What?" The word barely squeezed out as her own certainty tried to strangle him. He was finally able to shove her away. "Nera, no!"

She linked her hands tightly around his neck, despite how it must have hurt, clinging to him. "I want to hold you as I die. I want your eyes to be the last thing I see." She kissed him hard on the lips.

Anger washed over him. He turned his face away. "I said no."

She lifted her head. "You don't want that? Good, because I'm willing to fight too. I killed someone today. Someone who was terrified and wanted only to save his kids. And I'm glad!" Her eyes glittered with a hint of madness. "I'll kill anyone if it means I'll get one more second with you."

Giovanni stared back at her.

Nera shook him. "People want to take me from you? Then let's go for blood." Her eyes closed as she rested her forehead against his. Her next words were barely audible. "Even if it's your father's blood."

He'd considered killing his father over the years. He'd even attempted it before. Each time, he was the one that ended up broken, reminded of just how pathetic he was.

Giovanni's arms lifted to hold her again. He closed his eyes. "I'm scared," he admitted.

Her body softened as it rested against him. "Do you know what I'm scared of?" she asked.

Giovanni opened his eyes again. Ever since the accident, Nera's pupils had contracted almost to pinpoints, the black nearly disappearing, leaving more of her gentle brown. The only time they ever focused normally was when she looked at him.

"I'm scared that I'll leave this world regretting every moment that I wasted not being with you. I don't want any regrets." She sighed, searching his eyes. "Let me stay with you."

Giovanni let the warmth of her slide inside him to mingle with the fear. It hurt. Being with her would always hurt. He spoke the desire that had been clawing at him for days. "Marry me, Nera."

Her smile was blinding, but even it didn't remove the shadows from his heart. "Yes," she said. It wasn't the gleeful shout he half expected. She spoke the word solemnly, as if she understood the way she was embracing death.

Chapter 20

Vittore had already smoothed things over with the priest and used their connections to expedite the license. Giovanni was grateful. He'd wasted most of the week he'd been given.

Normally multiple steps would need to be taken in accordance with their faith. Giovanni was the son of the head of the Di Salvo family. Many would have expected his marriage to garner the fanfare that called for. Heredity didn't decide the next leader of their family. An arranged alliance instead of a marriage, like his parents had, would have garnered him more respect among the Di Salvos. Giovanni had resolved to consider such a thing once Nera left for France, back before she chased him out of the bakery, back before everything had fallen apart.

Instead he exchanged vows with Nera inside Tommaso's recovery room, with only Antonio and Enzo present from the Di Salvos, Tommaso himself crying, and Mylene glaring daggers in Giovanni's back.

His mother would have been happy to see them marry. Perhaps she did watch over them, if she had become the angel Nera had once called her.

Nera didn't cry, though her smile was subdued until after they exchanged rings. Then she held up her hand, her eyes searching for his, and Giovanni was unable to look away from what he saw there. He'd kept the bands simple, choosing a matching pair of soft platinum that still weighed down his hand. The material wouldn't scratch if scraped with a knife, and not adding anything that stuck out would be best for Nera. The bandage around her hand looked whiter below the gray ring.

When Giovanni kissed her, his nerves kept the kiss light and quick before they turned to accept their congratulations.

Antonio hadn't argued at all when Giovanni had told him his decision the day before. Over the years, Antonio had often pushed him to marry a daughter from one of the other La Cosa Nostra families, but when Giovanni told him he was going to marry Nera, he had nodded without saying a word.

Maybe, like Giovanni, Antonio thought Nera might not have long for this world.

Giovanni's free hand, the one not linked with Nera's, closed into a fist at the thought.

Tommaso's face was still blotchy when he accepted Nera's hug. "Be happy," he said, his gruff voice deeper than ever. He cleared his throat. "I know you are, but remember that feeling."

Nera nodded.

"Nera," Mylene said. The way she said her name wasn't a joyful sound.

Nera reached out to squeeze her hand anyway. "I want this," she said before turning away, tugging Giovanni with her.

Giovanni met Tommaso's eyes, accepting the nod he sent him before leaving the room with the others.

Vittore was waiting for him in the hallway.

Antonio escorted the priest away without a backward glance. Giovanni worried about his cousin's thoughts, but knew he'd tell him in time.

Vittore held out his hands. Nera hesitated, but released Giovanni so she could accept the gesture. "Welcome to the family," his uncle said. His fingers skated over her bandage as he gripped both of her hands in his. He leaned forward, kissing Nera's cheek before releasing her. His eyes cut to Giovanni. "I'll let your father know she's a Di Salvo now."

Giovanni's throat closed. He nodded, more to let his uncle know he had heard him than in agreement that things had changed at all. He watched Vittore walk away.

Nera linked her injured hand with Giovanni's again. She tugged him forward.

Enzo trailed behind them as Nera led Giovanni to her guest room. Giovanni probably should have taken her to his, but it was only a few doors away from his mother's.

He hesitated outside the door.

Nera smiled at him before she released his hand. "Come inside when you're ready," she said, entering the room without him. The door clicked shut behind her.

Enzo leaned against the opposite wall. His uncle wasn't a voyeur; he was a bodyguard. They still didn't know who was targeting Nera. Even with a locked door and a gun on the nightstand, the idea that they might be attacked while consummating their marriage was horrific in its possibility.

A wedding was a strange thing. Giovanni wondered how many people imagined the groom fucking the bride while they exchanged vows. During the length of a typical Catholic wedding, there was ample time to add in every detail.

"This was a mistake." Giovanni was surprised he'd been able to say the words aloud. His acceptance during the vows had been strangled.

"You think so?" Enzo smiled toward the door. "To me, she's always been a Di Salvo." The smile faded from his face, becoming something harder. "I won't tell you not to worry, Gio, but this is a moment. Treat it as if you might never get it again." Enzo's jaw clenched, and he looked away to stare down the hall. "Because you might not."

Giovanni entered the room, leaving his uncle in the hallway to guard them.

Nera was sitting on the edge of the bed. She'd slipped off her shoes, but otherwise remained dressed. There hadn't been time for a wedding dress. Nera had worn a flowing, cream skirt and a white blouse that matched the bandage on her hand. Her fingers tangled where they rested in her lap, and she stared down at the wedding band she now wore.

Giovanni crossed to sit beside her. Not too close. No part of them touched.

Nera was his wife now, and there was an expectation in the air, as if he was supposed to just take her. Giovanni was limp at the idea of it.

He'd listened to his father force his mother. Mostly through walls, but once he'd been in the room. He couldn't remember how old he'd been while hiding in her closet. He'd been scared, like usual, but he never hid there again. His father had reminded her she was his wife as he'd hurt her. As if it was her duty to be hurt by him. He still remembered the way his mother had cried.

Giovanni had come across them once, toward the end. His father's hand had been on his mother's throat as he'd called her his wife, and something inside Giovanni had snapped. The hatred in his mother's eyes had turned on her son as he'd approached, and she'd screamed at him to go away. "You're Giovanni Di Salvo, just like him. I hate you!" Her eyes had looked so hard. "You're pathetic. What could you do?"

Giovanni had been pathetic, just as she said. He hadn't followed when his father pushed his wife into her room. His father had killed her there that same day.

His mother had told Giovanni that she loved him right before she was shot in the head. Maybe she'd thought she was being kind by saying the words. Giovanni had already known the opposite was true.

"Giovanni?" Nera called. Her hand reached for him.

He pushed off the bed before she could touch him.

Nera remained where she was. "Talk to me," she said.

Giovanni began to pace as he tried to find words. Silence wouldn't be enough this time. "The quickness of the wedding. There was a reason."

Nera nodded. "To make me a Di Salvo."

"It was one path that would postpone my father's threat. And you said you wanted to be with me. But if you didn't mean—" He broke off, running his hands through his hair before forcing himself to face her. "It was giving you my name that I was rushing. We don't have to rush anything else. I'm not demanding sex."

Nera scrambled off the bed. "Are you suggesting our marriage be in name only?" She moved toward him, and he forced himself not to back away. Her hand trembled as it lifted to touch his face. "Giovanni, do you not want me?"

Giovanni couldn't lie. He wasn't certain he'd be able to have sex with her. "What if I touch you like I did once before?" The way she'd looked when she'd orgasmed had captivated him. That was something he wanted again.

He took the hand on his face within his, her bandages reminding him that she'd been hurt just the day before. He used it to lead her to the bed.

Nera pulled away as they stopped beside it. Before he could ask her why, she pushed him onto the bed.

Her hands moved to the buttons of her blouse, making quick work of them. She let the blouse fall to the floor. She still had a bandage on her arm, though she refused to wear the sling anymore. His eyes moved away from the bandage when she unclasped her bra and let it fall away as well.

Giovanni stared at her bare breasts. They were round and captivating, jutting out as far as the swell of her stomach. The bottoms brushed her skin, and he had the urge to cup her. He wondered if the skin there would be as soft as her stomach had been.

Nera wasn't immune to his staring. A bright pink flush stained her chest. She pushed her skirt and underwear down, stepping out of them.

Then she crawled on top of him, completely naked. Giovanni's hands came up, but everywhere he started to touch, his fingers slid across soft skin that made his chest feel too tight.

Nera's hands gripped his face, forcing him to look into her eyes. "I don't want a marriage in name only. It's our wedding night, and you, Giovanni, are going to come inside me. That's what I want."

Her lips weren't gentle when they met his. They weren't just warm either. They were hot and demanding as they slanted over him again and again.

His hands settled on touching her back as he tried not to overthink things. He wasn't forcing Nera. That much let his tension ease as he focused on her kiss. Nera bit his bottom lip, and his mouth opened to her tongue.

He enjoyed being kissed by Nera. Especially the way her eyes stared into his while she did it. Nera's eyes were everything. She was everything.

At the thought, his cock stirred. Giovanni lost himself in her kiss as he realized it would be possible to have an erection on his wedding night after all.

Chapter 21

Giovanni was her husband. The thought wouldn't go away as Nera kissed him over and over again. Devoured him, really.

The gray of his eyes was too calm. That calmness over the years had soothed her heart. It was familiar. Expected.

Nera wanted to shatter it.

His hands lightly pressed to her naked back, but they didn't caress her. Even his lips under hers were still, letting her take what she wanted. Letting her be selfish.

She didn't want to be selfish.

Her legs shifted in restlessness along his slacks, and she felt it. Proof that the desire between them didn't flow only one way. It was only a partial erection, but she would change that.

Being completely naked against him, while he still wore a full, black suit with a tie, was tantalizing. Air blew over her back where his arms didn't cover her, and across her bare ass, making her rock toward his warmth. His mouth opened to her tongue as his hands tightened around her.

She rewarded him for it, tangling and tempting his own tongue into stroking hers.

It wasn't enough. She wanted to touch him more.

Nera lifted her head. It hurt a little to brace herself on her hands, but she didn't show it. Even a hint of discomfort, and Giovanni would give in to worry over passion.

The maroon that she loved darkened the bedspread beneath them. It made the angles and planes of his face even more starkly focused. His hair was white in her vision, not the blond she knew it was. He'd trimmed it for their wedding, and the lower edges brushed his neck above his tightly buttoned shirt and jacket.

Her hands reached for him, her fingers brushing along his vulnerable neck.

Giovanni's breath shuddered at her touch. He stared up at her, as if unable to look away.

She lowered her head to just above his collar. Her tongue marked the spot before her lips settled there and sucked hard. Giovanni was hers. He shuddered as she sucked, making a mark that his collar wouldn't hide.

Nera sat up fully, which pressed his partial erection tighter against her. She enjoyed straddling him and gave in to the urge to shimmy. Her fingers trailed over his skin until she reached his collar and then his tightly cinched tie. She tugged a little, pulling it tighter and watching the gray of his eyes darken. Then she undid the knot.

She slowly pulled the silky cloth free. Once she had it in her hands, she leaned her body back on his lap, which thrust her against his building interest. Then she dangled the tie over the end of the bed, letting it fall to the floor.

Giovanni's hands lowered on her back to aid in the maneuver, then settled at her hips instead when she deliberately thrust against him. His elegant fingers pressed harder into her skin.

He still looked barely disheveled, even without the tie. He'd buttoned his black dress shirt all the way to the top. Her fingers caressed that top button before slipping it free. Then the next, all the way to where the shirt was tucked into his waistband. Giovanni hadn't worn an undershirt. She parted the gap in his shirt with her hands, sliding them over the tight skin of his chest and pushing the material to his shoulders, so that his jacket also slipped off.

Giovanni would never be thick with muscle or have a wide torso. She'd bared his collarbone, so elegant in the way it poked out and the way the skin dipped around it.

Nera lowered herself until her lips could skim over his taut flesh. She followed the path up to the skin at the top of his shoulder. There was a puckered scar there, from an injury long healed. If she shifted more toward his shoulder, she'd kiss over still healing scabs that spread toward his back, but it was his neck that interested her. She drew her tongue over his skin as she moved up the curve of it, then tested little nips of her teeth.

The skin where she'd already sucked had darkened. She sucked there again, wanting to make the hickey even darker.

Giovanni's grip on her hips pulled her lower body tighter against him, telling her he liked what she did.

He swallowed hard, and his Adam's apple bobbed, distracting her. She shifted her lips, kissing over it, and was delighted when it bobbed again.

She lifted herself so she could see his eyes. They didn't look quite so calm any more. But it wasn't enough.

"I want you naked like me," she said.

Giovanni's hands eased her off him, lingering deliciously against her skin before he released her to stand.

He pulled the bottom of his shirt out of his pants, undoing the last buttons before shrugging the black shirt and jacket off together. They didn't fall to the floor as her clothes had. He moved to a nearby chair, hanging them over the back. Then he bent and lifted his tie, hanging it over the jacket as well.

Her clothes were next to be picked up. Nera wanted to tell him not to bother, but she enjoyed watching his hands fold her skirt and place it on the seat of the chair.

Giovanni didn't turn toward her as he stripped off his slacks and underwear. Nera was disappointed at first, but his tight, pert ass was a gift from the angels. She'd found a new place she wanted to bite.

He folded the slacks as well. Her eyes slid up his bare back while he did it, finding more scars—long slices of discolored flesh and smaller, puckered marks lower on his hips. He placed his clothes on top of her skirt. His hand remained over the clothes for a moment before he turned to face her.

Giovanni was stunning. Instead of what society might regard as muscular, masculine perfection, he was lean and angled and sharp. His torso seemed longer because of it. She loved the way his collarbones stuck out. Even more than that, she loved the divots at his pelvic bone that led her gaze down to his cock.

It wasn't massive and hard and standing at attention. It wasn't soft and hanging either. His erection was still in progress, showing an interest that was waiting to grow, as if begging for her touch to help. The head of his cock only barely peeked out.

He could get much bigger than that. She hadn't seen it with her eyes, but she had felt it.

"Come here," Nera said, holding out her unbandaged hand.

Giovanni moved back to the bed. He made as if to crawl over her, but Nera pushed at his shoulder, making him lie flat. She stretched out over him, her weight pressing him down.

They were naked against each other, skin to skin from where her head rested on top of his chest down to their tangled legs. His arms came up around her back on their own. She listened to his heartbeat, a fast strum that told her he was anxious. His hands made small circles on her back.

His partial erection pressed into her stomach.

They didn't say anything. Giovanni's heartbeat started to slow. He had been right, in a way. If all they had that night was this closeness, it was joyful, comforting even.

Nera turned her head to press her lips to his chest. He was mostly smooth, with only spatters of hair. She let her kisses drift over and down, finding his nipple. Her lips closed around it, and she sucked hard.

The softest exhalation escaped his throat. Not a full gasp or groan, but a sound that said he wasn't unaffected. She switched from a suck to a bite, and his cock twitched against her. Yes. Giovanni liked things a little bit harder, edging toward pain.

She moved her face to his other nipple, laving it before biting down. His soothing strokes on her back stopped as his hands clutched at her instead.

Her own hands traced his sides as she shifted down his body, licking a path down to his navel, then thrusting her tongue inside. She couldn't help but to suck hard at the skin along his divots. They were hers, and she left her mark on his left side.

"Nera!" he called. His hands no longer reached her back, and they fell away as she kissed the top of his pubic hair.

The skin of his cock was silky as she rubbed her cheek against it. She lifted herself just enough to stare down at it. Her eyes flicked up toward Giovanni. He'd pushed slightly up from the bed and was watching her hover over him. His jaw was clenched, a tick building there as his hot, dark eyes stared at her.

He wasn't so calm now.

Nera braced herself with her bandaged hand, ignoring the discomfort because it freed her other hand to wrap around his cock. Giovanni's breath shuddered out of him as he became harder. She worked her hand down, freeing the head of him for her lips to close over. She sucked, her eyes watching his Adam's apple bob as he swallowed before squeezing his own shut.

Giovanni was hot and hard under her tight grip. His hands fisted on the bedspread below them as his jaw worked, and his hips below her trembled.

Her tongue slid over his slit. "You can thrust while I do this. Better yet, sink your hands in my hair. Use them to move me how you want."

His hands reached for her, but the fingers were gentle as they slid into her hair. He didn't grip her like he had the bedspread. His eyes had softened. "I can't do that," he said.

She took him deeper into her mouth, sliding down his cock until her lips met her hand.

"Nera!" he cried, his upper body curling forward. His reaction made her do it all over again, lifting until the wet tip of him was free before taking him deep in her mouth. She found a rhythm that made him start to shake. When her teeth grazed him, his fingers tightened in her hair, not as tight as she would have liked.

Realizing what he'd done, his hands left her. "Nera, I—"

He was trying to speak. She slowed, the red of him drawing her in like it always did. His torso fell to the bed as he panted. His erection was straining, and she realized how close she'd brought him. That wouldn't do. She wanted him inside her.

She crawled up his body until her slick entrance brushed over the tip of him. She'd gotten hot just from turning him on. His hands clamped onto her hips to force her still, and the hard grip made her shudder.

Giovanni's jaw had clenched again. His gray eyes seemed to shimmer up at her. It wasn't all desire there. Something else lurked inside that brought her hands up to cup his face. She kissed him, gently this time, before pressing her forehead against his. "It's okay, Giovanni. I want this."

His hips raised toward her at the words, pressing the tip of him firmly against her, but he stopped there, trying to force his body to relax.

"Giovanni?" Nera asked, moving against him.

He sucked in a breath, his eyes squeezing shut. "Wait. Don't move."

A smile slipped over her face at the idea that he was about to lose control. "You mean like this?" she asked, pressing down. They both moaned as the head of his cock slid inside her.

"Nera!" Giovanni's eyes opened. They stared into her from so close. "Is it supposed to feel like this?"

The sudden realization crystalized inside her. Giovanni hadn't had sex before. Nera wasn't sure how it was possible. He was so beautiful. The idea that she was the first to have him caused her to push down, taking more of him inside.

"Why? How does it feel?" she asked.

His jaw clenched beneath her fingers before a groan slipped out of his lips. His forehead slid against hers as he shook his head. His hands trembled at her hips.

Nera rocked against him, working him a little deeper. "I love you, Giovanni."

"Oh, God, Nera!" His hips thrust up as he pulled her hips down, burying himself inside her. Their breath mingled as their bodies shook, trying to process the feeling.

She'd had sex before, had even imagined it had been him, but nothing compared to having Giovanni inside her.

Nera stroked a finger over his jaw before bracing her hands on his chest. Then she began to move.

She lifted slowly at first, feeling the drag of his cock leaving her before she sank down to take him deep again. As sensation built, her body moved faster. Giovanni let her lead, his hands hot on her waist as she rode him.

Soon, each time she sank down, his body lifted into it. His shoulders curled off the bed with every stroke. She knew he was close.

"You can let go," she told him, trying to squeeze on the next downward motion.

The tick at the lower edge of his cheek throbbed, and he shook his head. His hands gripped her hard, stopping her from lifting. He rolled her to her back, further controlling her body. The idea that he was taking over sent a throb inside her, and she arched into him.

Giovanni pressed down harder and sucked a breath between his teeth. His eyes remained fierce on hers as he fought his body's instincts.

Nera tried to smile at him, but everything was too much. "It's okay. I want you to come."

Giovanni's hand rose to caress her cheek. "But you don't look the same."

He meant when he'd brought her to orgasm with his fingers, she realized. She'd never been able to orgasm from straight sex, but she didn't know how to explain that to him. But this was Giovanni. Her husband. She had to try. Nera bit her lip as another throb made her try to arch into him.

He controlled her thrust, but lifted afterward, separating their bodies enough to slip his hand between them. His fingers found where they were connected first, the soft brush there making her tingle and causing his breath to pant. Then he found her clit. He stroked it, and her body tightened.

"Ah!" Nera couldn't look away from his intense gaze as he studied her face.

The pressure softened slightly, becoming perfect. "Like this?" he murmured, but his finger was certain as he worked her clit.

Nera couldn't speak as heat consumed her.

"There. Nera, you're so beautiful."

She cried out as she lifted into him, wrapping her arms and legs tight around him as her orgasm swept through her.

Giovanni's eyes lost focus as his cock jerked inside her. He called out her name when he came. Her own pulses acted like they would tear her apart, and her inner muscles clamped down on him with each pulse, as if trying to drag out every last drop.

Giovanni collapsed against her chest. Her arms wouldn't uncurl from around him. Nera decided that was just fine, since he held her so tightly in return, as if he never wanted them to part.

Chapter 22

Giovanni was still buried inside his wife. Apparently orgasms made him tired. He'd fallen asleep cradled inside of her soft, warm body.

He'd come inside Nera. The reminder made him start to harden. He wanted to do it again, but the selfish thought prompted him to move away from her.

Nera's face looked peaceful as she continued to sleep. He brushed the backs of his fingers along her cheek, careful not to wake her. She'd been so giving. She'd used her mouth to take him from worrying he wouldn't get an erection to desperately trying to hold on to his control. It had almost been too easy to want her, the more he thought about how it was Nera doing it to him.

When she'd told him she loved him again, he'd almost come right then.

His hand drifted down to her lips. He wanted to hear her say it again. He doubted he'd get used to it, even after she'd said it a hundred times.

She'd told him to let go, but he hadn't wanted to use her like that. He'd seen her orgasm before, and he'd wanted her to do it again.

Nera had looked gorgeous as she'd ridden him. Warmth and affection had filled her face, but she hadn't looked like she did when she really and truly lost herself. He'd wanted to see her as desperate as he was, then sexily sated. Nera had to come first.

His touch had done it. Giovanni frowned as his hand paused on her arm. He couldn't help touching her now, but he'd barely done it earlier. Not until he realized she needed it. Nera needed his touch as much as he needed hers.

If he touched her more, would she obtain that expression he craved even sooner? She'd used her mouth on him. If he returned the gesture, would she end up chanting out her love as her body shook?

He had to shift his suddenly full erection away from her so he didn't poke her in the leg.

Why was it Nera? Why could simply the thought of her love make his body respond in a way he'd never thought it would?

He'd always known he loved her, though he hadn't equated that with a sexual love. Nera had been special to him. From the first time she had hugged him, her smile had dazzled him. It held no hidden secrets. Every time Nera saw him, she was happy. And he'd loved her for it.

He hadn't given her the words. Trying to speak at all was a struggle. Trying to say something that important...

He hovered over her. Maybe he could tell her in another way.

Giovanni pressed a soft kiss to her lips. He moved to her jaw next, kissing her there. Nera had trembled when he'd done the same to her neck the other day. He let his mouth trail there, remembering his own reaction when she'd sucked at his skin. His lips returned the gesture. Her skin was warm and salty and addictive as he sucked.

Nera gasped, her hands finding his head and pressing him harder against her.

"Giovanni?" Her voice sounded husky, like it was filled with dreams.

He wondered if she'd been dreaming of him. He lifted his head, seeing the dark red mark that he'd made. His own hand moved to cover his neck. The idea of carrying each other's mark didn't calm his erection.

Nera's hand found his cock, gripping him. "Already?" she murmured.

Giovanni pulled her hand away, pressing it against the bed. He was careful not to push too hard. He lowered his head to kiss the bandage wrapped around her arm.

Nera's eyes glittered with warmth when he met them. "I'd like to make you come again," she said

Their desires were the same. He resisted the way she tugged to pull free, dropping his gaze to her breasts instead. When she'd sucked and bit him there, the sensation had led straight to his cock. He decided it must be the same for her.

His hands were busy holding her still, so he used his mouth. The skin of her breasts was softer than her stomach as he kissed his way to the tip and closed his mouth around her nipple. Soft suction didn't bring forth the sounds he wanted. He bit down to her strangled gasp before soothing the bite with his tongue and then sucking hard.

Nera's voice cried out for him. He released one nipple to give the same treatment to the other, playing with pressures. Too hard, and she stiffened. Nera liked things on the edge between gentle and rough. It was difficult to find that balance; he just wanted to be gentle.

He loved the way she shivered when he kissed his way down her stomach. Everywhere she was soft, she was also sensitive.

He had to release her hands to part her legs properly. Her vagina was especially tender, he recalled from touching her before. He kept that in mind as he slid his tongue over her entrance. Her scent was different than he remembered. Perhaps that was because his own had joined hers.

Her legs trembled, but there were no gasping cries. He moved to her clit. That was the part of her that needed stimulation the most. It was magic, the way touching it made her orgasm. He licked it.

Her hands found his hair. Unlike him, she had no problem grabbing his head and pressing his mouth against her.

"Please!" Nera cried.

He used his tongue to stroke. Soon her thighs trembled and her hands pressed him against her harder. He switched to sucking, like he had with her nipple, and Nera's scream rang in the room as she convulsed.

Giovanni paused before continuing to suck her through the orgasm. There'd been no fear in her voice. Enzo probably understood that better than he did.

All the other Di Salvos had a lot more experience with women. Everything Giovanni knew, he had only learned from her.

When her body went limp, he crawled up to look into her eyes. She'd orgasmed more quickly with his mouth, but it was hard to see her while he used it on her.

Nera's hand shook as she brushed her fingers over his cheek.

Giovanni's finger had already found her clit. "I want to see it," he explained, beginning to stroke.

She already wore the expression he craved, the one that said she only had eyes for him. The one that made her quiver, that made her hands clutch at him.

She was more sensitive now, so he lightened his strokes. He moved in a swirl instead of the back-and-forth motion she had taught him, and her eyes dilated. Her hips lifted into his touch, and he wanted to sink inside her. To feel that thrust of her hips while he was buried within her. The need was almost painful, and he increased the rhythm of his caress. The shaking of her thighs returned, and he sealed her lips before she cried out when another orgasm rippled over her.

Her thighs closed around his hand, as if to keep him pressed against her as her body rode the wave of release. He waited for them to loosen before pulling his hand away.

Giovanni moved over her body to find her eyes had closed. He hesitated. The intensity of his erection had his heart trying to beat out of his chest, but he'd rather not use it if it would cause her any discomfort.

Her lashes fluttered before her eyelids lifted. Nera smiled as she wrapped her arms around his neck. "Why aren't you inside me?"

Giovanni's throat closed at that welcoming expression. Nera's thighs widened, and he settled between them. She was wet and warm against the head of his cock, and he pushed inside.

It was even better than before. The way she squeezed him. The leftover tremors from the orgasms he'd given her. Her hands, moving down to grip his ass and pull him against her. Giovanni clawed for his control, but then her knees lifted to draw his cock in deeper. His body shook as he searched her eyes.

"I love you, Giovanni. Let go."

The sound he made was of a man breaking. He lost control of his body as his hands slid under her, pulling her into his desperate thrusts. He couldn't let go of her to touch her. She needed to be touched.

He pushed her legs wider instead, needing their bodies to be closer as he worked his cock inside her. There was no space between them.

Suddenly, each thrust forward made her face have the same look as before. He tried to focus, but his own need overwhelmed him. His movements lost all rhythm. Each time he thrust forward, her body strained into it. Her head fell back and her mouth opened, but no sounds came out. At least, none he could hear over his own choked gasps of her name.

Nera's body clasped down on him, and he came in long, wild bursts. Nera's nails dug into the cheeks of his ass, holding him tightly to her.

When he could breathe again, air brushed over the sweat on his back, sending a chill through him. His arms shook as he lifted himself. "Are you all right, Nera?" He couldn't see her face because she'd buried it against him. Her nose rubbed along his neck as she tried to burrow closer. "I'm sorry." That he needed to apologize stabbed inside him.

Her head moved against him in a shake. He felt dampness and realized she was crying.

Numbness slid through him. He'd done that to her. "Let go."

Nera loosened her hold at his tone, and he pushed her away so he could see her face. She really was crying. His cock softened, slipping out of her as he tried to roll away.

She grabbed onto him. "It's okay!"

"You crying is not okay." Giovanni was furious with himself. He'd meant to pleasure her, not rut inside her like an animal.

Nera pressed her forehead to his, and he stilled. Her eyes were wet with tears, but they were still warm and affectionate as she stared into him.

"These are happy tears. I'm really, really happy." She laughed, brushing a kiss over his lips. "I've never orgasmed quite like that."

"You orgasmed?" Giovanni remembered the way she had squeezed around him.

"Couldn't you tell?" Nera searched his eyes. "You didn't hurt me. The opposite. It was like you were stroking my clit with your body instead of your hands." A flush filled her cheeks at having to explain it. "You didn't hurt me, Giovanni," she repeated.

Nera's eyes were wide and innocent. Nera didn't lie to him. He forced himself to accept her words. His fingers found her damp cheeks, wiping away her tears.

He wanted to hear her say she loved him again, but it wasn't something he should ask for. It was something she should give. Only when she felt it.

He rolled them over to take his weight off of her, resting on his side instead and tucking her into his body.

Nera's head found the space against his neck. Her breathing slowed, the warmth of it fluttering against him. It was when he realized she could peacefully slip into sleep with him there that the last of his tension eased.

Chapter 23

Nera woke up to color for the first time in forever, even if it was only one color. They hadn't switched off the lamps the night before, so she stared into Giovanni's face, turned toward her as he slept on his side. It was the most beautiful thing she'd woken up to in a long time.

She rolled away from him and headed to the ensuite bathroom. The dimmer on the overhead lights gave an almost comfortable glow to the space. She normally showered at night, but other things had taken her attention the evening before. Giovanni had lost control the second time. Giddiness filled her at the reminder. None of the stand-ins she'd tried had held a candle to being with the one she wanted. And he'd wanted her in return.

He'd only ever been with her. The very idea sent tingles over her skin.

The warm water of the shower was soothing. Realization dawned as she washed. Giovanni hadn't worn a condom, and she wasn't on birth control. Her hand slid up to her stomach. Even now, a part of him might be growing inside her.

Nera looked at him when she reentered the room. His face was often expressionless, but she'd only seen it relaxed in sleep once before. Her fingers itched to touch him, but he didn't seem to sleep often. She stared down at her unwrapped hand. She had kept the upper arm bandage dry, but the one around her hand had been impossible to avoid. The white strips holding the cut together had held up well enough. Maybe without the bandage, she would be able to cook properly.

She wanted to make her husband breakfast.

Careful to close the latch silently behind her, Nera came face to face with Enzo.

Giovanni's uncle glanced at the closed door behind her, lifting an eyebrow. "I take it you wore the boy out?"

Nera flushed as she remembered his uncle had been right outside all night. She tried not to remember any of the noises she might have made.

Enzo laughed at her embarrassment, waving her forward. "Come along."

Nera followed him toward the kitchen. A part of her was nervous to return. Giovanni had asked her not to the day before. The day they'd gotten married. It still felt a little impossible.

She studied Enzo's back. If he hadn't come to the kitchen after the attack, the marriage would never have happened. She reached for his arm, but he turned before her touch connected.

She glanced past him, but it was too early for the other Di Salvos to be hanging out downstairs. Her eyes moved back to his face, which was almost clear this close. "I never thanked you for the other day. Thank you. Really."

Enzo shook his head. "You saved yourself. I just arrived in time for cleanup, like usual."

He led her the rest of the way to the kitchen. To her surprise, Mylene was inside, already baking. She had only turned on the light over the stove, as if she'd been waiting for Nera to arrive.

The French woman snorted when she saw her. "To think, even marrying the man you always wanted didn't let you sleep in, ma choupette."

Mylene's normal term of endearment made Nera remember how it had sounded in a man's voice. Especially since there was an edge to Mylene's tone. Nera's hand closed into a fist, making the cut along her palm burn as she stared at the spot where a man had died. No bloodstain gave it away—Enzo was thorough—but she knew the exact spot.

"You came to make Giovanni something, didn't you? Your husband is a lucky man." Mylene pursed her lips in displeasure.

Nera let the disappointment roll over her. Mylene had been like a mother to her for a long time. She'd be lying if she said it didn't sting, but the French woman had always been annoyed by Nera's crush on Giovanni. "Yes. Would you like to help me?" she asked.

Mylene continued to cut fruit on the kitchen island. She stood with her spine ramrod straight. Her posture became more pronounced like that when she was angry. Tommaso often made her that way, but never Nera.

"I wish you could be happy for me," she murmured.

"Happy?" Mylene whirled around to glare at her. "When you're wasting your life?" Her hand still clutched the knife as she turned, and it waved between them in Mylene's agitation.

Before Nera could blink, Enzo had pressed the tip of his gun against Mylene's head.

The French woman froze, her anger draining away as fear replaced it.

Panic filled Nera. Enzo's typical smile had disappeared. "Enzo, don't!"

A tense moment passed as the Di Salvo soldier stared into Mylene's eyes. "Put the knife down," he told her.

Mylene's hand shook as she placed the kitchen knife on the counter.

Enzo slid it out of reach with his free hand before putting his gun away.

Mylene tried to glare, but she was too frightened to manage it properly. "You think I'd hurt Nera? She's like a daughter to me!"

Enzo shrugged, his smile returning. He ignored Mylene, focusing on Nera. "You were going to make something for Giovanni, weren't you, doll?"

"Nera! Tell him I wouldn't hurt you."

Nera's hand ached where she continued to clench it against her side. She hadn't told Mylene about the incident in the kitchen. Sadness filled her as she realized there would likely be a lot she wouldn't tell her. "It's his job to protect me," she whispered. She was grateful Enzo hadn't pulled the trigger.

Mylene made a noise in her throat and darted out of the kitchen.

Nera's feet remained rooted to the floor instead of chasing after her.

"Here, none of that," Enzo said, and he reached for Nera's hand. He eased her fingers open, staring at the long cut that had begun to bleed again. "You can't make anything that way," he said, tugging her to the sink. His touch was gentle as he held her hand under the cool water.

"Mylene wouldn't have done anything," Nera said, staring at the running water.

Enzo laughed. "I bet you thought the same of that French cook."

Nera's stomach lurched as she remembered how the cook's throat had sliced open so easily.

Enzo turned off the water, his touch gentle as he used paper towels to pat her dry. "Here, press it tight and the bleeding should stop."

Nera obeyed.

"You're too trusting, doll. It's okay. That's why you're good for Giovanni." Enzo leaned against the counter as he continued to smile at her. "I like you. As long as you never betray the Di Salvos, I'll always protect you." His smile faded, and his eyes had the same expression they had held as they stared at Mylene. "It would break my heart if I ever had to clean up after you. But I would. That's my job."

Nera swallowed as she stared back into those dark gray eyes. The eyes shared by all the Di Salvos. Even Giovanni.

Enzo's face softened as his gaze fell to her hand. "Has the bleeding stopped?"

She lifted the paper towels. There wasn't much blood on them at all. "It's fine."

"That's good. Giovanni would be mad if it got worse." His smile returned as he took the used towels from her and crossed the kitchen to throw them in the trash. He gestured toward the island. "What were you going to make for him?"

Nera's feet carried her forward. Mylene had been cutting up strawberries. Nera liked them, but Giovanni wasn't a fan. Strawberries were too tart for his sweet tooth. "Normally I'd make him panna cotta," she admitted. Her eyes cut toward Enzo to see if he'd react the way Antonio had.

Enzo's smile grew, but shadows darkened the gray of his eyes. "It's my favorite." His voice lowered at the confession. "I had some of yours the other day. It was better than any I've ever eaten, but it might not be good to make it again. Not yet."

"Antonio told me that." Nera remembered the way Enzo had tossed the name of the dessert at Giovanni's father. She studied him, her lips closing around the question that had risen to mind.

Enzo sighed. "Yeah. I can be reckless." He patted her shoulder. "Don't be like me. Giovanni would worry." He snorted again as his hand fell away. "Well, worry more. The Di Salvo name will help, but..." He shrugged.

Nera reached for the knife, deciding that finishing cutting up the strawberries would at least keep her hands busy as she figured out what to make. Her hand paused, hovering over the knife. It was part of a different set from the one that had been in the kitchen before.

"Giovanni thought it'd be easier on you," Enzo murmured.

Nera nodded, forcing her undamaged hand to close around it. She began to cut. Giovanni was wrong. Picturing red coating the new blade was just as easy.

Chapter 24

Giovanni woke up alone in bed. He'd slept deeply enough not to be disturbed by Nera leaving the room. He'd only slept that well once before, when he'd used her as a pillow. His body had been sexually sated then as well.

His hand slid over the empty sheet beside him, but it was cool to the touch.

He sat up, the sheet slithering to his lap as instinct prompted him to look toward the window.

A man that was more of a shadow sat in the cushioned chair in front of the shifting curtain.

Giovanni had slipped out of bed in the middle of the night to retrieve his gun from his suit jacket and place it on the nightstand. If he needed it against the shadow, he'd be dead before he reached for it.

Luka had been a highly skilled killer even when he'd been not much more than a child. Giovanni hadn't made things easy on him on the night they first met so long ago, but Luka had been better. Now,

Giovanni wasn't worried. If Luka had wanted him dead, he'd had ample opportunity to make it happen.

Antonio was going to be angry when he learned Luka had gotten through the Di Salvo security again. He already didn't like the man.

Neither said anything as he rose from the bed. Dawn had risen, and Giovanni's skin wasn't tan enough to hide the heat crawling up his neck as he padded naked to the chair. He slipped on his slacks but didn't bother with the shirt before turning to face the man who still hadn't said a word. Giovanni crossed his arms, covering part of one of his worst scars. It was one that Luka had given him on that long ago night, along with a good half of his others.

Delicate birdsong welcoming the morning filtered in from the open window.

Giovanni would have to start any conversation. He didn't like to talk, but Luka was worse. If he waited for him to start, they'd stare at each other forever.

This time, Luka surprised him. "Congratulations," he murmured, staring down at his inked hands, where they dangled between his knees.

The warmth along Giovanni's skin reached his ears. "You're not here for that."

Luka didn't look up. "But it's what's said, isn't it?"

Giovanni didn't ask how Luka knew about his marriage when most of the Di Salvos hadn't been told. He needed to speak to his father first, but the announcement would come later.

Luka was good at information. Even better at killing. The term 'assassin' fit him better than 'hitman.'

Giovanni didn't understand why the boy had allowed him to live so long ago. After the kidnapping incident with the Bratva, Giovanni had attempted to take out as many of the Russians as he could get his hands on. Giovanni Sr. had been furious and proud, the one and only time Giovanni had seen those emotions in his father's eyes. Sending Luka had been the pakhan's answer, and Giovanni had taken time to recover after their encounter. That was the longest that he'd ever stayed away from Nera. But still, he'd survived.

Luka pushed to his feet. "You put out feelers."

"The Frenchman?" Giovanni was still furious that someone working within the Di Salvo estate had been turned against them. After the cook had died, Enzo had found the man's children, already cold. Whether the cook had succeeded or not in killing Nera, he and his family would have died. Giovanni studied Luka. He hadn't even considered asking him about the incident. Luka never killed women or children.

Giovanni frowned. "Was it Ivankov?" he asked.

"Yes." Luka tilted his head and then shook it. "And no."

Giovanni's arms tightened. "It can't be both."

"He laughed while he ordered it," Luka admitted.

"Then that's a yes," Giovanni said.

"He said, 'I wish I'd thought of something this fun,'" Luka murmured.

The word 'fun' made Giovanni's flush fade. The air conditioner turned on, cold air brushing over his shoulders. "Who would Ivankov take orders from?"

Kiryl Ivankov had taken over the Bratva after Giovanni's mother had been killed. He'd murdered the previous head of the Lipin family, Giovanni's uncle, the one who had forced his mother to marry into the Di Salvo family.

Kiryl Ivankov hadn't had a reason to do it. He'd built his reputation on examples of the same. Of blood and death without purpose. Most of the Italian families agreed that the new pakhan needed to be replaced, but they also knew that attempting to do so might wipe out La Cosa Nostra instead. So a decade had passed with Ivankov remaining in charge.

Luka turned toward the window without answering Giovanni's question. That meant even he didn't know who was behind it.

"I might have need of your services soon." Giovanni's words came out softly. He was surprised they came out at all. His lips pressed together when Luka glanced back at him.

The morning sunshine dappled a new tattoo on the man's neck. "You're ready?" Luka asked.

Giovanni tried to say yes. Instead, he imagined his father's hand choking the air out of him.

"Be certain," Luka said, then slipped out of the window.

Luka excelled at what he did, but Giovanni Di Salvo Sr. was a force that blotted out all else. Luka was slight in stature, just as Giovanni was. They had a lot in common, despite being part of two different families.

Even if his father said the right things about his marriage to Nera, the path forward had already been set. If Giovanni wasn't ready to accept that, he should have sent Nera away.

He finished getting dressed. As he picked up his gun, he wished he had time to go to the range. Shooting would help to settle his nerves. Seeing Nera would do the same.

He tucked the gun away, though, and determined not to head to the kitchen. Nerves weren't always a bad thing.

Antonio was waiting in the hallway when he opened the door. Sweet-smelling smoke lingered in the air around him as his hand moved away from his inner jacket pocket. He pushed off the wall. "Enzo is playing sous chef to the newest Di Salvo."

Giovanni didn't need the explanation. He was content that his uncle prioritized Nera's safety over his own. Luka had breached their security, but the hitman was stealthier than anyone else he had known. He decided not to admit to having an assassin in his room as Antonio fell into step beside him to approach the stairs.

"So, about last night," Antonio said.

"No." Giovanni didn't look at his cousin. He had no intention of telling him anything.

Antonio laughed. "I wasn't asking for details. I just wanted to offer my expertise in case you needed some pointers."

Giovanni flushed. He remembered how he'd lost control all over again. He hoped that wouldn't continue to happen. Nera deserved better.

"No," he repeated. He could feel Antonio's gaze on him, but it was easy to ignore as they approached his father's office.

Antonio didn't hesitate to follow Giovanni in. Vittore waited inside as well.

Giovanni Sr. leaned back in his chair as he watched them. His eyes focused on Antonio, and he smiled in a way he always did at Giovanni's cousin. As if he would have preferred him for a son. "Good, you're here too. I have a few things to go over."

Giovanni listened to his father talk business. It was unusual for them to receive direct orders from him, as Giovanni Sr. let Vittore handle most of the Di Salvo interests. This was for the best since Vittore remained calm in the face of conflict.

As capos, Antonio and Giovanni had their own crews to run. That had been put on hold since the Bratva's hit outside the bakery, while they stuck closer to the house. Giovanni understood what his father was telling them. That time was over, and it was time to return to business as usual.

When his father had wound down, Giovanni forced his mouth to open. "I—"

"My brother already informed me," Giovanni Sr. interrupted. "Vittore says he supports the marriage. It's a waste, but I should have expected as much from you."

The words meant nothing to Giovanni. His father hadn't said what he needed to hear. "Does—"

His father still wouldn't let him speak.

"Enzo will keep an eye on the girl. He doesn't get queasy in the face of hard tasks."

Giovanni's heartbeat stuttered in his chest. The reminder wasn't necessary. Enzo had cleaned up after his mother's death. He'd refused to allow Giovanni to help. Enzo hadn't agreed with it, though, and things between him and Giovanni's father, his brother, hadn't been the same since.

Giovanni pressed his sweating palms against his slacks, the same ones he'd worn to his wedding. "I need to hear you say it." The words fell heavily into the room.

His father stared back at him. "She's a Di Salvo now. Nothing will happen." His eyes always looked darker behind his desk, where the light didn't quite reach them to show their deep blue. "Not without cause."

Giovanni's throat tightened. It was the best he would get. He forced himself not flinch at the simmering anger in his father's eyes.

His father studied him the same way he always had. "This marriage. Your war with the Bratva. You, Giovanni!" His father's gaze raked down his body. "You're lucky to have reached capo. Don't expect more."

Giovanni didn't bother to remind him that he'd given up on expectations a long time ago.

"And stay away from the Bratva," his father commanded. "This war of yours is over."

Vittore followed them out, shutting the door behind him. There was a crash inside that failed to make any of them jump.

Antonio's hands dug into his pockets. "That went well."

"Surprisingly," Vittore agreed.

"For fuck's sake, Vittore," Antonio muttered. "It's like he doesn't care that Gio was almost killed. Again."

Giovanni hadn't expected his father to care about that, but after the cook's attack, he doubted even the shootout outside the bakery had been about him.

"Be careful, Antonio," Vittore warned. He placed a hand on Giovanni's shoulder.

His uncle often did that. Giovanni always hated the weight of it.

"Don't worry," Vittore told him. "Nera will be safe with the Di Salvos now. Let's go let the others know before you two head out."

Giovanni's jaw ached as he held back his doubts. They still didn't understand why she had been targeted by the Bratva, and he was no longer being given leeway to find out. Not that the torture had led to answers.

"Will you be able to spare Enzo?" He studied his uncle's face.

Vittore squeezed his shoulder. "Gio, it's not necessary."

"There was the cook," Antonio said, his hand moving to the back of his head. "I, for one, find that hard to forget."

"He was not a Di Salvo. With him gone, there are no others in the house." His uncle frowned. "Except your wife's family. How is Tommaso's recovery?"

Antonio snorted. "He was shot in the chest. It'll take a bit longer."

Vittore's touch left Giovanni as he waved that aside. "Tommaso isn't the problem. He is a Di Salvo, despite everything, but I heard his woman refuses to marry him."

"Nera's family isn't a concern." He had little doubt of that. He didn't quite understand the relationship Tommaso had with the French woman, and Mylene had often glared at him when he'd come to the bakery, but she wouldn't hurt Nera.

And Nera was his only concern.

Giovanni decided to talk to Enzo himself. It was too soon to leave Nera alone.

"Then it's all settled," Vittore said, heading toward the stairs. "Let's make sure the family hears the news."

Antonio met Giovanni's eyes. "I know," his cousin murmured. His gaze slid to the closed office door. "But, Gio, there are other things that also need our attention."

The thrumming in Giovanni's chest reminded him that he could have made another choice. He wondered if he would be experiencing this same panic if Nera was an ocean away.

Chapter 25

Nera hadn't expected to see so little of her husband. He stood with her as Vittore gathered the other Di Salvos to officially introduce her. Nerves made Nera grateful for her overexposed vision for the first time. It kept her from becoming overwhelmed as the Di Salvos welcomed her to their family.

Giovanni hadn't stayed after, not even long enough to eat the breakfast she had made him, but the other Di Salvos hadn't let the food go to waste.

She'd been struggling to learn their names over the days since. Under the fluorescent lights of the kitchen, the white of her vision was exacerbated, and the olive skin, dark hair, and dark eyes of most of the men was difficult to differentiate. The older Di Salvo she had started to recognize, the one that had almost shot her, now stayed away.

Mylene constantly reminded her of how comfortable the kitchen had been at her parents' home. The French woman's attitude hadn't softened since the wedding. They often cooked together, but what was once familiar had become strained.

Nera was around Enzo the most often. Despite his warning, his company was comfortable. He reminded her a little of Tommaso, or the man Tommaso used to be. Tommaso had reached the stage of recovery where he tried to overdo things. He had already forced himself to his feet more than once, and soon after that began pacing his room. When Enzo sometimes had to leave for business, he made sure she stayed with Tommaso. Between the grumpy bear and Mylene, Nera herself was feeling stir-crazy, but she never asked to leave the estate.

Nera hadn't seen Giovanni's father again, but his other uncle, Vittore, had begun to seek her out. It seemed he was trying to welcome her to the family.

Most of the time, he visited with her around meals and was effusive in his compliments of her cooking. It was hard not to like someone that enjoyed eating. That was one of the things she loved about Giovanni, though he'd tried to hide his enjoyment. It was the moments when she thought she caught Vittore staring at her, though, that made Nera uncomfortable.

Three days after the wedding, Enzo walked with her toward her room. He didn't fill the space with chatter. He'd become more of a constant than Giovanni, and Nera didn't like it. She'd been out of sorts all day, and it didn't help that the lights around the estate had started a headache pulsing behind her eyes.

She hesitated with her hand on the handle of the bedroom door. "Where is Giovanni's room?" she asked. That was the part that got to her the most. She understood he had to work, but he hadn't been coming into the room to sleep with her.

"It's not you, doll. His father is keeping him busy, that's all." Enzo sighed. "Didn't you see his things? He moved them in here."

Nera nodded. She'd found the closet full of his suits, and his personal products were scattered around the bathroom. The smell was soothing, but it wasn't the same as his color. She hadn't seen his color for days.

Her stomach twisted at the thought, and her brow furrowed at the sudden pain. She shouldn't let herself get this upset.

"Get some rest," Enzo encouraged.

Nera pushed her way into the bedroom. She felt silly when her stomach cramped again as she was gathering clothes. Her hand covered the pain, and she realized it wasn't her stomach.

She'd started her time of the month. She told herself she wasn't disappointed. This gave her more time to have a talk with Giovanni, time she was going to need.

After checking underneath the sink, she folded toilet paper to stuff into her new clean underwear. She stared at herself in the mirror.

Something about getting her period always made her feel like a lost little girl. It wasn't that she hadn't known what to expect the first time. Her mother had explained it to her before she died, but her mother hadn't been there when it happened. And Tommaso wasn't her father; not really.

Mylene had only been working at the bakery for a short time when she'd found Nera crying in the bathroom. It had been the first time Nera had realized the French woman who seemed so angry all the time had a softer side.

Nera pressed her hand harder against her abdomen. She didn't often cramp that badly, but it had happened before. She breathed through the pain. First things first, she needed supplies. And as much as she liked Enzo, asking him to run to the store for feminine products didn't seem possible.

The Di Salvos needed more women around the house.

When Nera opened the bedroom door, Enzo raised an eyebrow.

"I need to talk to Mylene about something."

Enzo led the way as they retraced their steps down the hall. Walking eased the ache in her abdomen enough for her hand to drop to her side, though she was hyperaware of the toilet paper when they descended the stairs.

Outside Tommaso's room, the shouting going on inside was more than obvious. Most of the words Nera could hear were French curses. Tommaso didn't raise his voice. Despite her size, Mylene was the one with the bigger temper.

It was as if Tommaso knew his lack of reaction riled her more. Nera pictured the amused smile he often wore when Mylene was in a temper.

"We can come back later," Enzo said.

Only Nera couldn't. She rapped on the door. It took a louder knock before Mylene jerked open the door. There was no welcoming smile as the French woman stared at her.

Nera had also been wrong about Tommaso. Over Mylene's shoulder, she saw that he wasn't smiling as usual.

"Can I come in?" Nera asked. Doubt about how welcome she would be made her voice weak.

Mylene hesitated, then stepped back.

Nera didn't have to ask Enzo to wait. He took a place against the far wall before she shut the bedroom door behind her.

Mylene's arms folded across her chest. "This couldn't wait until morning?" she snapped.

Nera bit her lip, staring at the ground as she reminded herself that she was a grown woman. Frustrated tears rose in her eyes. "I was hoping you brought some... stuff."

Mylene's arms fell to her sides. "Oh," she murmured.

When Nera forced herself to look up, the French woman's face had softened.

"Sure," Mylene murmured. Then she glared at Tommaso, waving her hand. "See! This is a perfect example of things not being right." She went into the bathroom, opening the cabinets harder than necessary.

"Things have been busy. I just forgot, is all," Nera said, her hand moving to press against her waistband.

"What did you forget, Nera?" Tommaso asked, his voice as soothing as always.

It had never made it any easier to talk about womanly things with him. Tommaso was her comfort, a steady presence that helped to stabilize her life; her big, warm security blanket.

But Mylene had been the practical parent. The plastic bag in her hands crinkled as she shoved it toward Nera. "She's bleeding, Tommaso!" Mylene announced.

Nera took the bag. Despite Mylene's matter-of-factness, she still felt embarrassed.

"And because she's a prisoner here, she can't even go out for the things she needs. This is what I've been talking about."

Tommaso rolled his eyes. "You bought her those things, Mylene. Even when she lived at home. You babied our little girl too."

Mylene pursed her lips, but she didn't deny it.

Nera shifted her feet as she faced just how sheltered she'd been. It was one reason she'd been forcing herself to go to culinary school in France. Her lack of independence had begun to, well, not chafe exactly, but it had led her to self-doubt.

"Things aren't safe right now. It won't always be like this." It had been less than a week since she'd killed the cook, though Mylene didn't even know about that.

"You are among the Di Salvos now." Mylene sighed, her anger fading.

Her sad acceptance brought a deep sense of trepidation to Nera. "I love Giovanni," she told the woman who had been a mother to her. Her hand tightened around the bag of supplies. "I've always loved him."

"I know, ma choupette." Mylene met her eyes and forced a smile. "I know."

Nera couldn't hold her gaze. She looked toward Tommaso, but he smiled at her like he always did.

"You're hurting. I can tell. Go rest now." Mylene crossed to the door, opening it.

Nera said good night as she shuffled out. The door closed behind her, but the shouting didn't resume.

Enzo stared at the door. "She seemed less angry. What did you say to her, doll?"

Nera clutched the plastic bag harder in her hand. "The truth."

They didn't talk as she returned to her room. The warmth of the shower failed to soothe her, but at least Nera had what she needed. She took a pill from the bottle Mylene had given her, along with some pads, and curled up in the center of the bed, leaving the corner lamp on in case Giovanni came home. Her cramping eased enough for her to fall asleep.

When she next opened her eyes, it was to see the color she'd been craving. Giovanni must have been careful not to wake her as he'd crawled into bed. He looked peaceful in sleep.

Nera told herself not to wake him, but she leaned forward despite her inner protest. His lips were soft under hers. His breathing shifted, and she watched as his eyes opened.

Her hand moved up to stroke his face.

"Nera," he mumbled sleepily. She hadn't thought a new way of him saying her name would get to her like it did.

Nera kissed him again. She wasn't thinking. If she had been, she would have focused on how they needed to talk. Instead, she reminded herself what his lips felt like. He was her husband. Him being there in her bed made it feel more real.

Their lips parted so she could suck in a breath. She pressed her forehead against his. "I missed you."

She waited for him to say it back, but he was Giovanni. He didn't say anything, only wrapped his arms around her.

Nera knew better than to ask him where he'd been. Tommaso had told her all she knew about the Di Salvos. Giovanni kept that part of himself separate from her as much as he could.

"Sorry," she murmured. The words moved her lips against his, causing them to tingle. It made her want to keep kissing him, but she resisted the temptation. "I should let you sleep."

"You never have to apologize to me," Giovanni said. He kissed her instead.

Him initiating the kiss made her chest feel tight. His tongue was the aggressor, stroking against hers. Her hands wrapped around him to pull him closer, finding only hot skin. Even his ass was bare. He'd slipped into bed with her naked, and the reality of it had her pulling him more tightly against her.

The extra cushion of the pad between them made her remember. She was turned on, but she ached down there in another way, too, and she found the idea of trying to have pleasure around the edges of her pain confusing. She stopped tugging him closer as indecision ran through her.

Giovanni gentled the kiss before ending it. "We should sleep," he said, and Nera realized her body had stiffened against him.

His hand moved into soothing strokes low on her back. Nera hadn't realized how much that part of her had ached until his warm fingers made a little moan slip out.

It was his turn to tense under her hands. His breath whooshed over her lips as his hands paused.

"It's not that I don't want to," Nera started. "I kind of do."

Giovanni's eyes stared into hers. "Sex isn't an expectation, Nera." He swallowed. "Whenever it happens, I want you to want to completely." His hands resumed their gentle ministrations on her back. "No forcing yourself."

There was an intensity to his eyes that caused her to nod. "I just meant that, because of the bleeding, I wasn't sure—"

"Bleeding?" He rolled away from her, and the lamp on the nightstand flicked on. "Where are you hurt?"

Nera sat up with him, laying a hand over his chest, where his heartbeat thumped rapidly under her touch. "I'm not hurt." She swallowed her embarrassment. "I'm on my period."

The darker dusting of gray that spread up his neck was endearing. Giovanni's shoulders relaxed as he looked away.

"I mean, we still can." She shrugged as she stared at her hand on his chest. "But it might be messy, and I was cramping worse than normal earlier." It was like thinking about the cramping brought one on. Or maybe it was the tension in her body that caused it. Her other hand moved to her abdomen. "So, yeah. I wasn't sure if we should."

Giovanni's hand moved to rest over hers. "You hurt here?" he asked.

Nera slipped her hand out from under his. Giovanni's touch felt so much warmer than her own. She held his hand there when he would have pulled away. The warmth eased the pressure of the cramp, and she lay back down on the bed again.

Giovanni worriedly hovered over her. "We shouldn't if you hurt. Can I do anything?"

Nera hesitated, then told the truth. "I liked the way you were rubbing my lower back before."

He turned off the lamp and lay down next to her. She put herself in the circle of his arms. His hands began rubbing the small of her back as she laid her head against his chest. His warmth seemed to spread everywhere.

"Um, there was something we didn't talk about," she said into his chest.

Giovanni kept up his gentle massage as he waited for her to continue.

"I'm not on any birth control. And, well, we didn't use condoms. So does that mean..." She trailed off. Silence followed, and she lifted her head from his chest as she asked, "Do you want children, Giovanni?"

He remained silent.

"Giovanni?"

He blinked, and his eyes focused on her again. "I didn't consider it." His jaw tightened, as if he was holding something within him. It eased as his hand moved around to press on her stomach. "But I don't hate the idea if it's with you. How do you feel, Nera?"

She leaned forward, kissing him. Then her head settled against his chest. "Same. I mean, I'm obviously not pregnant yet, and with the danger and everything, that's probably good." His thumb brushed over her stomach, and she closed her eyes. "But same. So I won't go on birth control."

His hand pressed her closer. "Okay," he murmured.

Nera listened to his heartbeat as it slowed to a steady thrum that lulled her back to sleep.

Chapter 26

Giovanni woke feeling rested, even though he'd only slept for a few hours over the last few days. Nera's face remained relaxed in sleep on the pillow next to his. He didn't reach out to touch her.

When her body had stiffened against his during their kiss in the middle of the night, he'd lost his erection. He hated that she would ever force herself to have sex with him. Holding her in his arms had been more than enough for him, especially since she'd been in pain. The idea that his touch would soothe her had returned his body's interest, but he was in control of it, not the other way around.

Despite the fact that he'd tried to impregnate her without considering the consequences. No, he wouldn't touch her, not when the thought of impregnating her still flooded his mind. Her soft stomach rounded with child, a piece of himself growing inside her. Something about the image made his breath catch and his cock stiffen.

He'd thought the way he'd reacted to her on their wedding night was an aberration. And the time before that, when just her touch had brought him to orgasm. But everything about her made him want her.

He wondered how long it would take to get used to the fact that he was a sexual creature after all.

He was more like his father than he'd ever thought possible.

Only he wasn't, Giovanni told himself. The doubts tainting his mind helped to ease his desperate need for her, the one that made him so hard his cock actually ached. His breath shuddered out, and he softened as he continued to watch her sleep.

She'd thought a little blood would make him not want her. How often had he been covered in it during the nights without her? But no matter how many Bratva men he questioned, none provided the answers he needed. He'd showered in his old room before joining her in bed.

No, blood didn't bother him, but that it could be her blood, that was another matter altogether. He never wanted to hurt her. And if anyone else did, he would kill them.

His gaze traced her face. Unless she killed the person first. He was glad the cut on her hand was healing. The scab had been hard against his skin when she'd gripped him so tightly.

Nera woke slightly before dawn. Her eyelids fluttered before opening. There was a softness to her gaze as she took in his presence.

"Good morning," she murmured in a husky, sleep-filled voice that reminded Giovanni all over again that he was married. He tried to return the words, but no sound came out—mainly because Nera's lips had covered his in a soft kiss that made his lungs feel like they were collapsing from the overwhelming, not entirely unpleasant, emotions inside of him.

She sat up afterward, frowning down at herself. "I need to shower again, but I'd like to cook you something after. That is, if you'll be around long enough?"

Giovanni nodded, watching as she padded to the bathroom and the door snicked shut behind her. Nera hadn't pushed him about where he'd been. She'd never asked a lot of questions, even back when he used to show up at the bakery covered in bruises and cuts.

He rose as well, making the bed before slipping on the clothes he'd worn so briefly the night before.

When she left the bathroom, he studied her and found that her frown had left her features. She was looking at him with the smile that always made him wonder how someone could be so beautiful.

"Are you still in pain?" he asked, needing to be sure. If she hesitated at all, he'd try to get her to rest despite her desire to cook for him.

"No, I'm fine now. The cramping doesn't usually last long, at least not for me." Her cheeks flushed. "It'll be a few days until there's no blood, though."

Giovanni wished there was a way to convince her to not be embarrassed with him. It occurred to him she likely would have been too self-conscious to talk to Enzo about it either. "Do you have everything you need?"

Nera nodded. "Mylene gave me what she had. But if she hadn't, there's no way I'd bother you with this."

A numbness began at his fingers. He wanted to ask why, but he was afraid he already knew the answer. Nera had always seen him as out of reach. That was his fault. He'd acted that way with her ever since the kidnapping. He'd been too scared that he'd crumble if she became too close again. The numbness spread.

Nera blew out a breath and forced a laugh. "I mean, you're Giovanni. I can't picture you buying feminine supplies."

He crossed to her, his fingers sliding along her cheek in a caress that brought warmth to them again. "I want you to ask me. Anything and everything."

Only she hadn't even had a way to contact him, he realized.

He needed to fix that.

Her smile returned, so full of affection for him. "Thank you. Now, come on." Her hand linked with his as she tugged him toward the door. "If I can ask you for anything, then it's to let me feed you today before you go off again."

Enzo was out in the hallway, despite Giovanni telling him to get some rest when he'd returned. His uncle grinned at Nera's morning enthusiasm, and soon the two of them were chatting about possible things to bake as he followed them to the kitchen.

It was ridiculous that he was jealous of his uncle.

Nera studied him as she began pulling out ingredients. "You really don't have anything specific you'd like?"

Giovanni shook his head. He'd like anything she made. Nera knew his tastes better than he did.

She hadn't turned on the overhead lights. Giovanni had expected that. He studied the darkened bulbs, factoring through ways that he could have them replaced like he'd done at her home. The normal fluorescent bulbs tired out her vision and gave her headaches.

Security was most important, but it might be worth the precautions that would be needed to have workers complete the change sooner rather than later.

Anything to bring her comfort in her new home. Watching her in her element eased the tension he was so used to carrying. At least most of the Di Salvos were asleep and couldn't see his relaxed face. All but his uncle, who had seen him look so much worse.

"Gio!" Enzo's voice warned.

A sudden panic filled him at the tone.

The hand that clamped around his throat, slamming him into the wall, was one he knew all too well. But instead of the hatred that normally flooded him, all he could feel was panic.

Nera was with him in the kitchen.

A sudden, loud thump caused Nera to drop the baking sheet she'd been removing from the oven. Chocolate-filled croissants scattered across the kitchen floor.

She could barely see the red that brought her so much joy. A shadowy bulk of a man blocked his color.

"I warned you," the man growled at her husband, pulling him forward just to slam him into the wall harder.

Enzo just stood in the doorway. He didn't move forward to help.

Nera's hand closed on the knife before she could think it through. Before she remembered that she'd heard the man's voice before, seen that particular gray shape, she lunged with the knife.

A large hand knocked hers away. The knife clattered as it dropped to the tile. Pain spread across her cheek at the smack that followed, and Nera tumbled away from where the giant, dark shadow of a man was strangling her husband.

Giovanni hadn't even called her name.

Her hands and knees hit the ground with jarring pain. Her previously injured hand didn't hurt. It was still encased in an oven mitt.

"I told you not to continue your war on the Bratva," Giovanni's father continued. He wasn't even out of breath from swatting her away. "But you've killed more of them, haven't you? A capo of the

Di Salvos is more than a killer." Giovanni clawed at the hand pressed against his throat. "You must follow orders."

Nera still couldn't see much of his color. Just bits of red. Not nearly enough. Her hand that had gone for the knife shook as she stared at the fallen tray in front of her.

"Giovanni." Enzo's voice sounded calm. Cold. "He's turning purple."

Nera's mitted hand closed on the tray. Vague heat flowed through the covering.

"If my son can't be a strength, perhaps he'll serve as an example."

Nera stood, clutching the hot tray.

Enzo had taken a step forward. "Has Vittore—"

She shoved the tray hard into the side of Giovanni's father's exposed neck.

The man cursed, knocking the tray aside as he jerked back from Giovanni.

She couldn't let herself look at Giovanni, where he had collapsed to the ground. No, it was impossible to turn away from his father, who clutched at his burn and glared murderously at her, but the spreading maroon at the edge of her vision calmed her enough that she could curl her unencumbered hand into a fist instead of attacking Giovanni Sr. again.

To her surprise, he laughed. "I think I like your wife, Giovanni." His gray eyes looked almost bright in his face as he took a step closer to her. It was like the madness there lightened them.

Giovanni scrambled toward them on the ground.

It distracted his father from his path toward her. He kicked his son in the side instead.

Giovanni didn't make a sound, despite how it must have hurt.

"Don't touch him!" Nera shouted.

"You're loyal. I'll give you that." His father's hand darted out, fisting in her hair.

Nera bit her lip when he jerked her head back and pain radiated through her scalp. Giovanni's father wore a smile, but there was a hardness to it like Antonio often wore. He tugged harder, and she couldn't fully prevent her gasp of pain from escaping.

Giovanni lunged up from the ground, forcing his father back.

His father hadn't taken a chunk of her hair; he released her instead, smirking as he stared at his furious son. "Hmmm," he mused. "Maybe there's some possibility in you yet."

Giovanni shifted so he stood between them.

"Don't disobey me again." His gaze shifted to Nera. "It seems you have something to lose now." With that, his father turned away.

Giovanni's hand moved to the small of his back.

Nera lurched forward, holding it tight before it could close around his gun. His hand shook within her grasp.

They watched his father leave the kitchen.

Enzo's hand became visible as he turned his back to them, watching Giovanni Di Salvo Sr. ascend the staircase. His grip moved off his own gun. "Fuck, that was bad," he muttered. He glanced at them, but didn't meet Nera's eyes. "I'll get Vittore."

He left Nera and Giovanni alone in the kitchen.

"I'm sorry," he said in a rasping, aching voice.

Nera wanted to get him something that would help his throat, but she found that she couldn't let go of his hand.

Giovanni wrapped his other hand around her and pulled her close. His breath shuddered over her face as he pressed his forehead to hers.

It took longer than she would have liked for her own breathing to slow. Giovanni's broken voice continued to whisper an apology, over and over again, as the pounding in her own ears faded.

When her hand lifted to settle softly over his bruised throat, he stopped.

Nera swallowed as she stared into his eyes.

Giovanni pulled back slightly. His fingers shook as they grazed her cheek, which had begun to ache, she realized.

She remembered what his father had said. "Don't be scared of losing me. I don't want to hold you back."

Giovanni shook his head. "Impossible." The gentleness of his fingers made her forget the pain. "You saved me, Nera. You're always saving me."

Her breath shuddered in. "So you're not going to lecture me? Tell me not to put myself in danger for you? I attacked your father." It was as if saying it made what she had done even more clear.

Giovanni leaned forward, pressing his lips to hers. "Be who you are, Nera. I'd never ask you to be someone else."

She wrapped her arms around him, and it was only then that she remembered she was still wearing an oven mitt.

Chapter 27

Giovanni let Nera fuss over him, even though it made him feel even more pathetic. His father had hurt her, and everything within him wanted to kill the fucking man. Instead, he sat on a stool and held cloth-wrapped ice against his throbbing neck.

His father had never attacked him out in the open like that before. It was usually behind closed doors.

Antonio was going to be angry when he saw the bruises. Giovanni was grateful his cousin hadn't been there.

He remembered the absolute dread he'd felt when Nera had lunged at his father with the knife. The bruise his father had given her would only grow darker in the days to come. He swallowed, letting the pain of the movement loosen his thoughts.

Enzo didn't say a word as he leaned against the kitchen island and watched Nera, who was restarting her recipe from scratch.

Vittore hadn't come with Enzo. Giovanni's stomach sank. Or maybe that was the throbbing pain from the kick his father had given him while he was on the ground.

"Thanks for not shooting me," Giovanni murmured. He hadn't missed the way his uncle had also gone for his gun.

Enzo reached across the island, popping an uncooked chocolate chip into his mouth. "You sure it was you I wanted to shoot?" He made a face as he chomped on the semi-sweet chocolate. "Vittore is talking to him."

Giovanni wouldn't let himself be fooled. It wasn't just the Pakhan of the Bratva that had a reputation for being unhinged, but his uncles had worked for his father for a long time. The Di Salvos were thriving, in spite of the recent trouble.

Business was good under his father.

Enzo hadn't looked away from Nera. "She's really something," he murmured, grabbing another chocolate chip despite not liking the taste.

Nera acted before she thought, and her action was always for him, never for herself, both in her comforting touch and in the way she threw herself into danger.

"She's terrifying," Giovanni admitted.

Enzo grinned at him as he tossed another chocolate into his mouth. "That burn she gave your father will last a heck of a lot longer than the hickey you're wearing."

Giovanni's stomach clenched again. He wasn't sure if it was in fear or envy. He'd proudly wear any mark Nera gave him, but he doubted his father would feel the same if Nera's attack scarred his neck.

Nera stomped over when Enzo snagged more chocolate. "You're going to make yourself sick with those," she said. Her eyes wouldn't quite meet his uncle's as she began adding the chips to the dough she had remade.

Giovanni wondered if she'd also seen his uncle go for his gun. Nera had saved him more than once that morning. Guilt mixed with the love he had for her. It was a familiar combination, one he'd told himself he accepted.

Vittore strode into the kitchen then.

That his uncle's gaze went to Nera first surprised Giovanni. He'd never been able to read Vittore well. Giovanni studied him as his wife and uncle casually greeted each other. He'd been away for a few days, so maybe this sort of interaction was common.

Vittore built relationships with everyone. Giovanni should have been glad he was taking the time to get to know Nera.

Instead, his stomach throbbed with the remembered kick from his father.

"Are you all right, Nera?" Vittore asked her.

Nera forced a smile as she focused on the dough. Giovanni wished they were alone so he could tell her not to push herself. "Do you like chocolate croissants?" she asked his uncle, avoiding answering his question. "Or should I make something else as well?"

Vittore smiled. "They sound delicious."

She nodded, continuing to work the semi-sweet chips into the dough.

Vittore's eyes moved to Giovanni. "Your father is in a surprisingly good mood now."

Giovanni's neck ached, and he realized he had pressed the cloth with the melting ice harder against it.

"You need to take his warning seriously. No more Bratva." Vittore held his gaze.

Silently, Giovanni refused. Nera had been locked up for too long already. She hadn't complained, but he hated the idea that the Di Salvo estate had become a prison instead of a refuge for her.

"Let me do some digging," Enzo said.

Vittore narrowed his eyes at him.

"What?" Enzo shrugged. "I wasn't the one he told not to."

Giovanni's eyes slid over to Nera. His uncle had spent more time with her than he had. The idea of spending more time with her himself, even in a house where his father ruled, was pleasant.

"Your father has another job for you," Vittore warned him, and the steady warmth that had begun to fill him scattered. "But Antonio will remain relatively free. I'll see to it." Vittore reached out, his hand on Giovanni's shoulder heavier than ever. "Your father seems even more accepting of your marriage, if that helps."

Giovanni had seen that acceptance for himself. His father only ever respected strength, and that was something Nera had.

Neither of his uncles said anything more about his father attacking him. They never had. All of them knew what Giovanni Sr. was like, especially toward his son.

His shoulder relaxed when Vittore pulled away again. His uncle swept out of the kitchen, and Giovanni slipped off the stool. His eyes met Enzo's, and Enzo nodded. His other uncle would stay with Nera while he talked to Antonio.

Antonio wasn't going to be happy. For a few reasons.

Nera's hands stilled where she'd begun rolling out the dough. The side of her face he could see wasn't bruised, but he still saw the bruise in his mind's eye. He reached for her. Just a soft touch on the back of her hand.

"I wasn't quick enough, was I?" Nera said. "You won't have time for breakfast?"

Giovanni's hand lingered. "I'll come back to eat before I go."

Her smile was so very precious.

He forced his feet to move away from her, even though that was the very last thing he wanted.

Nera liked Enzo a lot more than she liked Antonio. A few days with Giovanni's cousin reminded her of that fact. It wasn't that Antonio didn't treat her well. Since the incident with Giovanni's father, his sarcasm had faded. He just talked way too much.

She'd been glad she hadn't had to face Enzo at first. She was angry with him for reaching for his gun a beat after Giovanni had reached for his own.

It made Nera want her own gun. Not only so she could shoot Giovanni's father herself if he ever touched Giovanni again; she wanted a gun that not even Enzo knew about.

She'd never considered learning how to shoot one. With her eyesight, it had seemed pointless.

Nera squinted against the overhead kitchen lights. Antonio had turned them on much sooner than Enzo ever had. At first, she'd thought it was because he didn't care if she was uncomfortable, but then she'd realized he did it before any of the Di Salvos filtered in for breakfast. Appearances were important to Antonio.

She didn't bother telling him that the damage had already been done. She'd overheard some of the Di Salvos talking about her. They hadn't all been aware in the beginning, but enough time had passed that not telling most of them apart had made her handicap more obvious. It had hurt to hear them questioning her usefulness, saying that, not only wasn't she someone from the family, but she couldn't even see. That she shouldn't have been Giovanni's first choice, or any choice at all, given that he was the son of the head of the family.

But she had been Giovanni's choice, and the reminder soothed her. It wasn't like the Di Salvos were saying anything that was untrue.

That didn't stop Antonio from throwing them out of the kitchen if he picked up on even a hint of their gossip. She'd thought Antonio used his humor to disarm people, and she hadn't been wrong. When Giovanni's cousin was angry, the other Di Salvos feared him.

Which made it even more disconcerting how often his genuine smile had been aimed at her lately.

"Need a taster?" he asked, coming up beside her as she stirred the soup she'd made for lunch. There had been more of a draft in the estate the past day or so. Winter must have grown chillier outside. She wondered if Giovanni was cold wherever he was.

Nera hesitated, but the hopeful expression on Antonio's face softened her. Just a little.

She blew on the spoonful she'd scooped for him until she deemed it cool enough.

Antonio surprised her by letting her feed him. His eyes didn't close in pleasure, but he studied hers over the spoon before he withdrew.

"It's good," he said.

Nera nodded. She didn't need anyone to tell her that her food was tasty, but the compliment never hurt. It was still a little early for lunch, but Tommaso had become even more stubborn about staying in his room. She began filling a tray for him so he couldn't use lunch as an excuse to wander. The man liked to act like he didn't have two holes in his chest that were still healing.

"I've been meaning to apologize," Antonio said.

Nera's hands stopped mid-reach as she stared at Giovanni's cousin.

"Over the years, I ragged Giovanni about you. I hated that he would go visit your damn bakery." Antonio's smile had fallen, and he glared as he mentioned the bakery.

Even Mylene had stopped asking her about the bakery. Mylene had stopped helping her in the kitchen altogether since the last time Nera had seen her, and she stayed quiet whenever Nera visited Tommaso.

"I thought he was around you out of pity. Or guilt. Or his hang-ups from what happened to his mother." Antonio scowled at the steam rising from the soup pot.

Nera didn't dispute his words. She knew Giovanni had visited for all those reasons.

"I thought you were all wrong for him. I want Giovanni to lead this family when his father... well, when it's time, but the Di Salvos have often thought he's weak. He's not fucking weak." Antonio bit out the words. "Marrying some Mafia princess would have added to his resume, or at least I thought so. You've heard about the arranged marriage expectation."

Antonio wasn't the first to mention it. Most of the Di Salvos muttered about it, and Tommaso had told her about it long before. It had been one of the reasons she'd been certain that she'd never had a chance at what she'd wanted. That talk had led her to losing her virginity to someone else.

Nera didn't regret it, not exactly. Having them both be clueless in bed would have made things far more awkward.

But she hated the reminder that, so far, they'd only had sex on their wedding night. She regretted stopping things when he'd come home the other night.

"I was wrong, Nera." Antonio's words pulled her gaze back to him. He was close enough that she could tell again that he had the same eyes as Giovanni. "The other morning wasn't the first time Giovanni's father has hurt him. Enzo and Vittore... well, they pretend it doesn't happen, and I take my cue from them. But you." Antonio's smile wasn't one of happiness. It glittered like the edge of a knife. "You tried to stab his father, and you fucking burned the shit out of his neck. Thank you, Nera."

And then Giovanni's cousin hugged her. It was a little too tight, and Nera stared at how white the ceiling became because of the lights.

He pulled away, no longer touching her. "All Giovanni has seen, all he's put up with, and then there's you. He deserves the happiness you bring him, and I'll do better to make sure he gets that for as long as possible." His hand moved up to press against the back of his head, where the cooks' assault had healed. "I mean, you can protect yourself, as you've more than proven, but I'm here to help. I promise."

"Thank you," Nera said, not sure what else to say. She finished ladling the soup in a bowl and placing it just so on the tray, mainly for something to do with her hands. Antonio was smiling at her in a way that let the words she'd been thinking escape. "Will you teach me to shoot a gun?" she asked.

Antonio stilled, but his smile didn't fade as his eyes searched her face. "It might not be easy, with your sight."

Nera appreciated that he didn't avoid saying it. "I'd still like to try."

He nodded. "Let's go down to the range after dropping that off, then." He didn't offer to carry it for her. She'd refused the last few times he'd asked. Instead, he followed along behind her.

She didn't see his face as he murmured, "It's a good thing I didn't know how fierce you were before the marriage."

Nera didn't like that he was back to teasing her, but she liked that word. No one else had ever called her fierce.

Mylene was pulling the door to Tommaso's room shut as they approached. She had her overnight bag over her shoulder and stared at the doorknob before letting go. When she turned, she wouldn't meet Nera's eyes.

"Goodbye, Nera," Mylene said, making a wide berth around where Nera stood with the tray.

Nera didn't miss how final the words sounded. She didn't turn and watch the woman leave. Antonio opened the door to Tommaso's room for her. For once, he wasn't talking too much. She kind of wished he would. He didn't come in with her, but closed the door behind her.

Tommaso had gotten dressed by himself. Nera didn't scold him. Instead, she set the tray down in the same place where she'd put his breakfast a few hours before.

"So you saw." Tommaso lowered his bulk to sit on the bed. He patted the space beside him.

Nera sat.

Tommaso hugged her. He'd been the one to hug her the most, ever since her parents had died. Mylene hadn't done it as often, even after she'd moved in and become like a mother to her. Giovanni was touching Nera more these days, of course, but quick and easy affection had never been his instinct.

And so, Tommaso had always given the largest, warmest bear hugs. "It's for the best, Nera," he said, his voice gruff with tears. "She wouldn't have fit this life."

Nera held him while he cried. He'd always been more of a crier as well.

Chapter 28

Giovanni couldn't find Nera. The kitchen was inviting, with the savory aroma of soup permeating the air, but she wasn't there. She hadn't been in their room either, and Tommaso had said she'd left his room a while ago. He'd also told Giovanni about Mylene.

Nera would be upset. Giovanni wanted to be with her.

He reminded himself that Antonio was with her. The sudden jealousy, like he'd felt toward his uncle once before, was less than helpful.

In the past, when Giovanni became frustrated or upset, he'd used the indoor range to center himself. Now he'd rather be with his wife, but he found his feet carrying him down the stairs anyway.

The muffled hiccup he heard as he drew near barely sounded like a gunshot through the soundproofed glass. Few people used the range, and he peered through the window to see who was there.

"That wasn't bad," Antonio was saying when Giovanni pulled open the door.

The whir of the target returning followed, and then Nera's voice, saying something in French before she shouted, "I completely missed, Antonio!"

Giovanni moved closer so he could see her in the enclosed aisle of the range. Her volume was partly because she was wearing ear protection, but she was also annoyed. He'd never seen her wear that expression before.

Antonio smiled at Giovanni before taking off his own headgear. "Yeah, but your stance was spot-on. I told you, being able to shoot will take practice. Now, give me back my gun."

Nera hesitated before passing him the weapon. Her freed hands reached up to pull off her own protection before her eyes latched onto Giovanni. The smile he'd been craving spread across her face.

"Giovanni!" Nera called in delight, running to him. No one besides Nera had ever run to him. She almost knocked him over in her exuberance.

Giovanni fell back into the table, the unused targets there scattering as his arms came around her to steady her. Nera's embrace squeezed him in return.

Antonio tucked his gun away as he sauntered toward the door. "I'll leave you two alone," he said with a grin, closing the door behind him.

Giovanni hadn't had time to ask about the shooting lesson before Antonio waltzed out, but he decided it was for the best. He'd wanted to tell his cousin not to teach Nera, which made no sense. Nera could do anything she wanted, even shoot. He just wanted to be the one to teach her.

He eased Nera back so he could see her face. "I didn't know—"

Nera kissed him. She stared into his eyes, and then her lips went from gentle to demanding. Her mouth was hot and giving as it slanted over his.

Giovanni's hands moved to her hair, loving the way it parted for his fingers when he buried them in it. "Nera," he murmured against her before devouring her in return. He wasn't certain which of their mouths parted first. It didn't matter when their tongues tangled and stroked each other; when her gasps filled his ears. Her fingers glided over his throat to graze the back of his neck. They made him burn.

He'd thought he'd begun to understand what it was to feel desire. The heat spread faster than he ever would have guessed, and he realized he understood nothing, and he didn't care. Not when it was Nera doing it to his body. She arched against him, cuddling his sudden erection between her thighs.

Giovanni broke the kiss, looking toward the ceiling and trying to swallow enough air to speak.

Nera's lips had found the sensitive skin on his neck. She nipped as her nimble fingers unbuttoned his shirt.

"Bedroom," he managed, swallowing his sudden groan as her teeth found his bared nipple. He liked the way she bit him a little too much.

Nera's head lifted as she dragged her shirt over her head. "I can't wait that long," she said, her voice like a breathless caress. Her bra quickly followed her shirt to the ground. Then she was tugging his hands to her bare breasts. "I need you to touch me." Her gasp as she dragged his hands over her nipples made his cock ache.

She captured his mouth before he could agree, as if she was worried he'd protest again. With her body shuddering under his hands, her tongue in his mouth, and her eyes focused so intently on his own, Giovanni didn't want to protest. He only wanted her.

And there was no way to misconstrue Nera's own desire. She wanted to have sex, and not out of any sense of duty. She gasped as she rocked against him, but the angle wasn't quite right to satisfy her.

The table beneath them groaned in protest over their weight. It hadn't been made for them both to climb on top of.

Giovanni shifted them away from it, pushing Nera against the wall instead. His hand moved under the elastic band of her skirt and into her underwear. She was already wet between her trembling legs. He dipped his finger inside her before dragging it over her clit the way she had shown him.

The pressure of her mouth eased as she clung to his neck and arched into his touch. "Giovanni, I—" She cried out as her body shook. His stroking sped up.

Giovanni felt like he was the one about to come. "You're so beautiful, Nera," he told her, resting his forehead against hers as his finger continued its work. He'd never get enough of being this close to her. Eventually her eyes lost focus as she gasped, and her orgasm took her.

He pressed her against the wall in case her legs gave out, wishing he could lift her against it instead. They'd probably both end up on the floor.

Nera's hands tightened around his neck when her eyes were able to focus again.

Giovanni lightened his strokes, loving the way she continued to tremble. "Again?" he asked.

Her hands moved to his slacks, unbuttoning and unzipping them. "I need you inside me."

Giovanni couldn't deny his own need, not when her hand had already wrapped around his erection. Her other hand dragged his slacks lower until she stroked his bare ass. He breathed through the sudden intensity of his desire, not wanting to come all over her skirt again.

She was pushing the skirt down, along with her underwear, until she was naked and trying to drag him down on top of her on the table that was sure to collapse.

He almost didn't care, but the idea that she might be hurt stopped him. His body shook as she continued to squeeze his cock. Each time she stroked down, the sensitive head was bared even further. He didn't think he was going to last.

"Giovanni?" she asked as he stiffened.

He was trying to think, wondering if he should just drag her to the floor from the start, since they were likely to end up there. But the floor was hard concrete. Even if she was on top, her knees might get scratched.

"Do you not want to?" Nera asked.

Her hand was still on his erection, which was proof enough of the opposite. Only her eyes were searching his, as if to find an answer.

Giovanni kissed her, hard and brief. "The table might break. I don't want to hurt you."

"Oh." She released him, turning around to brace herself over the table instead. The arch of her bare back was sexy as hell. So was the round curve of her ass as it rubbed against him and her legs spread. "What about this? It won't be our full weight."

He couldn't see her eyes from behind until she turned her head, looking at him over her shoulder as she arched against him. Giovanni bent over her to capture her lips, and his cock slid between her soft thighs. Her eyes seemed to burn as he did it, and then her hand found his erection again, guiding the head of his cock to her already slick entrance. She arched back, and he lost his breath at the first push inside. He wasn't even buried fully yet, but the brush of her ass against his stomach and the way she squeezed around him were almost too much.

Their lips parted, and he realized Nera was begging as she rocked, trying to take more. "Giovanni, please!"

He wrapped an arm under her body, pulling her into him as he thrust deep. Her hands shook against the table, and she continued to rock even though he'd stopped again.

Giovanni thrust into her a second time, but the way his balls swung against her had him pausing to suck in a steadying breath instead of doing what his body was urging. He wanted to keep pushing into her until he came, which wouldn't take long at all.

His other hand slid down into her pubic hair instead. The position made finding her clit a simple thing. His body shook as he stroked her.

Only his attention backfired. Her legs spread wider to give him more access, and she began using her grip on the table to thrust into him.

"Oh God, Nera," he cried out as his control shattered. He thrust into her again and again, the movement pushing her clit against his finger when he couldn't focus enough to stroke anymore. She was hot and wet and perfect. He no longer stared into her eyes; her head hung down as she pushed herself into his thrusts, taking him in deeper. But it was Nera's gasps filling his ears, her voice calling his name as her orgasm washed over her and she tightened around him, and that was enough.

Giovanni tried to ignore the broken sound that escaped him as his body curled around her, pulling her as tightly into him as he could while he came. He collapsed against her when it was over, but the table held. The room around them was too bright, their panting breaths too loud, as if his senses had sharpened.

He forced his arms to hold his weight as he slowly pulled out of her. Her shudder brought his gaze to where they had parted. She looked so wet and slick. He'd flooded her with his cum, and the thought of leaving his presence inside her kept him from softening.

Nera straightened from the table. When she turned, her eyes dropped to where his erection still jutted out from his pants. "Again?" she asked.

Giovanni swallowed as his body reacted to her. It didn't seem possible, but he didn't want to deny what his body and mind were urging him to do. He slipped off his jacket, laying it on the hard ground near her skirt. "It won't be soft enough," he admitted. "But I need to be face to face this time." His gaze dropped to her waist. "After I taste myself in you." He froze as he realized he'd practically demanded it. He searched her eyes. "If you want that."

She wrapped her arms around his neck, pressing against his erection. "I want you. All of you, Giovanni." And she was the one that dragged him down to the makeshift cushion.

Chapter 29

Giovanni hadn't been kidding about tasting what they had done. His hands pushed Nera's thighs wider as his head dipped down.

Nera's shoulders tensed against the silk lining of his suit jacket in anticipation, but Giovanni paused, looking up at her from between her legs. "Is this all right?"

She realized he'd taken her tension as a rejection. Her hands slipped into his hair, using it to push him closer. "Don't tease me, Giovanni."

The feeling of moisture leaking from her had her hands tightening on him. He'd come inside her. Thinking about it caused her hips to shift up toward him.

Giovanni's gaze had dropped. He stared at her so intently, still as a statue. Then his head dipped, and he licked up the moisture, using his tongue to push it back inside her.

Nera's legs shook. "Did you just—?" Her words broke as his tongue licked and plunged. He angled her hips up off the ground, as if wanting gravity to help his cum remain within her. Only his tongue wasn't stopping either.

The concrete ground was hard where her back pressed into it. After having his cock inside her, his tongue wasn't enough, but the hum he made as he continued to thrust with it shook her nerve endings. "Giovanni, I need…" Her words failed as only his eyes looked up at her, as if he couldn't lift his head. The gray of his eyes was so much darker than she'd ever seen.

One of his hands pushed beneath her thigh in a silent demand for her to remain tilted. Instead of shifting his tongue higher, he moved his other hand to stroke her clit. His knowledge of the pressure her body loved had the climax building fast. Her hips lifted into the plunge of his tongue as the fluorescent light above her seemed to spark. The sound he made as she came, one he'd never made, even when he ate a dessert he was really enjoying, drew out her own whimper.

His head lifted, and he crawled up her body. He was still mostly dressed, while she was sprawled naked and open on the floor. Something about the feeling was incredibly sexy, just like the desperate clenching of his jaw. His erection pressed against her entrance.

His forehead dropped against hers. He searched her eyes, his body trembling.

"Nera, do you want me to?" he asked. "Or have you had enough?"

All she saw was the dark red that was Giovanni. The too-bright whiteness of her world was completely blotted out with him that close.

Her hands found his pert, naked ass. She gripped it firmly and lifted her hips as she pulled down. His cock filled her, sending a shudder through them both.

"I'll never have enough," she admitted, staring into his eyes. "I love you, Giovanni."

He didn't look away as his hands held her legs almost too wide and he began to thrust. It should have felt a little uncomfortable, since she wasn't the most flexible person, but each thrust was like the time before. As if his pelvic bone was stroking her clit.

Her hands left his ass to clutch at the sides of his face instead, holding his forehead tight against hers so that his color never shifted, even as his rhythm grew increasingly erratic. She hovered on the precipice as he came inside her, the feeling of it hypnotic. Giovanni was everywhere inside of her—her mind, her heart, her body.

Nera was still so incredibly turned on. Her hips lifted, trying to work herself over his softening cock. A sob escaped her lips as frustration built.

Giovanni's pupils constricted as he refocused on her eyes. His hand moved between their bodies. It only took a few strokes to set her off. The sudden wave of sensation rushed through her, causing a tightening where he was buried inside her.

"Nera!" He rocked into her as he came again.

It was as if the pulsing inside her went on forever, but instead of shaking them apart, it pulled them even closer together. When the orgasm was over, twitches down below wouldn't let her forget the intensity of it.

She wanted to keep staring at him forever.

He eventually shifted himself up on his arms. They both trembled as he slipped out of her.

"The concrete is too hard," he murmured, helping her to her feet.

Her limbs felt boneless. Giovanni righted himself quickly, then helped her to dress. She felt stronger by the time she was sorted.

They both stared down at his jacket, where it remained on the ground.

Giovanni swallowed as his eyes shifted to meet hers. She dreaded the idea that he would apologize for their time together.

Instead he turned to the rickety table, lifting the gun she hadn't seen him set to the side. It looked similar to the one that Antonio had let her shoot.

"You wanted to learn?" he asked, his gaze moving back to the cubby where she'd shot her first gun.

"Yes. I'm not good at all." She hadn't even been able to see the black lines of the target, much less hit within it.

Giovanni offered her the gun. "Show me."

Nera took the weapon from him. She set it on the shelf in the cubby as she put on the eye and ear protection. The whirring of the immaculate target followed as she sent it to where it no longer meant anything to her field of vision.

Knowing that Giovanni watched her was comforting as she mimicked the stance that Antonio had shown her before. The way the gun bucked against her hand had startled her into nearly dropping it the first time. Antonio had encouraged her to use both hands to steady it. Her mostly healed arm burned a little as she controlled it, emptying another clip into the ether.

When she returned the target after, her results were about the same, despite how steady she had seemed. "Aren't I terrible?" She couldn't hear her own voice through the ear protection. She pulled them off, staring at his resting gun instead of at the pristine target.

Giovanni moved up behind her. "Why did you put the target so far away?" he asked.

Nera returned her eyes to the vague silhouette. "I need to learn to aim despite my handicap."

"The Di Salvos will protect you, Nera. If you need a gun, it will be because we have failed, and your enemy will be close." His body brushed against hers as he reached for the mechanism to move the target. He stopped the target much closer, where she could still make out the shape of a person. "Maybe this distance. Try again."

The target was nearly on top of her. Like the French cook had been, with only the kitchen island between them. The reminder of how she'd seen him lift the gun forced her to deepen her breathing.

Giovanni stepped back.

Nera reloaded the way Antonio had taught her, though she'd already been familiar with the process from watching Tommaso.

The world felt as muddled in sound as it was in vision when she pulled on the ear protection again. This time, with each squeeze of the trigger, the target fluttered from the impact. Her aim wasn't great, but she didn't miss altogether.

"Again," Giovanni said.

By the end of their session together, her arm ached, but her shots had become a continually tightening cluster.

"Enough." Giovanni accepted his gun back from her.

"Thank you," she said. "I feel like I'm making progress already."

Giovanni inclined his head, but he didn't praise her. He stared down at his gun before tucking it away.

"Can you get me one?" Nera asked.

His head tilted. "Enzo—"

"I don't want anyone to know." She bit her lip. Giovanni had said he trusted the two people who guarded her. "I'll use theirs when I practice. But the fact that I have a gun, I want it to be a secret between you and me."

Giovanni moved toward her. When his forehead touched hers, she could breathe more evenly. She waited for him to defend his uncle. To remind her that his father was the most important person to the family.

Only one person was important to her.

"You won't be reckless?" he asked instead.

Nera stared into the color that soothed her the most. She never wanted to lie to her husband. She answered him with a question. "Will you be in danger?"

The small smile that he only ever showed her spread across his lips. "I should have expected this." He linked their hands, pulling hers up to eye level. He studied the scab across her palm that had become almost raw from her work in the kitchen and now the indoor range. "I will get you one, Nera."

She tried to ignore the tightening in her stomach that underscored the question he hadn't answered.

Chapter 30

Giovanni was relieved when Antonio wasn't waiting in the hallway outside the indoor range. He suspected his cousin knew what had happened with Nera. Not having to face that knowledge immediately after was welcome.

Nera wanted to go back to their room first. Not for sex. As Giovanni listened to the shower running, he began to pace. His cock didn't stir, being more than satisfied at the moment.

The position behind her had been stimulating, but Giovanni preferred being able to see her face. The fact that he was with Nera did more for his body than any caress.

He was still surprised at himself, especially his reaction to knowing he'd left his cum inside her. The intense pleasure the idea brought him made no sense. He could easily imagine Nera's body swollen with his child, despite not being able to imagine the child itself.

Nera would be an amazing mother, but he'd be a terrible father. They weren't ready, despite the desires of his body.

She'd only just bled. He dragged out his phone to research a woman's most fertile time.

A flicker of movement out of the corner of his eye caused him to pause. He lifted his head to find Luka in the same chair as he had sat in the day after his wedding.

The sound of water running seemed even louder.

Giovanni pocketed his phone as he took in the man's presence. A smear of blood stained his shaved scalp above his ear, blending with the tattoo there. "Twice in so little time?" Giovanni asked. "People will suspect we're friends."

Luka stared down at his hands. "A mistake, the Di Salvo trying to hire me."

A coldness slid down Giovanni's neck. "The Di Salvo?"

The shower turned off.

Luka shifted the chair to face the fluttering window curtain.

Giovanni tried to remember if Nera had taken her clothes in with her. He removed his jacket, crossing the room as the door clicked open. He folded her in the jacket before she stepped into the room wearing only a towel.

Nera's eyes followed the movement in confusion.

Giovanni waited for her to look up before he cut his eyes toward Luka. He waited for Nera to follow the gesture. It took her a moment to see the silhouette facing away from her in the chair, but then she tensed.

"This is Luka," Giovanni said. "Luka, this is my wife, Nera."

Luka nodded, though he didn't look toward her.

"Nice to meet you." Nera bit her lip after the greeting.

Once he was sure it was securely around her shoulders, Giovanni let go of his jacket. "It's safe. Retrieve what you need."

Nera pulled the coat more tightly around herself as she hurried to the dresser. Her actions were quick, and she disappeared back into the bathroom to change.

Luka never once glanced her way. He always seemed uncomfortable around women, which was one key reason why he wouldn't kill them.

"Was the job for me or for her?" Giovanni asked.

Luka's hands tightened into fists. "Her. The soldier won't return."

"Anyone I know?" Giovanni asked.

Luka shrugged. He stood, digging a wallet out of his pocket. He tossed it to Giovanni.

Giovanni caught it, but didn't look inside. "I appreciate you bringing this to me."

"I wasn't their first choice," Luka warned.

Luka already knew the French cook was dead. He was warning Giovanni of someone else.

"How many?" Giovanni asked. The slow pound of his heartbeat felt as if it shook his entire body.

"At least one inside." Luka glanced toward the bathroom door. "That's all I got before he bled out."

Giovanni wished it was more. Not only had someone gone to the Bratva's pakhan, but they'd approached Luka directly. And that someone had been a Di Salvo. He lifted the wallet. "Is this the same person who spoke with Ivankov?"

Luka shook his head. "That was a call."

That wasn't a true denial. Luka didn't know if it was the same person.

Giovanni stared at the wallet in his hand. No soldier in the Di Salvo family would act alone—they would only act on orders from either his father or his uncles.

That the Bratva had targeted Nera made no sense from the beginning. That it was a Di Salvo instead made his marriage to her pointless, for her safety anyway.

Being with Nera was not pointless.

The bathroom door clicked again. Nera crossed to Giovanni's side, close enough that her now blouse-covered arm brushed the sleeve of his dress shirt.

Even though she was fully clothed, Luka's gaze dropped to his feet.

Nera's posture shifted, as if she was unsure whether she should be there. "I was just about to start dinner," she said. "Would Luka like something?"

Giovanni linked his hand with hers. "Stay."

Her shoulders relaxed as she nodded.

Luka's head lifted, though his eyes didn't settle on her. "Your soup was good," he murmured before turning to slip past the curtain.

Though his words surprised Giovanni, they probably shouldn't have. The man was more than capable of slipping into the Di Salvo kitchen unnoticed. If Luka had accepted the hit, Nera would have already been dead.

She was smiling when Giovanni's gaze traced her face. "He liked my soup," she said, delighted. "Is he a friend of yours?"

"Of sorts," Giovanni admitted. It didn't matter that Luka had once been intent on killing him. Or that there was little he himself knew about Luka's life among the Bratva. Their bond had been built on a recognition of their innate similarities, and a mutual hate for dishonesty. "You can trust him."

Her head tilted. "So you really trust three people."

Giovanni tugged on her hand, pulling her closer to him, close enough for him to feel the heat from her body. "No. I trust four."

Her free hand skimmed over his cheek. "That makes me happy. I love you, Giovanni."

The chill that had consumed him before had faded.

He'd never given her the words back, he realized. His jaw clenched shut.

"Any requests for dinner?" she asked, letting her hand fall.

Giovanni shook his head. He remained quiet as he followed her to the kitchen. His gaze took in each Di Salvo they passed, nerves raising the hair along his arms. Which one of them had also gotten orders to harm Nera? Or was it more than one? At least none followed them into the kitchen.

He enjoyed watching Nera in her element, despite the dark thoughts that distracted him. He'd designed her prior kitchen for her, and had tried to imagine her in it, but imagination had never been his strength. The way her pupils became pinpricks under the fluorescent lights reminded him that he wanted to change the Di Salvo kitchen to suit her as well.

Antonio strolled into the kitchen. "About time you two started acting like newlyweds," he murmured so only Giovanni could hear.

Giovanni didn't bother responding. At least his jacket covered the fact that his neck had already grown warm. He hadn't switched it out for another one after covering Nera in front of Luka, and he could smell her soap when he shifted to remove the wallet. "Luka brought this."

The grin dropped from his cousin's face. He avoided the streak of blood at the corner of the leather as he opened it to view the ID inside. "This is one of Enzo's men. Luka is killing Di Salvos now?"

Giovanni stared out at the soldiers lingering in the open area outside of the kitchen. "Only when they try to hire him."

"Why would one of Enzo's men try to hire him?" Antonio's hand tightened on the wallet, no longer worried about the blood.

"They wouldn't. Not without orders." Giovanni met his cousin's gaze.

Antonio shook his head. "You can't suspect Enzo."

"Can't I?" Giovanni murmured. There were only three people who could have ordered it. The idea that the uncle he felt so close to may have betrayed him was making him nauseous.

"He's been alone with her the most. If Enzo wanted her dead, she'd be dead." Antonio tucked the wallet away. "Let me talk to Enzo. Maybe the soldier is a traitor." His eyes slid to Nera, where she continued to cook. "Luka must have been appalled when he was approached with the offer. How is that kid? Still in love with you?"

Giovanni shook his head. "Don't do that."

Antonio shrugged. "He's worse with women than you are." He glanced at Nera. "Though that seems to have changed. Damn, Gio, you—"

Giovanni's glare cut his cousin off. "Be careful what you say."

Antonio's eyes softened as he dropped his teasing. "Well, it seems like you've accepted your body's reaction at least. I was a little worried."

Giovanni looked away, his mind still racing over the information Luka had brought him. More Di Salvos were gathering in the house than ever before, and he'd been around his wife the least often out of anyone for the past week.

Nera had told him she would only regret their time not spent together. If something happened, he was only making things worse. His palms grew clammy as he scanned more faces through the entryway than he could count. "There're so many," he mumbled. So many family members who could hurt the person he loved the most.

"Because they're anticipating your wife's dinner." Antonio's smile was forced. "She's better at baking, no contest, but they enjoy all her meals." He reached up for the top of the doorframe, doing his own perusal of those gathered. "Worried?" he asked.

"Terrified," Giovanni admitted.

"Good," Antonio said.

"What?" Giovanni looked at his cousin.

Antonio's smile faltered. "You care, Gio. More than I ever thought you'd be able to." He let his arms fall. "Let me handle the investigation. You stay with her."

Giovanni considered it. No part of him wanted to dissuade his cousin, despite knowing his father would see it as him shirking his duty. If his father was the one behind the orders, what did that matter?

"Better yet, act like the newlyweds you are. Take her out for once." Antonio's gaze found Nera. "Gems glitter brighter in the sun."

"She's not a gem. She's—" No one word seemed like enough. Nera was everything.

Antonio was smiling at him. When he met his eyes, there were no hard edges. "There's a restaurant I think she'd like," he said.

Giovanni's pulse thrummed. "You can't be serious."

"I think it's better than setting up another meeting. And if my questions turn up what you suspect, we'll need allies." Antonio looked toward the stove. "You don't think Nera can handle it?"

"I didn't say that." Giovanni remembered the last time he'd been in the kitchen. Nera had no fear, not when it came to protecting him. Somehow, that thought was even more terrifying than the unknown faces that were trying to kill her. As long as Nera was the one being targeted, she'd remain calm.

Giovanni understood that. Even so, he'd much prefer it if his family came after him directly.

"I'll take her," he agreed.

"Good." Antonio crossed to Nera.

Watching his cousin help her cook brought that same ache to his stomach that he'd experienced before, but Giovanni didn't join them. Instead, he continued to study faces, wondering if he really did only have three people he could trust.

Chapter 31

Nera sat in the bucket seat of Giovanni's car, using her hands to smooth down her skirt. She'd asked if she should dress up, but Giovanni had told her to wear whatever made her comfortable. That hadn't helped, but her long skirts with actual pockets were still her favorite thing in the world, so she'd worn the same as usual.

After shutting her door, he'd rounded the car to settle in behind the wheel.

Nera had only ever ridden in the bakery's van. The bright blue sports car that matched Giovanni's eyes, at least according to Antonio, was completely out of her realm. Giovanni waited for her to buckle her seat belt before the engine seemed to almost purr. She didn't understand why the power of horses was always linked to cars when they sounded much closer to lions.

The sky above was a steady light gray, with no clouds as far as she could see. The heat of the sun didn't quite reach her through the darkly tinted windows.

Giovanni pulled away from the house. The driveway was longer than she remembered. She took in the spread of plants in a garden that she also hadn't remembered. The sun had barely risen back when Tommaso had been shot.

The estate moved out of sight behind them. Nera wondered if one reason why Mylene had left was because she felt trapped. Nera felt better than she had all week, but it wasn't because she was leaving the house.

Her gaze moved over Giovanni as the world passed by outside the window. She'd woken up with him that morning, and he'd said he'd be with her until they closed their eyes again. A whole day with him. It felt selfish but exhilarating.

"Ready?" Giovanni murmured, his eyes shifting to her briefly.

She nodded, resting her head against the seat behind her.

Giovanni floored it.

He'd warned her earlier. In order to make certain no one followed them, he was going to go fast and make turns that might frighten her.

While she knew the scenery was flying by faster than she should have been comfortable with, Nera barely paid it any attention. She focused on Giovanni instead. She'd never seen him drive a car before. His face was as stoic as ever as he slid the car into the first turn, but there was a darkening in his eyes that hinted at his satisfaction over the control he exerted on the machine. He continued to race and drive in a way that someone else might have thought of as reckless. She took in a new side of him that she might have never known if their lives had woven together differently than they had.

He pulled into a garage with the final swerve, braking so the bottom of his car didn't scrape as they bumped up the ramp. A final maneuver into a parking lot, and she was almost disappointed it was over.

Giovanni studied the garage in the quiet that fell after he cut the engine. Then he slid out, coming to the passenger-side door to open it for her.

Nera liked the way his fingers linked with hers as they walked away from the car. The stairwell's dim lighting was soothing. It made his color seem to spread. Only their footsteps sounded as they went down the first flight of two.

She tugged on his hand. "Giovanni?"

He paused, his face turning toward her.

Nera tilted her head up and kissed him. She loved the barely audible gasp of surprise he made when her tongue stroked inside. A part of her wanted to push him against the wall and make him forget everything. She pulled away instead, watching the slight tick at the edge of his jaw that told her he wasn't unaffected.

She pulled him toward the stairs. His hand tightened on hers as they descended together.

A few blocks from the parking garage, and they approached a car that was vaguely familiar. The gray wasn't the same as the previous one Giovanni drove. "Is it red?" Nera asked, seeing the color in her memory.

"Yes." Giovanni unlocked the passenger door for her. "This one was Tommaso's. He sold it to Antonio some time ago."

The seat differed from the prior car. It connected with the driver's side as if it was one giant seat. If she'd wanted, she could slide next to Giovanni, where he sat behind the wheel. She did want to, but stayed on her side and seat belted instead. The leather was warm under her hands when she connected the metal clasp.

Giovanni pulled out into the street much more sedately.

Nera's thumb rubbed over the smooth seat beneath her. She'd never had sex in a car, but something about the feel against her skin made her want to be naked against it. "This car is different."

"It's from 1967," Giovanni said, turning down the first side street. "No GPS. Few know Antonio has it."

She remembered Tommaso liked older cars, but that wasn't what interested her most. "So you no longer think we're being followed?" she asked.

"Likely not," Giovanni said.

Her hand slid along the middle of the seat, closer to Giovanni. "Then maybe we can find somewhere to park, just for a little while?"

His hands tightened on the steering wheel. "Nera, I—"

She craved her lips on his neck as she watched his Adam's apple bob. She wanted to watch him do that while she had him in her mouth.

"It's not safe," Giovanni said. His right hand left the steering wheel, linking with hers on the leather seat. "Another time."

"It's a date," she agreed. "We'll go for a drive one night, when we don't have to worry so much." She stared down at their hands, not letting herself worry about how long into the future that might be.

The restaurant Giovanni parked in front of wasn't one she'd ever seen before. That made sense, since it wasn't near the bakery. It was a similar, older brick building like the one her parents had chosen for the bakery, with a striped canopy arching over the entrance and fancy lettering in the window.

Giovanni led her to the door, and a bell jingled invitingly as they entered.

The expressions of the people inside weren't as inviting.

One man, larger than even Giovanni's father, though maybe it was his long beard that made it seem that way, rose to his feet, his hands braced on a checkered tablecloth. "Well, I'll be damned. What the hell is Giovanni Di Salvo doing in my restaurant?"

The other men rose, and Giovanni stepped in front of Nera. "Taking my wife to lunch," he said. His back didn't block the man's dumbstruck expression. "If you'll have us?"

The man's eyes narrowed. "The Di Salvos declined my generous offer."

"My father did," Giovanni agreed.

The man gestured to the arched-backed seats in front of him. "Welcome," he said.

Giovanni gestured her forward, and Nera crossed the room, glad that the restaurant was dim enough that she could make out what looked to be a genuine smile among all the facial hair the man wore. She'd never seen a beard so long.

"Nera, meet Montrell Coronella."

She held out her hand. She'd heard of the Coronella family, mainly from Tommaso. The customers around the bakery only ever spoke of the Di Salvos. "It's nice to meet you."

His handshake was warm and firm. "Likewise."

They took their seats, and Montrell waved the other men out of the restaurant. "Take a break. All but you, Vespa." He sat back in his chair across from them.

A woman stepped up behind him. Her dark hair was pulled back in a severe bun, and she wore tight, black slacks and a crisply buttoned black shirt topped off with the crisscrossed straps of dual gun holsters. Her toned arms folded across her chest as she studied first Giovanni and then Nera.

"Are you hungry?" Montrell asked Nera, his voice mellow.

Even with nerves, Nera could always eat. She glanced at Giovanni. He nodded.

"We did come for lunch," she said. She glanced around the restaurant. Now that the Coronella men had cleared out, there was no one else at the tables. "You serve Italian?"

"What else?" Montrell's smile had an edge. "I may be a half-breed like Giovanni here, but we're both still La Cosa Nostra. Giulia!" he called.

An older woman with a riot of dark curls poked her head out of a door in the back. "Don't shout!" she yelled back. "I've still got ears."

Montrell looked properly scolded, and his voice lowered. "Make something for my guests, please."

The older woman's eyes pierced Nera before she disappeared back inside what appeared to be a brightly lit kitchen.

"So. The junior Di Salvo is married now. Congratulations." Montrell smiled at Nera, pulling her gaze to him. "I'm a bit surprised by your choice."

Nera wasn't sure how to take that.

"It's not a reflection on you," Montrell assured her. "I took Giovanni here as the type to marry one of the princesses, is all. Like I almost did." The smile faded from his eyes.

"Almost? Then..." Nera shifted her gaze to Vespa, who returned her look with a toothy grin.

Montrell's laughter could have shaken the room. "Vespa? No, but she's the best enforcer any family could have. And my capos know it, after the older generation tried to test her. Misogynistic pricks. No offense, Giovanni."

Giovanni's face lost every trace of warmth. "I'm not my father."

"No, but you're still ruled by him. I already killed mine."

Nera studied the large man, who spoke of patricide so matter-of-factly. The memory of Giovanni's father squeezing the breath out of him rose within her.

Montrell's gaze narrowed. "He deserved it. He married an Irish daughter, hated her and me, since I was half her, and then acted surprised when she ran back to her family after being treated like shit." His chair creaked under his weight when he leaned back. "Killing him kept the bloodshed minimal. Arranged marriages are archaic. Perhaps I'm lucky my half-Irish pedigree kept me free of it." He lifted an eyebrow. "As your half-Russian blood did for you?"

Giovanni shook his head. "It was always Nera."

Her breath caught at his words. When she faced him, his red outline seemed to blaze in her vision.

"Really?" Montrell's eyes widened. "A well-kept secret then."

Giovanni's jaw clenched.

From the kitchen, the sound of pans being placed and an oven opening drifted to them.

"Why are you here, Giovanni?" Montrell asked.

Giovanni reached for Nera's hand beneath the table. "My priority is Nera's safety. That may require some changes soon."

Nera squeezed his hand as she understood what he was saying.

Montrell stared at him. "The Coronellas aren't allergic to change, but I have to be honest. I see little advantage in us getting involved with the Di Salvos until it's settled."

"Agreed," Giovanni said. "This was simply a safe place to take my wife for a meal."

Vespa sucked in a breath, her face turning stormy.

Montrell laughed. "Your cousin is rubbing off on you. But I'll play. Giulia makes a delicious meal."

"Speaking of Antonio, he came across some interesting information. About the Albanians."

All traces of laughter fled from Montrell's face. He sat forward, his hand closing in a fist on top of the table. "This is your strategy?"

"Antonio was certain you'd be interested. I hope he's right." Giovanni's hand trembled against hers, but his face remained expressionless. "The type of man I could respect would want to know."

Montrell pushed up from the table, his feet carrying him to the windows.

Vespa glared at them before stomping after him.

Nera couldn't make out their strained whispers.

Giulia pushed into the dining room, carrying a large serving tray. She frowned over at the Coronellas, then approached the table. Two steaming plates were set in front of Giovanni and Nera, and another where Montrell had been sitting. Apparently Vespa wouldn't be eating.

Giovanni released Nera's hand beneath the table, but the older woman wasn't blind to it. She had a lovely set of dimples when she smiled. "It's nice to see a love match for a change," she said.

Nera flushed, glancing at her husband. His neck had darkened, likely red again to match his color. His hand came up to rest next to hers on top of the table, but they didn't touch.

"Eat well, my dear," Giulia said, patting her shoulder before picking up the tray again.

The gnocchi Giulia had made smelled divine in its white sauce.

"Montrell!" Giulia shouted at him. "Food!" She hustled back to the kitchen.

Vespa still seemed irritated as she and Montrell returned to the table. She scowled down at the gnocchi.

Montrell sat, unrolling his napkin. "I may be interested, Giovanni, but I can't decide today."

"Understood," Giovanni said.

Montrell reached for his fork. "Is there anything else you're here for? Or can we eat a delicious meal in peace now?"

"There was one other thing." Giovanni turned toward Nera. He wore the small smile that so rarely appeared, and her chest squeezed. "I'd like to buy a gun. A gift for my wife."

"For God's sake, Di Salvo!" Vespa's hands came down on the table, shaking the plates. "Your family must have plenty of guns. She should already have one."

"The food, Vespa," Montrell griped.

She straightened, continuing to glare at Giovanni.

Giovanni met her gaze. "This one, no other Di Salvo will know of."

Vespa's anger faded.

Montrell sighed. "Pick a good one, Vespa. Our gift." He smiled at Nera. "A late wedding present."

Vespa hurried toward the back.

Nera leaned toward Giovanni. "Thank you," she murmured into his ear.

The small amount of skin above his collar became even darker.

Montrell speared his first bite. "By the way, Nera, I love your auburn hair."

Giovanni frowned at him. "Don't flirt with my wife."

Nera enjoyed the Coronella leader's deep laughter as she began to eat.

The gnocchi was delicious.

Chapter 32

Dread filled Giovanni as he pulled to a stop in front of the Di Salvo estate. He'd always felt that way when returning home. After turning off the car, the more modern one they'd returned in, not the one with the bench seats Nera had coveted, he turned toward his wife. She continued to wear that soft smile, and there was no returning tension in her shoulders, as if she was truly content despite the danger that surrounded them.

Giovanni was steadily accepting the path that lay ahead for the family. Something had to change. It was as if happiness shimmered on the horizon, ready to disappear if he blinked. He'd much rather pursue the mirage than lose it.

After he opened the passenger door, his hand reached for hers. He'd had trouble not touching her in some way all day. That she seemed to enjoy it had only encouraged him. The slide of his skin against hers sent tingles through his fingers.

Besides her brief kiss in the stairwell, which had sent his stomach tumbling, they had done little that should make his body feel this way.

From the estate's entryway, the bright lights of the kitchen spilled out like a beacon. The few Di Salvos present on the ground floor shifted their eyes away from Giovanni as shouting could be heard from within the kitchen.

Giovanni would recognize his cousin's voice anywhere.

"I have my fucking limits!" Antonio was saying.

Nera's hand tightened around his own as they moved into the kitchen doorway.

To Giovanni's surprise, he saw both of his uncles inside as well, with Vittore holding up his hands in an attempt to calm Antonio. Whatever he had said must not have worked. Antonio shoved Enzo's chest, causing his uncle to crash against the stove.

"Antonio!" Vittore snapped. "That's enough!"

Giovanni stared at his uncle, whose usual expression had dropped into one of frustration.

"It's nowhere near enough," Antonio said, but he didn't lunge for Enzo again.

"This is not the place." Vittore moved to Enzo's side, placing his hand on his brother's shoulder.

"What is this?" Giovanni asked. He stepped in front of Nera as the gazes of his family swung to him. He stared back. Silence had sometimes worked in his favor.

Antonio waved at Enzo. "He fucking knew, Gio. About his man."

Enzo straightened away from the stove. "That's not exactly what I said." His head tilted as he smiled at Nera. "Welcome home, doll. Did you have a nice date?"

Nera nodded. "I did." Her gaze took in the spotless kitchen. "But I didn't think about how that would leave the rest of the Di Salvos without dinner. Shall I make something?"

Giovanni didn't release her hand, not letting her move past him.

Vittore's face gentled as he also looked toward her. "You're Giovanni's wife, Nera. That's not necessary. Don't spoil the Di Salvos too much."

"Don't use her to avoid the subject," Antonio said.

"I'm not avoiding anything." Enzo didn't lose his smile. "Giovanni knows where I was. He was there when I discussed it with Vittore."

"You," Giovanni agreed. "Not your man."

Enzo's hands clenched as he grimaced. "I found him there. At the Bratva's. Or what was left of him." His eyes cut to Antonio. "That's how I knew." There was something dead in his gaze as he returned it to his brother. "And I came home for answers."

Vittore frowned in confusion. "What are you saying, Enzo?"

"The boys have a reason to be asking questions. I'm telling you now, Vittore; I can't live with that. Not again," Enzo rasped. His uncle's expression was one Giovanni had only seen once before. The memory almost drowned him.

The numbness that had always come over him, ever since his father had killed his mother, returned. Even the warmth of Nera's fingers couldn't penetrate it.

Vittore sighed. "I think we all know who in the family would order a hit on a woman."

Hearing it said out loud made the memory of his mother's death recede. Heat ignited the acid in Giovanni's stomach.

"Giovanni," Nera gasped behind him. She trembled where she pressed against his back.

He whirled, the brightness of the kitchen somehow dimming and noise rushing into his ears. Nera was trying to shield him with her body, he realized, and his gaze pierced the gloom beyond the kitchen's entrance, making out the trembling gun in the hand of a member of the Di Salvo.

Giovanni wished time would stop. He tried to shove Nera out of the way, worried he was too late, as he'd always been.

The hair on the back of Nera's neck had risen, and a shiver whispered up her spine at a change in air pressure. It was from concern over what the men were saying, she thought, but her gaze was drawn toward the dim area outside of the kitchen.

She recognized the Di Salvo. His expression was the same as the first time he had tried to shoot her: terrified. Only Enzo wasn't there to knock the weapon aside. She fumbled for the small of her back, where Vespa had strapped the gun, but she still gripped Giovanni with her dominant hand and couldn't let go.

Nera called Giovanni's name as her instinct to shield him also kicked in, trapping her reaching hand as she pressed hard into his back.

Giovanni pushed her to safety as the gun in front of her steadied, and she tumbled toward the kitchen floor.

The sound of a gunshot didn't follow. The gun clattered to the tiles instead as a scream of pain was cut off. Nera turned her head, staring just beyond the kitchen entrance into the bulging eyes of the Di Salvo who had almost shot her twice. He was on the floor as well. Large hands had wrapped around his neck, and the man scratched at them with one hand as the other lay on the ground—limp, bloody, and unmoving.

"That is my fucking daughter-in-law," a voice growled above him.

Nera shifted her gaze up to Giovanni's father, the fury on his face choking out her own breath.

"No one gets to fucking touch her," his father said, increasing the pressure.

Nera watched as the man's scratching grew still. The older Di Salvo's eyes remained just as wide even though they no longer saw her.

Giovanni's father rose from the body, his gaze sweeping over the crowd. "She is a Di Salvo! She is one of us!" he barked. Then he moved to where Nera lay on the kitchen floor, holding his hand down toward her.

She willed herself to be steady as she let her father-in-law help her to her feet. His hand didn't linger.

Nera stared at the dead man, realizing she hadn't seen him much since the day she'd killed the French cook. "He almost shot me before." She couldn't quite wrap her mind around it.

"Did he?" Giovanni Sr.'s voice was soft as he moved past her.

Giovanni didn't make a sound as his father grabbed his throat, shoving him against the kitchen island.

Nera pictured Giovanni staring at her with dead eyes. "Don't touch him!" She forced her way between father and son.

His father let her. Stepping back, he glared at his son. "Learn to take care of traitors," he said. His hard gaze swept over her. "If you tire of my limp-dick son, come find me." He stalked out of the kitchen, calling over his shoulder, "Vittore! Enzo!"

Giovanni's uncles scrambled after him.

Arms wrapped around her from behind, but even Giovanni's touch didn't loosen the tension in her body. He breathed out her name as he pulled her against him, burying his face in her hair.

Chapter 33

Antonio stalked past Giovanni and Nera, staring down at the dead Di Salvo soldier. "For fuck's sake, there were four of us in the kitchen."

And still Nera was almost shot. Giovanni wondered if that had been the point. Killing his wife while she held his hand was the ultimate way to prove how worthless Giovanni was. The thought forced him to raise his head. He stared out of the kitchen, but the other Di Salvo men had scattered.

His father's fury had terrified them.

It wasn't anger Giovanni felt when he clutched Nera against him.

"I should have killed him before," he said. The dark marks on the dead man's skin made Giovanni's own neck throb. He'd wanted nothing more than to kill the soldier when he'd realized he had almost shot Nera the first time. At that point, Enzo had stopped him.

"Go on," Antonio said, tilting his head toward the stairs. "I'll take care of this."

His cousin probably thought he needed to fuck his wife to prove she was alive. His father would have dragged her somewhere to fuck her afterward, if she was his. The thought made him remember all over again that it was his father who had saved her.

Nera's words echoed in his mind, protecting him after he'd failed to do the same. She didn't tremble against him. No, her eyes were fierce when she lifted her head. As her gaze traced over his skin, some of her tension eased, as if being with someone like him was enough.

Smudges darkened the skin under her eyes, evidence that she was more tired than she had let on.

"Make Enzo clean up," Giovanni told his cousin as he led Nera away.

It wasn't long before their bedroom door clicked shut behind them.

Nera tugged free from his grasp. Her hands slid his jacket off his shoulders. She set it over the back of the chair, then returned to him, her fingers loosening the top button of his shirt.

Giovanni stilled her progress. He moved closer, pressing his forehead against hers as he closed his eyes. "I can't, Nera." He swallowed, unable to look at her. "I don't have an erection." He doubted he'd be able to become aroused. Not when he kept envisioning her lifeless in front of him.

"You think this is about sex?" she asked. Her touch lifted to graze his neck above his collar. "I'm not thankful your father was there. Giovanni, he hurt you again."

At the tone of her voice, he opened his eyes.

"Your push is what saved me. You made sure I was out of the way, putting yourself in the crosshairs instead." Her finger slid to the pulse in his neck. "And yes, I want to touch you. I want to feel the warmth of your skin. The beat of your heart. It's okay if it's not more than that." Her hands moved back to the buttons of his shirt.

Giovanni didn't stop her this time. Instead, he watched the miracle of her, still full of life, in front of him. She undressed him. Then he did the same to her.

That he remained flaccid no longer embarrassed him. Her eyes never dropped to it.

Giovanni was careful to set both of their guns close to the bed. Within easy reach. Then he rolled toward his wife, gathering her in his arms.

Her warm skin felt right against his. Her head found its place against his chest, and her legs tangled with his, as if she needed as much physical contact as possible.

Nera listened to his heartbeat, and he listened to hers.

Giovanni loved her. He wanted to say the words, but like usual, they wouldn't come.

Nera never struggled to find words. "I love you," she said, increasing the ache in his heart.

Giovanni didn't want to admit to the heat in his eyes. His jaw worked open and shut and open again. "Why?" he asked.

Nera's ear remained pressed to his chest. "I used to think you came to the bakery out of pity. The poor, orphaned girl who also struggled with her sight must have been so pitiful to you."

Acid burned in Giovanni's stomach. "No."

"I did think it. I convinced myself I couldn't expect more." She leaned up, her lips brushing against his forehead. When she pulled away, she wore the smile she'd always given him. "And I wanted more. More of the way I seemed to be the only person you looked at. More moments where only I understood what you were thinking." Her hand shifted, and her thumb traced his bottom lip. "More of that little smile that you only ever directed at me. Giovanni, I don't need you to protect me. I only ever wanted you to love me."

His throat constricted.

"I know you do. I don't need the words." Her head found its place again. Her arms wrapped around his back, holding him close. "I love you."

He still didn't understand, but that no longer seemed to matter. His heart slowed as he listened to her breathing, recognizing when it shifted into the deeper pattern that came with sleep.

Giovanni didn't want to sleep. He didn't want to miss a single second of her being alive. Hours passed as he continued to watch her.

There was no numbness in his fingers, so when they began to tingle, the feeling confused him. He imagined them moving over her skin, and the urge to follow through caused the tingling to spread. He wanted to touch her, to memorize every inch of Nera's form. It was more than a want. His hands needed to etch every part of her into the recesses of his mind.

He resisted the need. Nera was exhausted. Sleep was necessary to her wellbeing.

His fingers began moving along her back without his permission, smoothing soft little strokes up and down her spine. Which was fine, he told himself. The caress would be soothing, and he would limit himself to that. Even just trailing his thumb along her skin filled him with her warmth.

Nera was warm and whole and alive. The mental image of her lying before him, broken and lifeless, faded as his touch spread outward from her spine. When his hands shifted over the top of her shoulders, his thumbs finding the beautiful arch of her neck, her breathing changed. He'd woken her.

Giovanni started to apologize, but he didn't really feel sorry. Not when her sleepy eyes opened and her lips tilted up in welcome.

His hands continued their path down her arms, making it to her elbows. He had to unwind her arms from around him to roll over her, resting the backs of her hands on the pillow before returning to where he had paused. Nera's forearms were strong, the nearly invisible hair along her skin soft even though her skin felt firm. He slid his hands under hers on the pillow, studying how his were slightly bigger, even though he'd never considered anything about himself large.

"Giovanni?" Nera's tone held a question with a sliver of concern.

He paused as he slid his palms around to press against hers, looking into her eyes. "I need to touch you. Is that all right?"

Her fingers curled between his, giving his hands a gentle squeeze. "Touch me as much as you want. I like the way it feels." Her fingers uncurled, not keeping him trapped.

Giovanni resumed his progress. His hands skimmed down the undersides of her arms. Her skin there was more sensitive to his touch when he kept his pressure light, so he pressed slightly harder to stop her ticklish tremble. The faint stubble of hair in her underarm rasped under his touch, and she had a small, dark circle of a mole just underneath the left one. His thumb stroked over it, and she drew in a breath.

He shifted to touch her shoulders, his fingers curling over to brush her back before reaching her neck. His hands could encircle it, but he hated that image and moved up to her ears quickly. The soft lobes were attached, and her tremble returned as he rubbed them between his fingers. Nera's ears were sensitive. He skimmed the firm skin behind them.

Then his hands slid into her hair. It was disheveled, and he was careful not to tug at it when knots burdened his progress. His fingers massaged her scalp before he slid them out, mapping over her gorgeous forehead next. Her eyes closed, and he skimmed delicately over the lids, appreciating the tickle of her lashes. The top of her nose was hard and bony, while the flared nostrils were soft. Her cheeks were even softer. Then his thumb skated over her bottom lip, and he felt a sudden throb in his cock.

It surprised him. He hadn't been considering sex with her. When her breath escaped in a sudden gasp at his thumb's repeated stroke, he had the urge to kiss her. He denied it, continuing his journey down her chin. He only used his thumb to slide down her neck, since he'd hated the way his full hands had looked against the skin there.

Nera's body arched into his. He stilled, waiting for her to lie back again before his hands flattened on her chest and slid down the top slope of her breasts. He paused above her nipple, deciding to curl his palms around the plump sides instead and down. When his fingers moved underneath, he found her skin hotter there, where the underside of her breasts had pressed against her. The heat made the proof of her life undeniable.

His hands crossed her stomach, which was almost as soft as her breasts had been. He liked the rounded feel, imagining the comfort of resting his head there, and the way he could feel it press against his own stomach when he was inside her.

His slight hardening had become an erection.

Giovanni ignored it as he continued his progress. The skin below her stomach was nearly as hot as the underside of her breasts had been. He paused at the top of her pubic hair, which was darker than the auburn color that suited her face so well. Nera had begun to tremble, and his nostrils flared as her scent reached him.

He moved his touch to the tops of her thighs instead; his touch hadn't been about sex when he'd started. His own ache had grown, becoming more difficult to ignore. His cock jutted out from his body, and pressing it into the bed brought no relief.

He focused on her body, but that only brought more heat. His hands couldn't cover her entire thigh. He found the almost invisible hair there soft again. Her thighs shook as his fingers skimmed down their insides. His palms curled to cup her knee, hard with bone. The lower part of her leg was smooth but firm, as strong as her forearms had been.

The most delicate veins rose on the top of her foot. Her toes weren't painted, but the nails had been clipped short. Her second toe was as long as the largest one. He brushed his thumb along the tips before sliding each of his hands under the very bottom of her. Nera's feet had a high arch that was as sensitive as her ears and neck had been. She laughed as he stroked there, and the sound shot through him.

Her legs parted, and her feet shifted as if she wanted to move them away. He added a deeper pressure as he stroked, and the end of her laugh turned into a startled moan.

Giovanni wanted to moan with her. His erection reacted as if it had been her hand that had stroked it instead. He clenched his jaw to keep any sound inside as he rubbed the arch of her foot again. Her scent became stronger as her legs slid wider.

He looked at the center of her, which he had skipped over before. His hands skimmed up the insides of her legs before his thoughts could focus. Nera's breathing had grown erratic, and so much louder. As it filled his ears, he found the softness of her thighs before moving higher.

He parted her so he could study her, as he'd done before. He'd been worried about exploring her incorrectly in the past, but he no longer felt any concern. When he rubbed his thumb along her slit, which was already soaked, her trembling grew stronger. Nera's breathing turned into gasps. She was sensitive here as well. And the warmth of her was unlike anything else he had touched.

Her clit above looked swollen and enlarged compared to the first time he had seen it. He finally dipped his thumb inside her before brushing over her clit.

Nera nearly came off the bed. Giovanni rested his weight on one of her thighs and used his free hand to keep her still as he drew circles around her clit. He watched her face as he did. Studied the way she bit her lip but then let it go in order to moan. Her head writhed as he continued to stroke. A flush darkened her cheeks before her body tried to arch and she climaxed.

Sensation shot through him as she cried out her love for him, so very alive. Too much sensation. His ass tightened and his mind blanked as he climaxed with her. He hadn't known that was possible. She hadn't even touched him. His face pressed to her stomach, and his arms wrapped around her waist.

His cock softened as they both caught their breath. He started to worry that she was disappointed, but then Nera's hands found his hair, slipping through the strands gently and removing the slight tension that had gathered within him. "I love you so much, Giovanni."

"Nera." Her name was like a prayer. "I love you."

Her hands paused as she sucked in a breath.

Giovanni felt incredibly light. He crawled up her body until he could lower his forehead against hers and wrap her tightly against him.

"I love you, Nera," he said again, because he could. "If you died, I would follow. I don't want to be without you."

Her eyes shimmered with tears.

He kissed her. Long, drugging kisses that he hoped wouldn't allow her to worry. When he lifted his head, her cheeks were damp, but no moisture remained in her eyes, only a blazing brightness. Her hands pushed at him, and Giovanni rolled to his back on the other side of the bed, letting her rest on his chest, expecting her head to find its spot there.

Nera sat up instead. Her fingers traced over his face. "I want to memorize you as well. You're so beautiful, Giovanni." His skin tingled as she skimmed over it. "Like these cheekbones. Amazing." Nera's lips followed, brushing the top of his cheek.

He tried to hold still as she progressed along his body. His sensitivity grew with every caress, every brush of her lips. Nera didn't just touch and kiss. Her words praised each part of his body that she reached. She was the one to gasp as her breasts dragged over the top of his thighs on her way down.

His erection was straining and desperate between them. She ignored it, as intent on mapping all of his body as he'd been with hers.

Giovanni enjoyed having his feet touched as much as he'd enjoyed touching hers. When she slowly worked her way between his legs, it already felt like too much. He couldn't have that. The need to be inside her was too strong.

He grabbed her, dragging her under his body as he settled against her heat. Already the tip of his cock was easing into her, and he froze, searching her eyes.

Nera's hands dug into his ass. "Please, Giovanni," she begged.

Her warmth surrounded and squeezed him as he buried himself inside. Only then he couldn't part from her to thrust. He breathed through the intensity he was feeling, lowering his forehead against hers as he rocked instead.

Giovanni never wanted it to end. That moment of euphoria would be amazing, but this was what he craved. The heat and essence of her made him feel complete.

"I'm yours, Nera," he said, staring into her eyes. "Always."

For once, she was the one without words. She captured his mouth, kissing him instead. Her tongue was wild as it thrust inside his mouth, and suddenly rocking into her wasn't enough. His body moved on its own. Her closed legs made each thrust feel like it slid through a tightly gripped caress. It was intense for her as well, and her whole body shook each time he surged inside. Her kiss fell away as she began to gasp and moan against his mouth. They moved together, his love for her tightening to an impossible burst.

Giovanni emptied himself inside of her, hoping to always be a part of her, for as long as they would be granted.

Chapter 34

Nera pulled Giovanni into the bathroom to shower with her. While his hands soaped her body, the flush all the way up to his ears was more obvious—and more adorable. They didn't have sex again. They didn't need to. What they had shared had already sated them both.

He watched her as she dressed afterward. She'd been wrapping her new gun holster around her waist so she could tuck his gift in at the small of her back.

Giovanni's hands skimmed over the thick band. "Is it comfortable?"

Nera was too aware of it to call it comfortable. "Vespa recommended it. With my long skirts, a thigh holster would trap a gun. This one allows for easier access, but can still be hidden beneath my waistband." She stepped back, pulling on her skirt. When her blouse followed, it hung loosely enough that the gun wasn't obvious. She always wore loose and comfortable clothing. Remembering the way Giovanni had fallen apart just from touching her, she had no worries over needing to dress more sexily.

She turned her back to him. "Can you tell?"

When his hands brushed her hips, she realized how sensitive she still felt. "No," he said. His touch dropped away as he finished dressing.

Giovanni looked good in a buttoned-up suit, but Nera preferred him naked. For the first time, they'd spent over twenty-four hours in each other's company, and she wanted more.

The way he stared convinced her he felt the same. She remembered the way he'd whispered his love to her. They were words she never thought she'd hear out loud. The gift was precious and freeing.

"Yesterday, you took me with you to a meeting," Nera said. "You talked about things in front of me. Does that mean I can ask questions about your business?"

Giovanni stepped closer, his hand reaching up to brush her hair off her forehead. "No secrets between us. Unless knowing hurts you." His hand fell away. "If it's ever too much, speak up."

Nera doubted it ever would be. She'd watched him carve off someone's ear. His father had strangled someone practically next to her. She still wanted to kill him for touching Giovanni, but she wasn't wrapped up in emotions about the deaths themselves.

As long as Giovanni lived, she was fine.

"You're going to talk to Vittore again today, aren't you?" she asked.

Giovanni nodded.

"Because of what he said about your father being the likely one behind the attacks." The sentiment had come moments before Giovanni Sr. had saved her life, but that wasn't why it had rung false. She grimaced. "Your father would never hire someone. He'd kill me himself."

"He killed my mother." Giovanni stared into a middle distance. "Vittore and Enzo were there. They didn't stop it." He swallowed. "Vittore agreed it was necessary."

"Enzo seemed upset in the kitchen. Do you really think he'd hurt me?" Nera had a hard time picturing him shooting her.

"My uncle follows orders."

Nera remembered Enzo's warning. There'd been a blank look in his eyes when he'd reached for his gun after Giovanni had done the same.

"All Di Salvos follow orders. From my father or Vittore."

Nera moved to Giovanni's side, grasping his hand. "You believe Vittore is behind all the attempts to kill me."

Giovanni frowned. "It has to be him, but I don't understand why. I plan on asking him."

"I'll come with you."

Giovanni hesitated.

Nera intertwined their fingers, liking the way they connected just right. "It's the same for me. There's no life without you." She squeezed. "So together."

He took the first step toward the door. "Antonio will be relieved."

Nera smiled. "He hates babysitting duty," she agreed, waiting for Giovanni to open the door. He had paused again, his eyes locked on hers, as if memorizing the look in her eyes.

Worry festered inside her despite her resolve.

Once they opened the door, Antonio pushed off the opposite wall, wearing the same clothes as the night before. She expected a knowing smirk, but he simply studied Giovanni. A smear of blood stained the stomach of his dress shirt.

Antonio joined them as they headed up the stairs leading to the offices above.

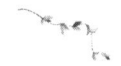

V ittore wasn't the only one in his office when they arrived. Enzo was staring at him from beside one of the chairs, breathing hard as he glared. His eyes cut to Nera, and his hands clenched. "You shouldn't be here, doll."

Giovanni's hand tightened around Nera's.

Vittore laughed. "And why not? She's the topic of conversation." He raised an eyebrow at Giovanni. "Did you come here to accuse me as well?"

He maintained his silence, feeling the heat of Nera's presence at his side.

Vittore rose from his desk to perch on it facing them. "I was the one that encouraged the marriage. Why would I want your wife dead?"

Antonio closed the door behind them before leaning against it, folding his arms across his chest. "That's our question."

Giovanni waited, letting the silence of the room draw out.

Vittore broke the silence first. "I thought this marriage would be good for you, Giovanni. Nera's family owns the bakery that your mother so loved. The two of you could run it together."

"That would never happen," Nera said from beside him. "Giovanni is a Di Salvo."

"One who has always hated the family. After what happened to his mother..." Vittore sighed. His eyes held the pity he had always directed at Giovanni. "Sharing his mother's blood set him apart. The other Di Salvos saw that. He had so many bruises as a boy. They weren't all from his father."

Giovanni remembered the way Nera would run to him when he showed up at the bakery after a beating. Whether the bruises were from fists large or small, she'd never asked questions, but her smile and touch would soothe him as her parents patched him up.

"A pleasant life with a woman such as her would suit you. Especially since you were responsible for her losing her sight."

Giovanni's throat tightened at the truth of the accusation.

"I'm not blind," Nera said.

Vittore shrugged. "Near enough, from what I've seen. You never recognized me, no matter how often I visited the bakery. Even since you've been staying here, I've watched you struggle to learn the names of the Di Salvos that greet you every day." He smiled at her gently. "I bet Giovanni is considering restructuring the lighting in the kitchen to make it easier on you."

"This isn't about that," Giovanni managed to say.

"Isn't it, though?" Vittore's tone hardened. "That kidnapping was a turning point for you, Giovanni. You and the girl."

Antonio shoved forward. "Because it had to be. The Di Salvos were at their worst back then. A fucking boss that won't lift a hand to save his son?"

Vittore studied Antonio. "He had another son."

Antonio glared at the wall.

Vittore's eyes held the same regard for Antonio that Giovanni Sr. often showed. "A son far more promising, and not just because he wasn't made between the legs of a Bratva whore."

"Careful," Enzo warned his brother.

"Me? I should be careful?" Vittore spat. "I had already lost one brother over a woman. Then you went and made the same goddamn mistake."

Enzo closed his eyes. "I should have been the one to pay for it."

The image of Enzo hovering over his mother's body rose in Giovanni's mind. His uncle had said taking care of it was his responsibility and had sent him away.

"My mother was never a traitor," Giovanni said. He'd never truly believed it.

"No. Your father jumped to conclusions." Vittore's gaze moved to his brother. "And those conclusions protected Enzo."

"I never wanted protection," Enzo said.

Vittore ignored the words. "The Bratva weren't happy when they heard the news of her death."

"For God's sake, that's why they kidnapped Gio," Antonio said. "They thought he'd turn."

"He'd become old enough to be a soldier, and they knew he hated his father." Vittore's lips twisted. "Instead of turning him, they hurt the only thing Giovanni still cared about." His eyes slid to Nera before returning to Giovanni. "The result of their mistake made me see you. Really see who you could become, Giovanni."

"He became a damn fine killer." Antonio's eyes gleamed with pride as he finally met Giovanni's gaze again. "And that's not just bias, as your brother." The term, said for the first time, fell between them. "All the Di Salvos started to think so. Hell, Gio, you've been getting rid of the Bratva left and right ever since."

"Marrying Nera actually helped his reputation further, which I hadn't factored in," Vittore's expression looked almost rueful.

"They like that he bucked tradition and married for goddamn love." Antonio shook his head. "I even admire him for it, and I was one of the ones urging him the other way. They don't respect her yet, which pisses me off, but him, that's another story. They respect him."

"Not like you Antonio. As it stood, the capos would have voted for you in a heartbeat." Vittore's fingers curled around the edge of the desk. "Giovanni's recent strength has been swaying them, though."

"You're wrong," Giovanni said. He was pathetic and weak. All the Di Salvos knew that.

Antonio's teeth flashed. "They've realized you're fucking ruthless, Gio. Hell, they're a bit scared of you, what with how many Bratva you've tortured lately after Nera..." Antonio trailed off with a frown.

Enzo glared at Vittore. "You set the Bratva on her."

"Of course I did!" Vittore slammed a hand on his desk.

Heat flooded through Giovanni.

"And it was all working perfectly," Vittore continued. "Our brother even threatened the girl." His eyes went soft with pity as he looked at Giovanni. "I thought for sure you would kill him then, but he left your mother's room alive. I saw that you still weren't ready." He sighed. "But you would finally act if his threats for Nera continued, if he was the one behind her death."

"But he saved her," Giovanni murmured.

Fury filled Vittore's face. "Does that wipe out everything from before? He killed your mother!"

"Because of you." Enzo's hands shook as he stared at his brother.

"To protect you!" Vittore shook his head, bringing himself under control again. "The past doesn't matter. We need to consider the future." His expression became calm, calculating as his eyes returned to Giovanni. "Giovanni Sr. has become increasingly unstable. He'll eventually kill Nera. You know that in your heart."

"Hell, he'll kill Gio first," Antonio said. "Even Nera's seen that truth."

Nera's grip on Giovanni's hand tightened.

Enzo frowned. "You were always the one protecting him, Vittore. Why not just say something if you want him gone?"

"It can't be me. I have no desire to lead." Vittore's lips twisted. "There's a certain quality I lack. Antonio already proved he has it." He smiled at him before switching his gaze to Giovanni. "I wanted to provide Giovanni with the same opportunity, to make up for doubting him before."

Antonio's eyes narrowed. "But why play games with a woman's life? Especially after she became a Di Salvo."

Vittore snorted. "A woman can never be a true Di Salvo. Both your mothers proved that."

The way his uncle looked at Nera was so much worse than the way his father ever had. Giovanni's hand dropped from Nera's to his gun.

Enzo's face paled as he stared at his brother. "Inessa never broke from the family. I was as much at fault for what happened."

Vittore's eyes were cold as he shook his head. "All women are dispensable. That's the one thing our brother understands." His gaze moved to Giovanni again. "He'll soon treat your Nera the same."

"*You* treated her that way!" Antonio shouted.

"Only to goad Giovanni." Vittore Di Salvo's eyes were nearly as dark as his father's had often seemed. "That will stop, as long as you're willing to act."

Giovanni returned his gaze. "You want me to kill my father."

"It's time," Vittore agreed softly.

He didn't need to hear any more words. Giovanni pulled his gun and shot the traitor in the head.

Chapter 35

Nera stared at Giovanni's remote expression as he stared down at his uncle's body. She took a step forward, intending to give him her support.

The door opened behind them. Giovanni's father took in Vittore's empty eyes and the gun in Giovanni's hand.

Panic filled Nera as his father lunged for him. They slammed into the wall with his father's hands already around his throat.

"Vittore!" Giovanni Sr. screamed. "You killed Vittore?"

Antonio rushed to stop him. A punch to his throat sent him to the ground.

Giovanni tried to kick, tried to scratch, but his father's weight kept him pinned as he struggled to breathe.

"I needed him." His father released Giovanni, watching him crumple to the ground. He pulled his gun.

Nera reached for her own, the handle catching on the elastic band of her skirt.

"Look at her, son." Giovanni's father's anger had faded from his voice. His eyes glittered darkly as he watched her aim at him.

Giovanni's were wide with fear.

"You take from me. I take from you," his father said.

Nera pulled the trigger. Nothing happened.

His father laughed. "I did like you."

"Nera!" Giovanni screamed, scrambling against the ground.

The gun fired.

Something slammed into her, and she went flying backward.

"Goddammit, Enzo!"

Nera looked at where Enzo lay. Blood began to spread across his stomach.

"You've cost me both my brothers." His father dragged Giovanni up, his arm wrapping around his throat as he held him tight to his chest. "I should have killed you long ago."

Giovanni clawed at his father's arm.

Nera pushed to her feet, staring down at the gun in her hand.

"Maybe this is better." His father squeezed. "You can die knowing just what I'll do to your sweet wife. Your punishment will be quick, but hers won't."

Nera fumbled with the safety latch that Vespa had shown her, raising the gun.

Giovanni Sr. laughed. "You're fucking blind. This will be the sweetest end for you, son, if she shoots you herself."

Giovanni's hands stopped struggling, but his color hadn't faded. His red outline was clear.

Nera took her shot.

"No!" Antonio croaked, rushing toward where they fell.

Nera dropped her gun, telling herself that she could still see red as she approached them.

Giovanni coughed, and her legs gave out. He was the one that crawled to her. His arms trembled as they wrapped around her, but his chest was so warm.

"For fuck's sake," Antonio muttered from where he'd collapsed against the wall. "She shot him in the head."

Satisfaction filled Nera, the warmth of it chasing along the path of Giovanni's caresses. His father would never hurt him again.

The Di Salvos buried two men, not three. Enzo was in a wheelchair at the funeral, but Antonio's surgeon expected him to fully recover.

All the other capos appeared ill at ease as they approached Giovanni. It was to be expected, since they assumed he'd killed both his father and his uncle. He let them, deciding it was safest for Nera.

Her hand squeezed his, reminding him she was near. She rarely left his side, present even at the meetings with the capos. They'd mainly told the truth. He wasn't certain what the Di Salvo family had made of it. He still didn't fully understand what his uncle Vittore had hoped to gain from his plan.

His father had always wanted him dead.

The vote for a new leader was scheduled for the day after the funeral.

Nera forced Enzo to rest after they returned to the estate. Giovanni followed her to his uncle's room. Enzo's smiles hadn't returned yet, though he often appeared flustered when Nera fussed over him.

Enzo had taken the bullet to save her life. Giovanni would always be grateful for it.

He didn't follow Nera from the room. She hesitated in the doorway, her hand resting on his arm before she closed the door behind her.

Giovanni didn't worry about her safety. Antonio never left her alone. His cousin had become almost as protective of her as he was. Or his brother. Giovanni needed to be sure.

Enzo's eyes were warm on his. "The killings were justified, Giovanni. I stand with you."

Giovanni nodded. "Thank you for saving Nera."

"She saved herself." Enzo's hand hovered over his stomach as he sagged into the bed. "Been a while since I've been shot. I don't like it, but anything for her." His eyes went distant. "She doesn't look like your mother, but sometimes she reminds me of her."

Giovanni's eyes closed. His strongest memory of his mother was of her smiling or laughing in the bakery.

"Life would have been easier for your mother if she wasn't as fierce as she was. The way your father treated her... Well, you know." Enzo's breath shuddered from him. "I didn't force her the way he did. I loved your mother."

Giovanni studied his uncle. "Is Antonio my brother?"

"Your father fucked his mother, but she was more than willing." Enzo sighed. "Don't be hard on Antonio for keeping this from you. He only knew because his mother was a piece of work."

"I'm not angry with him." Giovanni could never be. He knew enough about what had happened with Antonio's mother to understand his brother had protected him back then. His doubt lingered over the term. Giovanni had never been much like his father. In fact, he had far more similarities to the man who lay in front of him. "Am I his brother?"

Enzo's brow furrowed at the repeated question, but then his eyes softened. "I'm sorry, kid. I've thought of you as mine, but your mother was already pregnant when we first..." His cheeks reddened.

Giovanni accepted the explanation. In a way, it made it easier. His mother had treated him like he was his father's son. After realizing how it had been for her, Giovanni had understood.

It was still hard to accept that his mother had despised him, but at least it wasn't over a falsehood. He studied his uncle. Perhaps she had loved someone.

He moved to the door.

"Giovanni," Enzo called after him. "I'm proud of you. You'll lead the Di Salvo family well."

Giovanni left his uncle to rest.

He found Nera in the kitchen. She squinted against the bright lighting as Antonio pulled something from the oven for her.

No other Di Salvos lingered nearby, not after seeing Giovanni. If they hadn't been afraid of him before, they were now. Just like they'd feared his father. Giovanni didn't see a need to change their minds any time soon. That fear would provide Nera with protection.

If that's what she wanted. "Nera," he said, and the tension around her eyes eased as she turned to him.

She'd told him his color was the reason her aim had held so true. Giovanni knew it was all her determination. Nera would always be the one to save him.

He crossed to her. "What Vittore said." His hand brushed flour from her cheek. He'd never asked her about the life Vittore had weaved for them.

Antonio laughed as he set down the baking sheet. "You're going to have to be more specific, Gio. That crazy bastard said a lot of things."

He studied his brother. "The men of this family may fear me, but they also fear you."

Antonio's face became blank at the change of subject.

"And you're older," Giovanni continued. His gaze moved back to Nera. "There's your parents' bakery. Antonio could lead the family. The capos may decide that."

Antonio glowered at him. "I think I liked it better when you weren't so outspoken."

Nera laughed, moving closer to Giovanni. "Giovanni's perfect as he is. And so am I." She kissed him softly. "I will be an amazing wife to the Di Salvos' next boss."

"You already are," Antonio said, turning toward the stove again.

Giovanni struggled to see himself as the next head of the family. The Di Salvos had never seemed to accept him. But he silently agreed that Nera would help him become stronger if he was chosen. He kissed his wife again, lingering this time in her embrace.

Chapter 36

Giovanni woke up alone. His hand slid over the sheet next to him. It had already gone cold.

Nera had woken before dawn again, thanks to her deeply ingrained habit. She'd brought him awake in the most pleasant of ways, he recalled, as heat slid up his neck at the dreamlike memory, but he'd fallen asleep like he usually did when he was sexually sated.

He'd gotten home too late the night before, and he didn't feel content until he was next to her. Late evenings and insomnia were no longer the norm for him. Nera brought him a contentedness that he was learning to trust.

But last night, his presence among the capos had been necessary. Nera had wanted to go with him, but Giovanni drew a line when he knew blood would be spilled. It wasn't because she wouldn't be able to handle it. He was the one that was weak, and old habits were difficult to break. He'd always want to protect her. More so now.

The Di Salvos had already become used to Nera attending their meetings among the capos. She'd been present when they voted for

Giovanni to lead. Not everyone in La Cosa Nostra had seen his strength, especially not among the other families. He'd more than proven himself since, and the violence had delayed the combined meeting of the families. There might be a few hard feelings among those finally present.

Nera would bring her gun.

The urge to see her drew him out of bed despite the few hours he'd slept.

Tommaso's presence in the kitchen was no surprise. Nera's guardian had rejoined the Di Salvos as her bodyguard once he'd healed.

Despite Tommaso freeing up their time, Enzo and Antonio also helped Nera in the mornings, whenever they were able. Their presence that morning was ridiculous, since they'd had late nights as well, but Giovanni no longer felt any jealousy toward their time with her.

Nera sensed him like usual, her smile full of warmth and affection as she crossed to him. Changing the lights had been a simple project, and she no longer squinted as she baked, or anywhere else in the house. She wasn't shy about kissing him in front of the other men. He pulled her closer, loving the press of her body along his. He wondered when it would start changing and resisted pressing his hand against her stomach.

She had only had her period once more since they'd been married. She didn't seem to notice that it had been more than a month since it'd last happened. Giovanni remembered it well because of the pain she had experienced. Rubbing her lower back helped the most. He'd been looking forward to pampering her again, but the time had never come.

There'd been reason for her distraction. The Bratva were particularly angry with them at the moment, but Giovanni wasn't willing to stop his assaults until their leader fell. They may have targeted Nera because of Vittore, but they'd targeted her all the same. That was one reason for the meeting with the other families.

That and the Albanians, which Coronella would need help with.

"Goddammit, Gio, take her back to your room for all that," Antonio said with a laugh.

Giovanni flushed as he pulled away. Nera's panting breath made him want to kiss her again, but he resisted until she pressed her forehead against his and whispered, "I love you."

He lost himself in her as he turned her toward the kitchen entrance.

And nearly bumped into Luka, who was definitely not looking at them.

Nera laughed as Giovanni's hands fell away from her. "Good morning, Luka," she greeted him, even though he still didn't meet her gaze. "The chocolate croissants just came out of the oven, and we have panna cotta leftover from yesterday."

She'd made it for Giovanni again, even though he'd admitted to her that it wasn't his favorite. It was too mixed up with his mother. He preferred her chocolate croissants, and she spoiled him with them too often.

"Would you like some?" she asked Luka.

He nodded.

Nera fed him each time he came by, and she smiled at his quicker than usual agreement. "Which one?"

Luka's face went blank.

She laughed. "I'll bring you both."

Luka caught Giovanni's gaze when she crossed the kitchen. He tilted his head.

"Bring it to the office?" Giovanni asked her, catching her quick nod. He never called it *his* office. Not because it had once been his father's, but because he shared it with Nera.

Luka still didn't say anything after they were alone. Giovanni knew Luka didn't have an issue with the Di Salvos targeting the Bratva. His own relationship with the Russian mafia was complicated. Giovanni waited patiently, knowing how difficult finding the words could be. Luka no longer appeared in their bedroom when he visited. Giovanni appreciated the gesture, though it was likely due to Luka's own discomfort.

Despite that, Luka appeared much more often in the kitchen than the office. He ate Nera's food as if it was the first of its kind. Perhaps, for him, it was.

"I need help," Luka admitted, his hands closing into fists.

Giovanni didn't hesitate. "Tell me."

Nera knocked before she entered the office. Giovanni's expression was not the one she was expecting. Even though he trusted Luka, and considered him a friend, he normally maintained his stoic expression around the man.

He didn't wear that now. His flush had reached his ears. She loved when they darkened like that.

Luka took the desserts she had brought. Both portions. He was quick to exit with them.

"Is everything all right?" she asked, closing the door behind their guest before crossing to Giovanni's side. When he looked embarrassed like that, the urge to touch him became irresistible, and her hands moved to his top button.

"I wasn't expecting his question," Giovanni murmured, still lost in thought. She managed to undo half his buttons before his gaze flew to hers.

Her lips grazed his delicious collarbone. "Was it that difficult of a question?"

He shuddered under her shifting caress.

"I don't consider myself an expert." His slight inhale was a reward for the way she nipped at him. "Nera." Her name always sounded best coming from him.

She sat on the edge of the desk, unbuttoning her own shirt. Her interest in whatever Luka had come for waned as Giovanni's eyes followed her progress.

They'd never had sex in the office. His mouth opened, as if he would deny her.

"I love you, Giovanni," she murmured, knowing what it would do to him. Her love for him was better than any touch she could give him.

He rose from his chair, kissing her as his hands found her stomach. He loved the plump softness of it, and often stroked her there. This time, his hands were achingly gentle.

"I love you." His words were almost too low to hear, but Nera reveled in them all the same. Giovanni swallowed, lifting his head. "No recklessness. Even if I'm the one in danger, you can't shield me."

Nera shook her head. "I can't promise that. It's instinct." Her hands moved into his hair, wondering what had gotten into him. "We're strong together. You don't have to worry."

He shook his head, but he could no longer find his words. His lips replaced them, continuing to be gentle until she became the aggressor, turning it into so much more.

Thank you for reading Broken Protector, book 1 in the Gentle Sinners series. Please consider leaving a review to help others find Giovanni and Nera's story.

Did you also develop a soft spot for Giovanni's uncle, Enzo? If you'd like to read more about his past with Inessa, you can find a short story written in his POV at the below link:

https://dl.bookfunnel.com/xrtz0ybsyi

Also By Amber Warden

Gentle Sinners mafia series
Broken Protector – Giovanni and Nera
Broken Captive – Luka and Alina
Broken Worth – Montrell and Beatrice
Broken Resolve – Antonio and Vespa

The Last Shot Tavern Series
Finding Comfort – Trenton and Celia
Finding Nerve – Blake and Katie
Finding Instinct – Nicholas and Erin
Finding Hope – Malcolm and Jami
Finding Emotion – Damon and Skylar

Standalones

No Longer Faking

Undeserving of Wings

Neighborly Repairs
Fix My Closet
Fix My Sink
Fix My Locks

Amazon Author Page

https://www.amazon.com/~/e/B09R682NNK

About the Author

Amber Warden started reading romance earlier than she probably should have. Before long, she was anticipating the steamy scenes and skipping to the good parts. She loves dreaming up new book boyfriends and lives out her fantasies in her stories. Her main hope is for those reading to take away the feeling that they are more than enough for anyone.

When she's not writing, she's reading shoujo manga, playing otome games, and listening to her favorite J-rock music.

She'd love to hear from her readers:
amberwardenauthor@gmail.com

Instagram @amberwardenwrites

Facebook @amberwardenauthor

https://amberwardenauthor.mailerpage.com

Made in the USA
Columbia, SC
12 February 2025